MERCILESS STARS

CANDACE ROBINSON

For those who wish to fly

ONE

SILVER

Annihilate. Teeth and claws. Tear flesh. Blood. Death.

Those five phrases repeated inside Silver's head. They were the phrases her sister, Afton—the queen of Ketill—had told her for as long as she could remember. It was for the safety of their home—their kingdom.

A man wriggled in Afton's grasp. He hadn't spoken a word since arriving—none of the three guards sent by the King of Enare had. When the other two guards, who now lay dead on the marble floor, attempted to chain Afton's wrists, they'd wound up shredded to pieces by Silver and her sister.

Running her tongue across her teeth, Silver wiped them clean of blood as best she could. The two sharp rows of teeth had already retracted into her gums, leaving only her permanent ones in their wake. But the earth's magic still coursed through her, aching to unleash again.

"King Thorin's betrothment letter said it was up to me," Afton growled near the man's ear, her pitch-black eyes boring into him, her long white-blonde hair swinging forward. "Then you so graciously, or should I say *ungraciously*, changed your mind when I said I would take my time to think about it."

His hand shoved at Afton's chest as he attempted to slip

out of her grasp.

Not one to easily give up, Silver thought.

"Wrong answer." Afton thrust her head forward with a snarl, her razor-sharp teeth ripping the man's throat open, slicing through his neck and spine until his head thumped to the stone floor. Thick crimson pooled out from both open wounds.

Another head to add to the collection of traitorous skulls in the tunnel below the castle. All he had to do was *wait* and let Afton decide on an answer to the king's proposal. Silver's sister didn't murder for the sake of murder, but in times like these, it was necessary.

From an early age, Silver had learned several things—Afton would always choose for herself, and she would not let anyone ever control her. Those were just a couple of the reasons why Silver loved her sister.

When Afton was ten years old, she ended their cruel parents' lives, making her queen—the youngest ruler in Ketill's history. Silver had never once yearned to be queen—she'd only ever wanted to help her sister continue her legacy.

A stir and a stomp of boots *thump-thumped* from behind her. Silver whirled around, ready to attack again if she must.

Javan, Afton's guard, rounded the corner, carrying his cane in one hand, his lips pursed. "Looks like you two have made quite the mess, haven't you?" He pinched the bridge of his nose as his gaze swept across the crimson-smeared floor and walls.

Afton wiped her bloody palms against the skirts of her viridescent dress and picked up her mace. "So we did. You should have been *guarding*."

"You allowed them access without me knowing. I just found out from an outside guard." He ran a hand through his salt-and-pepper hair. "This isn't going to bode well with Enare. You know very well things have been falling apart over there for years."

"It seemed to bode well for me," Afton spat.

This is true…

"King Thorin is going to react," Javan snapped back.

"You're not my father."

"I'm not your friend either. I'm your *guard*."

Afton glared, her eyes full of icy daggers.

Javan took a step forward, arms folded over his chest, his hazel gaze resting on Afton. "Silver wouldn't have done this if you hadn't influenced her."

"We all know Silver is your favorite and you would love to see her on the throne." Afton's scowl deepened.

He gave an exhausted sigh. "I've never once said that about Silver, have I?"

Javan always thought of Silver as the gentle one, the proper one, the one who cared for everyone. That might be true, but sometimes blood was required over picking and gifting a bouquet of flowers. Sometimes the bouquet needed to be drenched in blood.

"You know I'm right here, also standing in the room," Silver said to break up some of the tension.

Both hard stares turned on her.

"Or not." Silver held her hands up, taking a step back. "I can be a ghost if you wish. But Afton made the correct decision—the guards were planning on taking her against her will." She pressed a hand to her chest, where her scar was visible just below her neck. As a young child, she'd been burned by her sister. It wasn't Afton's fault—it was their parents'. Afton always said their parents lay dead in the darkest pit of Torlarah. Silver hoped it was true and prayed they were suffering.

"Mm-hmm. I'm still sure there was a better solution," Javan grumbled.

"Get this mess cleaned up. I expect to have their hearts fully cooked for dinner." Afton rolled her eyes at Javan and sauntered out of the room.

A solution... That was what they needed. Javan's age was beginning to show at times, and although he was still strong when necessary, he was using his cane more often. Afton wouldn't replace him while he was still breathing, but she needed to have a guard prepared for when the time was right. Someone trustworthy. Silver stared at the dead bodies and closed her eyes, trying desperately to think of a plan. If she could keep her friend's soul in human form in this world, then she would have a permanent solution. King Thorin would send more guards when his didn't return, and Afton would need someone besides Javan. To make her friend—Keelen—whole, Silver would need to dig deeper into the dark magic of the earth to conjure him to stay. Even then, she didn't know if it would truly work after her numerous failed attempts over the years when he'd been a raven.

Silver stepped out of the room into the soft lighting reflecting off the walls. Lifting her skirts, she rushed after her sister, across the plush carpeted hallway. She pushed her black hair behind her shoulders, letting it fall to her waist. It only took a moment before she found Afton walking farther down the hall. She picked up her pace and skirted around her sister before stopping in front of her.

Speckles of crimson coated the bodice and skirt of Afton's gown. "I think I may have a solution for King Thorin and his control of Enare." Silver's chest heaved and she peered down, catching sight of her own thin dress smeared in blood.

Afton arched an obsidian brow, contrasting drastically with her light hair. "The foolish guards he sent are dead. Now, excuse me."

She grabbed Afton's wrist, and her sister gently removed Silver's fingers.

"I need to use the wax," Silver hurried on. "After you bathe, I want to show you something."

"Silver!" Afton stared at the ceiling before resting her dark eyes back on her. They mirrored Silver's black irises with a white pupil in the center—eyes that no other in their kingdom had ever been blessed with, ones that couldn't even be altered by magic. "You don't have to ask me to use the wax, but I'm tired. We can discuss this betrothal issue later. If those guards had been patient, they would have learned my answer was yes. I've grown tired of receiving these letters from Thorin the past four months. But my plan hasn't changed—I'll still destroy the king. Ketill will never be united with Enare under him. From 'our betrothal,' Enare would be ours once he's dead."

Afton brushed by her, sauntering past the sculpted statues without true faces, their cerulean bodies standing in different elegant dancing poses. Silver didn't go after her. She smiled to herself—her sister would see.

Silver clenched her filthy skirts, not bothering to change dresses since the fabric would only get messy again anyway.

She hurried to the end of the hall and opened the door to Afton's study. In the large space sat a desk, completely organized, with a stack of papers and an inkwell and quill resting atop the wood. Shelves of books hugged the walls, some with decaying split spines or fraying edges, others appearing as if they'd never been opened.

A massive cauldron hung in the center of the room from a metal chain, the peach wax kept bubbling by an invisible flame. The power came from the land. Afton and Silver didn't need the cauldron to use the magic, but with the wax brewing and alive, it was like an amplifier—making them stronger within the castle walls and more prepared for enemies. The liquid stayed churning due to the remedies she and Afton would retrieve from herbal sellers. Despite the cauldron always bubbling, no matter what she did, Keelen could never stay for long.

A thought struck her—Afton had wanted the hearts for dinner. *Damn it*. While trying to hurry, she'd forgotten to return to Javan before coming to the study. Lifting her skirts, she ran down the hallway to the meeting room where the bodies still lay.

Silver sighed in relief, her hand at her chest. "Thank the spirits."

It shouldn't matter which heart she used, so Silver grabbed the broad shoulders of a shorter guard who weighed the least. Silver pulled him halfway out of the room when Javan rounded the corner, this time leaning on his cane as he walked. In his other palm rested several sharp tools for him to dig out the hearts for the cook to prepare.

He stopped, a single eyebrow arched in suspicion. "What are you trying to do?"

"I need to borrow this guard for a bit. Can you help me?" She smiled wide, pleading. "And in return, I'll make things easier for you." She moved to one of the other bodies, magic swirling inside her. Flexing her fingers and extending her claws, Silver dove her hands into the man's stomach with a sickening squish, then up and under his rib cage. Cradling the warm organ in her palm, she casually pulled it out and repeated her motions on the second body. She held out both wet hearts, revealing the bloody muscle, to Javan. *Drip. Drip.*

"You girls can do all that but can't manage to lift a body with magic?" Javan asked, incredulous.

"Perhaps one day I'll be able to." She placed the hearts on the table and walked back to the body she'd been dragging. "All right, help me bring this one to the study."

Javan slowly ran a hand across his jaw but nodded and set down his cane. He grabbed the dead guard by his limp legs.

They exchanged no words as they passed the portraits on the wall and the statues decorating the hallway. She struggled with the guard's bulky shoulders, hefting them higher.

Once through the already-open door, they carried the body inside and laid it down beside the cauldron.

Javan stood there, unmoving, his brow furrowing.

"That will be all for now." Silver shooed him out with both hands so she could concentrate.

"You do know not to eat raw hearts and other organs, correct?"

"Trust me, you'll love the outcome of this." She grinned, knowing it might take some of the work load off of Javan. "But I need to focus alone."

"Uh-huh." He still didn't budge.

"I've got it. Just go."

Javan gripped the bridge of his nose and exited the study, closing the door gently behind him.

Finally, alone.

Silver tapped her chin and scanned the room—the three chairs, the desk, the bookcases, the floor, the body. She swiped the few things from the desk to the floor, then realized the top wouldn't be long enough. *Damn.* Hurriedly, she restacked the papers on the desk in a way that wouldn't be noticeable to Afton.

Taking one of the large ladles from the chain of the cauldron, Silver stirred the peach-colored wax in a clockwise circle.

At the age of eight, Silver had used her magic to shape a raven out of wax after Afton killed their parents. She then brought the raven to life, but it was no ordinary bird. She'd placed a soul of a young human boy within the raven—Keelen, the name she'd given him since he'd been unable to recall his—yet she could never figure out a way to make the wax hold its shape for long. No matter how many times she created a new raven, him staying remained temporary.

No one had ever known about Keelen besides her—even Afton. He was her secret, and now he wouldn't be any more if she could make him a permanent weapon. Sometimes, when she tried to bring him to life, the wax refused to listen. Sometimes it was for days, sometimes weeks, but this time it had been months.

Silver's heart pounded beneath her rib cage while she thought that the wax may not listen to her once more. Or perhaps Keelen didn't want to come back—perhaps he was tired of being reshaped into a raven and falling to pieces.

Each time she located Keelen within Torlarah—the afterlife—he could never remember his full story when she carried his soul out, only his age. He had been ten when she was eight. Although he was dead, he aged as she did, and she couldn't explain how it was possible. But it was.

Silver blew out a breath. She was twenty now, stronger, and could dig deeper into the dark magic. With the right necessities, and her power at its full potential, this would be the time for him to stay.

Or so she hoped.

"All right, hands and mind, let's do this." Using a ladle, she spread the boiling wax onto the floor and drew up a wind to cool the liquid into clumps. A glittering iridescent smoke curled around the wax, turning it more malleable. Her hands absorbed the warmth of the wax as she smoothed its texture, the wax's herbal scent filling the room.

With precision, she pressed her fingertips to the smooth texture and dug her digits in. She shaped, folded, weaved, and formed it as best she could. Silver didn't know what he should look like—he'd only ever been a raven before—so she entrusted the magic to cooperate with her in making him complete.

A soft *clink* sounded from outside the door and Silver stood, brushing her hands down the front of her dress before opening it.

Resting on the carpet, she spotted a silver dagger—ornate jewels and engravings decorated the handle—waiting for her. Javan was being generous, even though she didn't mind using her hands.

After shutting the door, Silver went and knelt beside the guard's dead body. She carefully used the sharp tip of her new gift to pluck out each of the violet eyes so Keelen would be able to see. Then she cut out the tongue for him to taste, and a heart for him to live. Organ after organ came next, and she wondered if she should have used all three bodies to find the strongest variety, but these appeared plentiful enough. She tucked each one inside the wax and covered them with thick layers—even the eyeballs were hidden.

Silver had missed Keelen, but she was also tired of seeing him die over and over because her magic wasn't strong enough to keep him whole. She'd been selfish, bringing him back time and time again. And down, hidden beneath the bloody muscular layers of her heart, was something—an emotion that could only also be considered selfish on her part.

Because, she loved him…

Why was she thinking about her heart when she needed to focus on *his*? Silver broke through several dark barriers, tugging at threads, all while feeling as though she was falling. Her breaths increased as she searched for Torlarah's fog. Farther. Farther. Before her, something thick and white drifted toward her. There it was. She went deeper. A faint heartbeat pulsed in front of her, then she could sense his familiar essence. She latched onto him and pulled, darkness rousing around her, within her, struggling to tear itself away. But she yanked harder, drawing the shimmering pearl up and out of Torlarah before placing the soul inside the wax.

Silver pressed her palms to the now-hardened chest, one hand right over the other. Closing her eyes, she shallowly pumped the area and whispered the word that would bring him to life. "Awake."

She opened her eyes. Smooth tan skin coated the wax body, silken to perfection. "It worked," she breathed.

Bones would be beneath the new layer, as would muscle and nerves. She'd never seen him with skin—he'd always had the waxy sheen while a raven. The guard's organs, along with the dark magic, changed that. His new flesh was without hair for the time being, but it would grow as blood now pumped through his veins.

Silver's heart caught in her throat as she continued to stare at him. He was beautiful. She hadn't known how he would look, but it wouldn't have mattered as long as he was there.

She waited and waited, the ends of her fingers tapping together. "Perhaps it didn't work."

Then his chest rose and fell, and his eyelids slowly opened to bright violet irises, like lavender under warm sunlight.

His head slowly turned toward her, his neck popping, and his body appearing stiff.

"Hi, Keelen." Silver grinned.

He didn't smile in return, his voice seemingly trapped in his throat.

Silver's brows lowered as she studied his face, his expression. He'd never looked like a man before, and she couldn't remove her gaze from him. Her heart beat harder while she continued to stare at his features—his strong jaw, his high cheekbones, his bright eyes.

"Hi," she repeated, breathless. Perhaps he didn't understand her. It was possible she'd made it so he didn't speak her language this time, though that had never happened before.

"Hello," he finally said, voice deep, cradling his lower lip between his teeth. So human-like. "Do I … do I know you?"

Her anxious beating heart plummeted as though sinking to the bottom of the sea, buried beneath the grains, too deep to find.

"You don't remember me?" Tears pricked her eyes, but she bit the inside of her cheek to pull herself together. "I'm Silver. You always remember me. I brought you here from the afterlife—Torlarah. Keelen is the name I gave you before."

Squinting his eyes, surveying her, he shook his head. "No, I think I would've remembered the color of your irises, the whites in the middle of them."

Maybe this was for the best—she wouldn't have to be attached to their friendship, her *feelings* for him, if he didn't remember her... "I've known you for a while. You were always a raven before, but now you're like me."

He shakily held up his hand and inspected his fingers. "One, two, three, four, five." His chin lifted, and his expression was questioning. "How?"

"I gave you a man's heart using a bit of magic." She didn't tell him how dark the power was and that there had been a chance he wouldn't have come to life at all.

Even though she knew she shouldn't, Silver wanted to press her palms to his new skin, run her fingers up the length of him. She reined in that temptation and held out her hands to him. He stared at them for a moment before placing his on top of hers. Smooth, not a single callus.

Keelen stumbled a bit as she brought him to standing, then maneuvered him to one of the plush chairs across from the writing desk.

Inside the closet, Silver found a stack of blankets and grabbed a wool one. She padded to the chair and wrapped the blanket around his naked form. It was hard for her not to peer down, even though she'd touched every inch of his body, but that was before it had become flesh—*real*. And she already knew the length between his thighs would please any woman, though she hadn't planned on creating it so perfectly.

He slumped back in the chair and spread his legs apart to where she caught a glimpse of his manhood. *Quit reminding me.* She flicked her gaze away and hurried to adjust the blanket better as he rested his head against the blue velvet. He breathed deeply, not saying a single word. She stood in front of him, blinking rapidly, waiting to discuss *something*.

Keelen released a low chuckle, his gaze softening when his eyes met hers. "I still can't remember much, only dying as a raven … numerous times. Yet I don't specifically remember you, or this place, or an afterlife either."

"That's because you weren't formed correctly before. I wasn't strong enough, and I should have used human organs."

She paused and thought of Keelen when he'd been there last. "Do you remember flying in the garden at all? When you were a raven?"

"No, Silver." He shook his head and pulled the blanket tighter at his chest. "I can't remember."

"Oh." At least he was saying her name. She liked the way it formed and sounded coming out of his new mouth.

"Only the pain. The dying."

Silver's heart dropped to her stomach, and she scooted closer to him. "With every fiber in me, I won't let you die. Not unless you choose it, but I have something I need you to do. I placed organs inside you and used a specific magic that should hopefully keep hold. You will age, you will live, and yes, eventually, you will die. I know I didn't give you a choice in what you look like. So, I will give you this opportunity..." She hadn't expected him to feel this way. Keelen had never remembered his past life, but he did always remember being with her, then the dying. He'd said it felt like flames were licking off layer after layer of flesh, yet to see her again was always worth it.

"I don't care what I look like. I don't care if I'm a raven, a man, or something else." His jaw tightened, but he wasn't focused on her. "If I do die again, I don't want you to bring me back."

Silver blinked—the old Keelen would have disagreed. She leaned forward and placed her warm hands in his, letting his cool fingertips absorb her warmth. "I won't bring you back." It was a lie.

The door cracked open, the sound reverberating off the walls. Silver whirled around and straightened.

Javan stopped in his tracks as his gaze settled on her. "What is this? I heard voices."

"Leave!" she shouted. He wasn't supposed to come in just yet.

His hazel eyes shifted to Keelen, then to the wax, and

finally to the torn-open body. "You've been using dark magic?" he rasped, his hand covering his mouth.

"It isn't dark if I'm only giving life." She didn't understand how that could be considered *wrong*.

"It's forbidden." He knelt and ran his fingertip across the leftover wax on the floor. "You know this."

"Afton will allow what I've done when she sees the usefulness of it."

"How long, Silver?" he seethed. "How long have you been doing things like this? How are you going to explain this to your sister?"

"Um, a good while?" She winced.

"Damn it. You saw what the magic did to your parents!" Javan cradled his face and dug his fingertips into the skin.

"They were like that even when they didn't dabble with the darkness," she forced out. "Trust me, he's good. He's going to be Afton's new guard, and she will need him for Enare. You won't be able to look after her forever."

Javan's head whipped up and his spine lengthened. "What is she planning, Silver?"

"She's going to marry Thorin as per his request." Silver didn't know the full story of what was to come, and Afton would have to be the one to explain the rest to him.

"Something isn't right here." Javan lightly bounced his fist against his mouth. "Afton wouldn't be so easily swayed."

"Will you help me remove the corpse? I'll go and talk to her." Silver peered down at herself, finally taking notice that she was drenched in even more scarlet.

"I've got it—I'll get everything cleaned up here." Javan batted her away. "Just go take *your guest* to one of the vacant rooms while I figure things out in the weapons area."

"I don't think you can." Silver inspected his cane on the floor.

"Silver, I have a limp. I'm not missing appendages. Now go," he grunted.

Not wanting to continue arguing, she helped Keelen to his feet and closed the door behind them. She glanced up, taking stock that Keelen was about a head taller than her.

His eyes locked onto hers. "So you have things you want me to do…"

"Yes, but you need to rest for now."

As they walked down the hall and turned down another, he wasn't stumbling anymore. Silver let go of his waist as he followed her with long strides to one of the guest rooms. She opened the door to a space that held a jewel-embedded wooden wardrobe, resting across from a bed. Tall ivory posts, encrusted with triangular-shaped obsidian, were at each corner of the mattress.

"Are you hungry?" she asked as Keelen sat on the bed. He inspected the ornate stitching of the blanket while she pulled him out a tunic and pants from the wardrobe. "I bet you're starving. Even I'm starving after the day I've had."

"Famished."

Silver tossed him the clothing. "Get dressed and don't go anywhere." She didn't wait for a response as she headed out of the room and down to the kitchens to gather something to fill their bellies.

Steaming chicken and an assortment of wonderful smells filled her nose when she entered the kitchens. Silver approached the counters, where Ragan stood squeezing lemon juice onto roasted meat. She collected pastries, fruit, bread, and slices of chicken, placing them on a plate. Ragan's deep mahogany eyes watched her while one chestnut-colored eyebrow rose, seeming to take notice of the blood on her. He was used to seeing her drenched in crimson, usually after she went out hunting in the woods with Afton. It had been three months since he'd started working at the palace, and Silver had sparked a friendship with him almost immediately.

"You're going to eat all that by yourself?" He smirked and swiped a lock of brown hair off his forehead.

"Maybe." She laughed before turning to go back to the guest room. Ragan was Afton's sole lover since his arrival, which had taken Silver by surprise since her sister had never opened her heart to any other man. Afton had always let them know beforehand that, besides a tumble, there would be nothing more. With Ragan, that changed.

Silver ascended the long staircase and returned to Keelen's room. He was fully dressed and staring at the candles. His legs were stretched out and crossed at the ankles as he rested against the headboard.

She handed him the plate of food while stuffing her mouth with a jellied pastry. As he bit into a plump strawberry, she remembered how, before, he preferred to snap up spiders with his beak.

Once he finished devouring his meal, his eyes started to flutter.

"Try resting for a bit." Silver helped him under the blankets and pulled them all the way up to his chin, then tucked it around his body. "How do you feel?"

"As though I can't move," Keelen drawled.

"Sorry about that." Silver laughed. Perhaps she did overdo it. She loosened the blankets and rolled them down to his chest. "I have something I want to ask of you." Her hands fidgeted as she waited for him to answer.

"What is it?" He eyed her warily.

"I know you heard me mention to Javan about you becoming my sister's guard. Afton needs a new one soon, and I was wondering if you would do it. She would refuse anyone else, but I know I can get her to listen to me about you. I trust you, even if you can't remember me. Besides, you always had knowledge about weapons in the past—that has to mean something."

"I'm not sure I can lift a weapon at the moment." He paused. "But I'll see."

Silver took that as a yes and relaxed.

"This doesn't belong to me." His hand was at his chest, over his heart, his long fingers seeming to thrum in sync with the organ's beat.

"Just because it wasn't yours before doesn't mean it isn't now." She shrugged, taking a deep swallow and forcing herself to smile. Did he hate her? Because all she could think right then, while holding his gaze, was how much she loved him. "Rest and let your body learn itself while you sleep. Goodnight."

He didn't say it back. He *always* said it back.

Silver's shoulders slumped and she fought back tears as she left the room. An ache formed in her chest—she was truly a stranger to him now.

TWO

AFTON

Afton relished in the bloodshed of her enemies, especially
when she was provoked. King Thorin's guards had reached for
her with chains, knowing good and well what she and her sister
were capable of. Perhaps they hadn't believed the rumors.
Perhaps they didn't know the magic she could conjure inside
the castle walls was more potent than anywhere else. Perhaps
they had been fools. All of them.

The guards had been silent when they arrived with the note
from their king in hand. Shani—one of her outside guards—
had brought her the envelope, and Afton then granted them
entry into the meeting room. Before, she hadn't allowed it, but
she was growing tired of receiving these letters from Thorin.

Afton peered at the light green color of her dress, now
ruined by crimson speckles. Such a shame. It was an exquisite
gown, after all, the way the material swished around her and
hugged her curves. Her wardrobe was filled with others just as
bold, just as beautifully deadly.

One of the servants had already unlaced her gown and left
Afton to herself. She peeled the silky material from her body,
letting it pool to the floor before stepping into the tub. The
water's warmth lit up her skin as she lowered herself inch by

inch into its depths, the liquid caressing every part of her body. In that moment, she wanted to explore herself, press her hands between her thighs, rid herself of the stress from earlier. What if she hadn't been at the castle? What if the guards had gotten to her sister? Silver was as strong as Afton, but she still could have been hurt—or worse, *killed*. She couldn't focus on relieving herself while her thoughts continued to turn to Enare.

King Thorin would remain an issue. The territories were separate for a reason, but that didn't stop Enare's villagers from slinking into Ketill and stirring up problems. They'd been a direct threat, yet now their bones resided with the growing collection in the tunnel. Chance after chance had been given, but after today, she knew it wouldn't end unless she did something more drastic.

Afton didn't know much about the newly-crowned king who had stepped into his father's role six months ago. Thorin's father had been a tyrant, and based on today, his son had taken after him. If the king wanted to woo her, he should have come himself and attempted to talk to her, not send letter after letter insisting that she travel there. Today had been more of a demand. And if anyone was going to make demands, it would be her.

The truth was nothing could tempt her toward Thorin because her heart already belonged to another. Ragan. He'd staked a claim on the organ and had somehow pierced past the layers, lightening the darkness within her. Yet, she couldn't avoid Thorin any longer.

Shaking away the anger coursing through her, Afton grabbed the vanilla soap bar and scrubbed herself clean. If Thorin wanted a betrothed, then he would get one. One who would rip him apart, remove his head, hands, and feet, then take over his territory. And not because she was a greedy monster, but because his territory had been in ruins for far too long. It was why some of the villagers were the way they were. Once she gained control, she would rebuild Enare.

By joining the two clans, Thorin would want Afton's territory for himself. That would never happen—it would only lead to the destruction of her people. As for the other surrounding territories, they could do as they damn well pleased—provided they remained on their own turf.

Reaching for her dagger, Afton picked and cleaned the debris from her nails. She sighed as she peered down at the clash between red blood and white soap, life and death entwined, swirling around her.

There wasn't time for her to relax, not when her body was still humming with energy. What she needed was to find a true escape. There wouldn't be time for a long interlude, since she had to follow through with her plan the following day. But it would be enough.

Afton needed to find Ragan now. When the spark between them had begun, she didn't love him—she'd never fallen for any of her past lovers. Before, Afton had always believed that to love was to yield, and she'd never wanted to yield. She'd wanted to loathe it, wanted to deny it, call it weak. Yet she'd chosen to give in. And she couldn't stop their first meeting from rising to the surface.

Silver stood chatting with a man whose back was turned to Afton. He was tall, broad, his brown hair pulled back with a leather strap. Her body heated just from looking at his backside, then she realized what he was. A stranger in her kitchens, with her sister.

"Who's this?" Afton asked, her tone clipped.

"His name's Ragan." Silver beamed, waving Afton closer. "Jeanette brought him here for us to meet, to see about him taking over some of her shifts in the kitchens."

The man turned to look at her, and Afton blinked. His face was one of the prettiest she'd ever seen. Strong jaw, defined lines and angles, long lashes above deep brown eyes.

"You must be Afton," Ragan said, his voice low and deep. She scowled at his easy use of her name.

"What do you think?" Silver grinned.

Afton thought that perhaps he should leave and never return. Instead, she asked, "Can you make tarts?" Anyone who worked there needed to know how to bake them for her sister. Silver wouldn't have cared, but Afton did.

"I can make anything you want." His lips tilted up, his eyes not lifting from hers.

"Then start now, and I'll come back to try them later. If they suit our tastes, then you can stay." She whirled around and trudged toward the front of the castle, refusing to glance back, before she invited him to her bed. He might be pretty enough to take for the night, but that would be all.

Afton had been so wrong about that… Those damn tarts had led much farther than she ever would have expected.

For now, she would have his naked skin against hers before returning to her duties. Throwing on another gown with a plunging neckline and a slit on one side of the skirts—this time red to go with the bloody theme of her day—Afton headed out of her room. Her boots dug into the plush carpet as she walked past the rows of statues, ones that Afton had made Silver hide behind when their parents' moods would take an even darker turn.

She brushed off the familiar fury that still rose in her chest when thinking of her parents. Afton grasped the wooden handrail while descending the onyx staircase to the wide sitting room below. New silk pillows decorated the purple velvet settee, and not a speck of dust covered the marble floors or any of the decorations.

The clanging of metal reverberated through the walls near the bottom of the stairs. She already knew it was Javan in the weapons room. He grated on her nerves, ever since she was a small child. Because he had done *nothing*, while her parents had done *everything*. And the everything her parents had done to her and Silver didn't have an ounce of goodness hidden within. Deep down, a minuscule part of her knew Javan had tried to do better once Afton murdered her parents. Though she had never forgiven him, and never would, she couldn't kill him either. Silver loved him too much. Besides, he'd proven his loyalty to the two of them time and again.

Afton lifted her chin, picked up her skirts, and kept her footsteps light as she walked past the weapons room. She was certain Javan wouldn't want to follow her to see where she was going.

The energy from the earth strummed a fast and furious song within her, the magic practically yelling at her as the wax churned upstairs. Her digits twitched, wanting to draw it in, and she extended her claws, then retracted them, to calm it. The magic quieted while she walked down the narrow hall, once covered in the past royals' portraits. Now they stood bare—she'd burned the paintings, destroyed the faces of the queens and kings who had been no better than her parents.

Afton itched for her mace, but she'd left it behind in her room. Her fingers brushed the dagger hidden in the secret pocket of her dress. With a smile, she ran her sharp nails across the wall to signal Ragan. A shuffling came from the kitchens, and she knew he was in tune to her every movement.

As she rounded the corner, her hand dropped from the wall, and she sauntered into the wide space. The scent of roasted meat and buttery rolls filled the air. Copper pans hung across one of the walls, and white powder covered several of the gray stone countertops. Ragan stood in front of the stove with his back turned—he didn't even glance behind him when she neared. Afton's heart swelled as she folded her hand around his neck and pressed her nails to his skin, digging in, but not deep enough to draw blood, just right where he liked it.

She couldn't pinpoint when and how her feelings for him had changed. Perhaps it was while sitting beside him on his porch out in the woods as they gazed up at the merciless stars. Or maybe it was how he'd never once asked her why she hadn't kissed him on the mouth. Yet she had pressed her lips both ferociously and tenderly to every other inch of his flesh. It may have even been his lack of fear for the darkness of her heart, for he knew what she'd done to her parents, her enemies.

"Hello, Afton," Ragan rasped.

"Hello, Ragan," she whispered in his ear and removed her fingernails.

"I've been thinking about you all day." His movements were swift, lifting her so fast that he already had her seated on the counter with his strong body positioned between her legs. White flour coated the front of his apron, and flecks of it had gathered on her dress from the counter.

A brown lock of hair had escaped the leather tie he always wore, and she swiped the strands behind his ear. Her body heated as his piercing gaze locked on hers—those eyes were what had first drawn her in. Not the shade, it wouldn't have mattered the color, but the intensity, the loneliness— something she'd wanted to unravel. And then she'd wished to stay instead of leave.

"Did you request hearts on this fine evening?" he asked silkily, his lips pressing soft kisses to her neck.

She reclined her head back to give him better access as she drew him in closer by the waistband of his pants. "Is that all you have for me?"

His mouth left her flesh and he stepped back, making her viciously desperate for his warmth to return. He moved toward the stove, where two cooked organs rested on top of a tray, though there should have been three... But she wouldn't question Javan now, not when flames were licking across her body with a sharpening need for Ragan.

Scooping the hearts up, he plopped them on a plate and handed the organs to her. The brown outer layers looked positively delicious, not a hint of rawness in sight.

"I suppose I'll share one with you." She smirked, lifting the warm meat to her lips and taking a bite. As the piece slid down her throat, magic shook within her, hard, fierce, like an earthquake about to shatter the ground. *Perfect.*

Afton held the organ toward Ragan, and he smiled as his teeth sank into it. She set the meat back on the plate and placed her hands on Ragan's back.

"Do I want to know how you obtained these?" He grinned while chewing.

"I'll tell you the story after."

"After what?" Ragan leaned forward, his eyes on hers.

"This." Afton tugged his hips toward hers and pressed her lips to the center of his throat—the same place where her nails had dug in earlier.

"Then let's not waste time," he groaned, his length hardening deliciously against her.

She still didn't allow her lips to caress his mouth as she skated them behind his ear, then under his jaw. Even though she'd never kissed a single lover, she yearned to do it with him. She would give him her first kiss eventually, but not today.

Ignoring that want—that *need*—she unbuckled his pants. Her fingers trailed down his lower stomach, then slipped beneath his waistband, so close to touching his hardness.

A loud clatter sounded, making Afton protectively push Ragan to the side to look past him. Her claws extended, her hidden teeth lowering. Shani stood frozen, staring at her, with her gray eyes as wide as saucers. Afton's gaze drifted to the two metal trays on the floor.

She hopped from the counter—any heat burning through her extinguished.

Ragan groaned, knowing he would need to get back to work. "Later? In the gardens?"

Afton wanted to—was about to say fuck it all—yet she needed to remain focused. "I've got some business I'll have to take care of for a few days, but after that? I'll do anything you want in the garden. And perhaps, I may confess to you more of my secrets if you tell me more of yours."

His gaze pinned to hers, the edges of his lips tilting upward. "I like that idea."

She turned to Shani, who had scooped up the trays. "You're lucky you walked in when we were still dressed."

Shani's face flushed against her brown skin. Afton chuckled and headed back to her room.

Throwing open her door, she grabbed the trunk from beneath her bed and packed it with a couple simple dresses. As soon as the sun rose in the morning, she would leave Ketill.

First, as the world grew dark, Afton needed to stop by the cottage outside the castle for a few supplies. The idea brewing inside her head was better than any she'd had in a long time. But she couldn't execute this plan on her own—it would require her sister. Afton hated asking Silver for help when it could put her in danger.

For this, though, it was necessary.

THREE

SILVER

As Silver left the castle, cool air stirred around her, disheveling her hair. She wiped at her eyes—perhaps a little too roughly. Keelen wasn't the same, yet she trusted him with her whole heart. His memory had to be buried somewhere within himself.

Afton deserved the same protection she'd gotten from Javan for the last twelve years. Besides their parents, there had been several incidents in the past that proved people couldn't be trustworthy. Her parents' old guards had attempted to murder Afton within her first month as queen. Javan, Silver, and Afton had ended them together. The bones of those guards still resided in the tunnel below the castle. After that, Afton refused to keep any other personal guard except for Javan.

To all of Ketill, Silver was the younger sister, the one with the scarring. And it didn't matter—she wore her scars proudly.

Like her sister, she had a dark side—everyone did, whether it remained hidden or not—and hers would often surface when she caught wind of someone spreading lies about Afton. Sometimes, she would incite rumors about the gossiper. Silver had no qualms about doing so—she would always protect her sister.

The setting sun illuminated the cobblestone path, catching brighter on the steps leading down to the meadow. Silver descended them and peered out at the field, blooming with ivory edelweiss flowers aglow in the fading light. The sweet scent they gave off drifted past her with the gust of the wind.

Midnight would be waiting for her in the meadow. He always waited for her. His onyx hair and knowing dark eyes shone brilliantly under the pale hues of remaining light as she spotted him.

His gaze met hers then, yearning for the same thing she did.

Silver rushed to his side and hopped atop his firm and steady back. "The sun's going down," she whispered, stroking his head, "so are you ready for our gallop beneath the moon?"

In understanding, Midnight let out a whinny and threw his head back.

She laughed, lacing his mane with her fingers and holding tight as he lunged into a canter, the cool wind dancing through her hair. When Javan had given Midnight to her as a child, it was one of the happiest days of her life. Midnight had been so small then, frail and underfed, but she'd nursed him to health with Javan's help.

The entrancing woodsy scent of the outdoors enveloped her as Midnight stomped his hooves against the grass, skirting around the edelweiss. Out of all the horses in the stables, Midnight was still her favorite. He would roam around the castle on his own, never once choosing to flee. Midnight's hair appeared pure obsidian in the darkness, allowing him to practically become night itself. All he needed were specks of stars sewn into his coat to resemble a night sky.

As she rode her horse beneath the silvery moon, its light casting shadows across the field, she thought about Keelen resting in the palace. He was patient, kind, funny—at least the one she knew before was. And even though she hadn't known what his true face looked like, she'd loved him anyway. She still did…

A strange feeling washed over Silver as she thought about where things could lead while Keelen was Afton's guard—his new lips brushing against her sister's, him kissing down her throat, his hand drifting higher and higher up her thigh. With a tug of his mane, Midnight came to an immediate stop, a soft neigh his only protest.

"Enough," she told herself, pressing her eyes tightly shut. "Enough. Enough. Enough." What in all the spirits was wrong with her? Afton was in love with Ragan. "Stop being a fool. He's been in his body for less than a day." Perhaps it was a sign, telling her to go and discuss him with Afton.

Blowing out a breath, she was almost certain that Afton had bathed, gone to Ragan, and was back in her room, possibly writing in her diary. That was how well she knew her sister.

Silver's body shivered against the cool night air, a sudden gust of wind lifting her thin gown around her legs. Hopping off Midnight's back with one swift movement, she led him into the stables where Shani was pouring small buckets of water into the troughs.

Shani glanced over her shoulder, her long dark braid falling to her waist, and smiled. She mouthed a "hello" while Midnight trotted to his trough to drink.

"You're working late," Silver said. "Go relax for the evening."

Shani batted her away and released a silent chuckle. After Silver's parents removed Shani's tongue, and took away her vocal cords by forcing a concoction down her throat, no words could be heard from her any longer. Even now, Silver shuddered at the thought of how Shani must have felt as her tongue was yanked forward and sliced clean off.

Giving her one last smile, Silver headed back toward the castle. She passed through the entrance, the high vaulted ceiling with its sparkling black chandeliers above her. A hint of honey hit her senses, and her stomach twitched at the sweet delectable aroma.

One quick stop first.

Silver padded her boots against the marble floor to the kitchens, where she found Ragan topping off pastries with golden honey. And appearing … a bit rumpled. His chestnut hair was still pulled back into his leather strap but several locks were loose. She rolled her eyes.

"Did you at least wash your hands?" she asked, snatching a tart from a ceramic plate. Not that it mattered what his answer would be as she shoved the sugary dessert into her mouth. She practically salivated while chewing the treat.

"Unfortunately, that wasn't necessary." He smiled, his shoulder nudging hers. Silver never would have guessed her sister could fall for anyone, not until Ragan. She knew he'd loved Afton early on—it was in the way his eyes followed her sister, the way he chewed on his lower lip while studying her, the way his fingers rubbed against one another when she stood close.

Silver wondered what that would be like, having someone love her back equally… Besides her sister. But that was a different sort of love.

She then thought of Keelen. A raven… Now a man…

Taking a deep swallow, Silver's heart beat wildly in her chest. She grabbed another tart, then another and another. No one could control who their heart would beat for, the blasted organ would do as it wished.

As she peered up at Ragan, she thought again about him and Afton, knowing he hadn't told her sister the words. Silver placed a hand to Ragan's face, his warm cheek dotted with flour. "Confess to her all you feel," she said gently. "Your heart deserves to hear her words in return."

"Perhaps I'm waiting for her to tell me first." He smiled again and handed her another tart. "One for the journey to your room."

"You know I can't refuse that." She bit into the dessert and wandered out of the kitchens toward Afton's room instead. Her sister would never eat sweets, not even when they were younger and Silver had tried to share.

"You know not to take those," Afton whispered.

"Just try one." Silver shoved the blueberry tart forward.

"No." Afton gently moved Silver's small hand from her face, then her voice came out softer. *"You eat them, Silver. And bring the dolls with you. Hide them before our parents take those away too."*

Silver would try and sneak her dolls into Afton's room to play, but her sister would only sit and watch, as if staying alert to protect them. The dolls were made from hay or weeds since neither were allowed to have such *nonsense*. Most of the time, their parents kept her and Afton separated, trying to prevent them from bonding, always pitting them against each other. None of it worked. After Afton finally found a way to murder them, she had already become more of an adult than anyone in the castle.

At night, Silver would look up at the stars which studied her in return. She'd realized that while a bit of darkness existed in everyone, the glistening diamonds were the true merciless ones because they remained up there watching and doing nothing as people suffered. In one of her favorite dark tales, the stars didn't belong to the people of her world—they belonged to another realm known as Valgmyr, where a single villainous king ruled, awaiting his perfect match, while bringing destruction on each person who entered his kingdom.

One night after gazing up at the stars, Silver had decided to dip into the darkest part of the magic within the wax to create a live raven by placing pebbles inside. It was a shot in the dark, but it had worked. On subsequent tries she'd used leaves or animal hearts. She'd seen her parents utilize these things when they conjured black magic, though they'd never brought something to life. Silver had somehow known she could control the darkness, that she wouldn't become what her parents had. And although her spell worked, it had always been temporary. She supposed Keelen's memories were temporary too.

As a raven, she remembered the way Keelen's waxy skin felt against her fingertips and the stories he told her. She'd never introduced him to Afton, fearful that her sister wouldn't allow her to use the wax anymore if she discovered what kind of darkness Silver had used to give him life.

Now, running her hands down the skirts of her dress, she noticed the mud caked along the hem. Silver ignored the brown stains and knocked on Afton's door. A rustle came from inside before the door swung open.

"*What?*" Afton's blonde hair was pulled back in an erratic knot on top of her head. Her stiffened shoulders relaxed. "Oh, it's you. I thought you were Javan."

Silver pressed her hand to the door and pushed it open the remainder of the way. "Oh, hello, Afton, fancy finding you here." She bit the inside of her cheek and smiled. "I come bearing gifts."

Afton cocked her head and blinked several times, appearing skeptical while studying Silver's palms. "Your hands are empty."

"To be clearer, it's in another room." Her heart slammed against her rib cage, as if telling her to stop. A part of her still feared that Afton might do something to Keelen since Silver had brought him there with dark magic. But she was older now and she would make her sister understand.

Afton's dark brows lowered and she shook her head. "That can wait. I was actually going to come looking for you." She tugged her hair free of the tie and started to braid the front while leaving a sheet of it hanging in the back.

Stepping away from the door, Silver waved her sister to follow. "I need to show you this first. Trust me, it's important."

"You're acting strange." Afton gritted her teeth. "Besides,

the things you say are important rarely are."

"It's not food." Silver sighed and smiled. "Just come on. It won't take long."

Afton rolled her gaze to the ceiling but followed Silver down the halls to Keelen's room. One of the servants was dusting the statues and iron butterflies on the wall.

Pressing her fingertips against the metal handle, Silver peered over her shoulder. "Try not to get angry. Your study got incredibly messy, but it should be all clean now."

Afton's brow remained furrowed and her lips pursed as though she was ready to start removing heads, appendages, and hearts from someone.

At least it wouldn't be Silver's.

As she opened the door, Silver's heart accelerated, and she wished she could make it stop. Her duty tonight was to arrange fate, not think about herself.

"I have a guest here," Silver whispered.

Afton's gaze scanned the dusty room before settling on Keelen's sleeping frame, her nose wrinkling upward. Silver scanned his pale skin, defined chin, strong nose. He was just as beautiful as when she'd last seen him. Silver wondered what it would be like to bed him, what kind of lover he would be, and the thought caused her cheeks to heat. There had never been a time where Silver had lain naked with anyone. She would rather tear the life from an enemy using her teeth and claws than be with some of the males in Ketill. Yet she'd always been curious, so she'd kissed a few, but nothing had gone much farther.

Silence gripped the room. Afton tapped her foot, waiting for Silver to continue.

Before Silver could shatter the quiet, Afton yanked her out into the hall by the arm. The only other sound besides the air slipping out of Afton's flaring nostrils was Keelen's soft snoring.

"What is this?" Afton asked, not bothering to keep her

voice low. "You show me a man in a bed as though I've never seen one before?"

Silver placed her hands on Afton's shoulders. "He'll be your new guard. Your weapon."

With a scoff, Afton shrugged out of Silver's loose grasp and glanced back into the room. "*Mine*? My mace, my hands, and my teeth have done well enough over the years. Besides, I already have Javan."

"Javan isn't going to be around forever."

Afton ran a hand across her brow and squeezed the bridge of her nose. "Where did you pick up this vagrant? Or did you get him from a pleasure house?"

"No, I didn't go there. I made his body from the wax and used organs from one of the dead guards… And brought his soul here…" she breathed, taking a step back.

Silver watched as Afton's eyes became the thinnest of slits—she knew that look all too well. The vein along her sister's neck beat like a drum.

Moment after long moment passed before Afton finally spoke through clenched teeth. "You didn't just conjure with the land's magic, did you?" Her dark irises expanded, swallowing the white outer layer, making her eyes almost entirely black. "You dipped into dark magic, am I correct?"

Silver didn't hold an ounce of fear, even though Afton had never used the hard, icy stare on her before. Afton had never once, on her own accord, hurt Silver. Only when their parents had forced her. After their parents died, Afton never raised a hand to her again.

If it were anyone else besides Silver, Afton would have used her teeth to bite through their throat, then snap their spine to remove their head and yank out their skeleton. This was strictly forbidden. Dark magic could lead to losing oneself forever. Silver was always careful, though, and she couldn't explain it, but she was somehow able to weave through the menacing parts that wanted to latch onto her.

"As I told Javan"—Silver straightened so she was as tall as her sister, staring her straight in the eyes—"it's not dark with me. It's never been dark."

"So you're telling me this isn't your first time! That *you've* done this *before?*" Afton seethed, the walls around them vibrating from the stirring in the magic she'd summoned. "Silver, I should rip your head and appendages from your body right now, or I should take you to the dungeon. Have you even thought about where you pulled his soul from?"

"I took it from Torlarah," she said slowly, trying not to wince as the magic pulsed harder, seeming to bend the walls. "And I promise you, he isn't evil. He doesn't remember me this time, but I've brought him here again and again in raven form with the wax."

"That doesn't mean anything!" Afton snapped. "Torlarah doesn't just have good, Silver. *Everyone* goes there once they die." She rested her head against the wall, biting her lip to the point where a drop of blood blossomed to the surface.

Her sister was right, but Silver could feel his heart each time she roused Keelen. It wasn't a tarnished one. There was hurt in there but not hate. "Please, be with me on this. He's my friend, and I trust him as much as I do you."

Afton exhaled loudly, relenting, the strength of the magic lessening around them. "This isn't the end of the conversation. But I have a more important matter at hand at the moment. I have a demand."

"All right." Silver arched a brow, her interest piqued. Perhaps Afton wanted her to kill more enemy guards, go out and hunt with her hands for a wild beast's heart, decorate the tunnel with the skulls and bones resting there.

"Two things actually," Afton started. "First, I need you to come with me now. Next, you will accompany me to meet King Thorin very soon."

Silver pursed her lips. "You don't plan on actually following through with marrying the toad, do you?" She assumed Afton would go to the kingdom, kill him, and be done with it.

"How dare you speak about my future betrothed like that?" A wicked grin—with her teeth bared, the second sharp set lowering—spread across Afton's face. "When we arrive to see King Thorin, I'm going to need my sister to pretend to be me."

FOUR

KEELEN

Rustling stirred outside Keelen's room, and he immediately recognized Silver's high-pitched voice, followed by another female with a deeper tone. Then came silence, the voices gone. It might have been her sister Afton. He hadn't met her yet—wasn't sure if he really cared to. Even though he'd sort of agreed to guard her. But what the fuck did he know about weapons or protecting someone? Silver seemed to think he could, though.

Pulling himself forward to a sitting position, Keelen stared toward the ceiling at the hanging chandelier lit with eight bright flaming candles. If he was still wax, the flames could have easily licked away his flesh. Fuck, they could still do that now. Leaning against the headboard, he tapped his fingers together. It was a squishy sort of feeling compared to his old waxy skin—his last death came to mind. Keelen's peach wings had melted first while he was flying indoors somewhere, the rest of his body following suit, breaking apart and turning to liquid. He'd never once had hands in any of his wax raven lives.

Silver had said she'd drawn him out from Torlarah—he couldn't remember that. Or his past human life. None of it.

Including Silver. Not her tangled, long dark hair, not her wholly black wide eyes, or her pale skin, or her full red lips, not the raised scar on her upper chest. Crimson had coated her clothing and skin, but he hadn't questioned it. All he'd been able to focus on was his new form.

And her face...

Keelen tried to recall past conversations between them. She'd said they'd been friends since they were younger. Perhaps she was lying. He knew he was twenty-two and if she'd pulled him from Torlarah, then how could he age and not remain the same as always? Unless by bringing him here, he aged as though he were still alive? It didn't make a lick of sense.

He was supposed to be resting, wasn't he? She didn't really say, but he wasn't the least bit tired anymore. His body was no longer weak. The room around him was spacious, decorated with two wardrobe cabinets and four paintings of gnarled and twisted trees hanging on the walls, each one depicting a different season. Colorful flowers for spring. Luscious green for summer. Dying and changing leaves for fall. Ivory snow for winter. How could he know this world and its seasons but not *everything*?

Pressing a hand to his smooth chest, Keelen felt his heart pump against his palm, beneath flesh and bone. The bloody thing within his rib cage hadn't truly been his, but someone else's, before Silver had inserted it, as if she'd been playing at being one of the gods. None of it belonged to him—not his eyes, not his organs, not his flesh, only the barely-there memories. A darker question tugged at his mind: were his thoughts really even his? He shook that off. They *had* to be.

Inhaling, he took in a lingering scent of not only the blood, but roses—Silver. The metal odor had overpowered the flowery scent, but he'd smelled it beneath the scarlet.

Keelen leaned forward, stretched his arms, and wiggled his toes—he preferred this body over a raven's. It was easy to move, to grasp things, to do almost anything he wanted. Except fly.

Movement from the wall drew his attention. A shiny blue and green circular object with six fluttering legs—a beetle. Keelen's tongue rubbed the roof of his mouth before licking his lips—he was still famished. With one swift motion, he leapt from the bed, his feet thumping across the floor. Leaving the insect no time to escape, he scooped it up in his palm and dropped it into his mouth. The *crunch crunch* echoed within his skull. He closed his eyes and sighed at the delicacy, the saltiness, the crispy zing of its taste. This was no comparison to the exceptional meal from earlier, but it was better than nothing. There was something familiar about the insect, as if he remembered plucking them up with his beak, but the memory remained locked away, the key hidden.

"You'll remember, Keelen," he said to himself. *Keelen*. It was the name Silver had given him, and he … liked it.

He peered down at himself—a too-tight tunic and too-long trousers. It was as if the damn pants were meant for a giant. With rhythmic motions, he tapped all his new digits against his cheek. "To stay, or not to stay." He wouldn't remain in this cage of a room—he would go seek out Silver, demand answers.

Keelen thought of Silver and her smiles... Her wide eyes watching him… *Forget that*. Silver was out of the question, and he resolved to explore the castle instead.

Keeping quiet, he pulled open the door. *Creak*. He jumped back and cursed under his breath at the door. Each time he tugged the fucking thing open little by little, it made that same blasted sound. There was no point in continuing this nonsense, so he ripped it the remainder of the way open and stepped out into the hallway. He looked both ways, hoping Silver wasn't lingering around, but the hall was empty.

As he walked down the corridor, Keelen studied the blue statues with their eyeless and bare faces, their strange curving poses. His pants brushed the carpet, and if he could cut the trousers with his teeth, he would.

Keelen turned down the next hallway and struck a hard body. They were the same height and build, but deep lines creased the man's face, and one of his hands gripped a cane.

Javan.

"And just what do you think you're doing?" Javan asked, his hazel eyes glaring. Before Keelen could step back, Javan's hand wrapped around his shoulder, his strong fingers pressing in. A combination of tobacco and old leather wafted up from the older man. His graying hair was carefully slicked back— all nice and tidy now. "Silver just left you?"

"I'm only having a look around," Keelen said. He wrenched his shoulder from Javan's firm grasp and leaned against the wall.

"No, you're not," he snapped, yanking him back. "And stay off the walls."

The vein in Javan's neck pulsed. Keelen arched a brow when something inside his chest seemed to swell and writhe, as though there was a dormant energy resting there, now coming alive. He tried to recognize what it was, yet the anxious feeling swarming through his blood burned it out. Had this happened to him when he was there before?

The rush slowly pulled back, though it didn't completely vanish. It still *tick-tick-ticked* inside him, like a pocket watch declaring time rushing toward something important.

Javan's hard gaze scanned Keelen up and down, not softening in the slightest. "I see Silver didn't dress you properly. Come on then—we need to chat." Turning on his heels, Javan motioned him to follow.

Keelen did so, but stayed cautious. For all he knew, this man wanted him dead. From how he'd acted earlier, it was a strong possibility.

Something small and black floated against the wall in his periphery, like an illusion. A spider, spinning a silky web, crawled with featherlight motions, almost rhythmical, beautiful. All Keelen's previous attention on Javan faded. He inched closer to the wall, a predator going in for the kill. With a swing of his arm, he snatched the spider up, then shoved it into his mouth.

Javan's nose wrinkled in disgust, not missing Keelen's movements. The man held up a finger while Keelen finished chewing and swallowed. "Don't do that again."

"And why not?" Keelen bit his lower lip, skimming his fingertips over the curve of one of the statue's faces.

"Stop that!" Javan knocked Keelen's hand away, as if disciplining a child. "Your behavior is abnormal."

"Is there something wrong with that?" He searched for another spider, but only a few empty cobwebs rested in the corners. Damn.

Grunting, Javan shook his head and continued down the carpeted hall. A tense silence stretched between them. Questions continued to knock at Keelen's skull, so he broke the quiet with an invisible blade. "Do you remember me from before?"

"What? Are you dense?" Javan stopped in front of a door. "Today is the first time I've met you. Have you been here before?" His eyes narrowed, and his hand clenched the head of his cane.

"I don't remember for certain." For some reason, he didn't want to tell him everything Silver had said. A part of him wanted to … protect her? Why?

"Humph." Javan opened the door and entered some sort of study with a narrow space in the back that appeared to adjoin another room. Several clocks made from silver and gold, their metal insides exposed, gears moving in a synchronized mechanical dance, hung on one of the walls. Across from them was an oval mirror—ornamental winged fae framed the glass.

"Sit." Javan pointed to one of the black velvet chairs with glistening silver arms and legs. "What do I call you?"

Keelen didn't take a seat. Swallowing, he tried to stir up his real name. Nothing. Not even a possibility slithered forth. It didn't matter, because for some reason, the one Silver had given him was the one he wanted to keep. "Keelen."

"From what Silver mentioned in the study, she made you to be a guard for Afton." He scanned Keelen up and down, clearly unimpressed. "Do you think you can do that?"

How should he know? For all he knew, he wouldn't even be able to wield a fork. As he thought about thrusting a sword forward, another twitching tugged at his body, the rush of something strong, pressing and crushing. He placed his hand against his ribs, his chest heaving.

"You feel it? The magical current from the earth?" Javan's eyebrows flew up, and he watched him as though trying to see inside him.

"I think so." His voice came out unsure. Was that what he was feeling?

Javan rubbed a hand down his forehead and sighed. "As I'm inspecting you, I don't see how you could protect anyone, regardless of your size or what you're feeling." He shifted forward and lifted Keelen's chin, turning his head with his wrinkled hand. "You look as though you haven't seen a day of sun in your life, you're missing *all* your hair, and I just saw you eat a damn spider in the hallway. Not to mention, your slouch is awful. Straighten your spine, pull back your shoulders."

Keelen rotated his arms forward and backward a few times, then stood tall. But it wasn't enough. Javan placed a hand to Keelen's upper chest and another at his lower back, making his spine pop. Keelen drew in a sharp breath. His posture was now in a perfectly straight position.

Javan removed his hands. Keelen slouched again.

"No!" Javan shouted.

Keelen scowled and straightened once more, holding his breath so his body wouldn't slump again. Then he slowly took breaths while staying in position.

Javan paced in front of Keelen, his arms folded across his chest. "As Afton's guard, I remain straight at all times. You will do the same. When you're eating, when you relieve yourself, when you're sitting." He paused and held Keelen's gaze. "Even when you're sleeping. Understand?"

"Even if I'm with a woman and we're—"

"Don't talk about that with me."

"It was a serious question." Keelen smirked, remaining straight. "Besides, I can't control what I do in my sleep."

Craning his neck, Javan's hardened stare became harder, if that was possible. "Those are the rules."

Keelen didn't like these fucking rules. Then Silver's smiling face slipped into his mind again. And damn it, for whatever reason, something pulled at him to do it for her. Not Afton, not Javan, but Silver. He tried to shut that emotion off, squeeze it until there was nothing, yet he couldn't do it. "I'll think about it."

"You're lucky I didn't slit your throat when I first discovered you. I'm only doing this for Silver, but do know this, any sign of untrustworthiness will end in your blood spilled."

"I'm not here to harm anyone." *Truth.*

Javan took a seat on the edge of his desk and massaged his temples. "So much work to do. What weapons can you use? Do you even *know* what a weapon is?"

Keelen tapped his fingers against his cheeks, recalling, recalling. Still no Silver, but a few images slid forward—him in raven form carrying twigs in his beak and scrawling notes with them dipped in ink. "I know what they are. I'm sure I've held one." Maybe?

"That doesn't count." Javan didn't believe him. "Do you want to go to the weapons room now or in the morning?"

"Now?" Keelen asked, realizing it was late. "You aren't tired?" After the rest Keelen had gotten earlier, he couldn't sleep, not even if he wanted to.

"I haven't slept in a long time," Javan said, opening the door. "And not just because I've been guarding Afton."

Keelen frowned, wondering what he'd meant by that. Since he wasn't going to hunt down a pair of scissors, he rolled up the legs of his trousers and followed Javan.

They descended the long staircase, Keelen's fingers gliding across the ornate wooden handrail. Obsidian chandeliers dangled above the sitting room, and dark purple velvet furniture shimmered in the candlelight. Animal skulls decorated the walls between the flickering flames. The opposite walls displayed paintings of skeletons wielding weapons, kissing, dancing. He arched a brow at them as he rounded the corner to where Javan stood in front of large metal doors with black curving handles. Javan pulled the door open, and Keelen's gaze met a small table and chairs, then nothing but weapons. Weapons everywhere, covering every surface of the towering walls, stacked in corners of the windowless room. Closing his eyes, Keelen breathed in iron, leather, and sweat, the scents at once familiar. He'd seen this room—he knew he had.

Swords, hatchets, chains, maces, mauls, katars, and war hammers hung on the walls. All shapes and sizes. So many options to choose from. So many weapons that could bring an enemy to their knees. His fingers itched to touch each one.

Keelen recalled these weapons, this room, but still couldn't remember hearing Silver's voice or seeing her. He tried to imagine a younger Silver with a rounder face, same dark eyes, smaller stature, and a tinier voice. Nothing.

Javan grabbed a hatchet from one of the walls and handed it to Keelen. "Show me your throwing game."

Across the room stood a wooden monstrous-shaped figure with claws, carved fur, and triangular ears. Keelen rotated the hatchet in between his hands, wondering what the fuck he was supposed to do with it. Training his eyes to where he wanted the weapon to go, he took a deep breath, the thrumming of the earth flowing through him, and he let the hatchet fly. It struck the wooden creature's chest, where its hidden heart would've been.

Apparently I'm damn good with a weapon.

Keelen grinned at Javan. The man didn't say a word, didn't change his neutral expression, as he handed Keelen a dagger next, followed by an iron throwing star, then a bronze chakram. Every weapon hit its mark, right where he'd aimed. He didn't know if it was all him, or if it was from the magic he was somehow drawing in. Either way, he was what Silver had wished him to be. A weapon. The perfect guard.

Taking two more hatchets from the wall, he spun them in his hands and let them soar at the same time. They landed perfectly, directly beside each other in the chest of one of the statues.

Javan pressed his lips into a tight line. "Silver really did use the darkest of magics to create you, didn't she?"

FIVE

SILVER

"**H**urry up!" Afton hissed. "I don't want Javan knowing about this yet."

Javan was trustworthy but if he didn't agree with Afton, he would ask too many questions. Silver never understood why Afton was constantly on edge with him. Perhaps it was the fact he'd worked for their parents first, but he never once defended them after Afton took the crown. He became her guard as though she'd always been his queen, and Silver had known he would be loyal to them and their territory. Even in the past, he wouldn't have been able to defeat their parents if he'd tried, not when he couldn't feel or use magic—the energy they'd used was pure darkness.

Before leaving the upper levels of the castle, Afton had collected her mace, and Silver had strapped one to her own back.

As Afton led her down to the tunnel, Silver regretted not telling Keelen they were leaving. But he'd been asleep, deep in slumber with heavy inhales and slow exhales. She wondered if he was dreaming, dreaming about his past life, dreaming possibly about … her.

Javan would never be pleased about her using dark magic

to conjure Keelen's soul there. That sort of power was a fairytale to most of Ketill. Outside the castle walls, some of the people could draw a little earth magic but nothing like Silver or Afton could do. Once she'd met Keelen, using darker magic had always been worth the risk to bring him back, just as she would do if it had been her sister.

Silver rubbed her hands together to warm them in the cool hallway. "Are you going to tell me what's going on now? You refused to tell me earlier about why you said *I'll* be pretending to be you. After hushing me, as though I'd screamed the words across the territory, you said you would discuss it later. Well, here we are … later." Silver's eyes had almost popped out of her head in surprise over the request. If she had to pretend to be Afton, that would mean seducing Thorin. Seduction was an art form that Silver knew nothing about.

They reached the mouth of the secret tunnel hidden beneath the castle. Afton lit a torch and handed one to Silver. Ignoring her question, she simply lifted her skirts and descended the stone stairs.

"Hmm. Hmm. *Hmm,*" Silver pressed as she followed her sister down the decaying steps. The narrow walls brushed her shoulders as she trekked toward the bottom. Their torches illuminated the darkness, the shadows from the flames dancing along the walls.

"All in due time." Silver could hear the smile in Afton's voice. "Now hush and stop being aggravating." Afton adjusted the mace at her back. The weapon was the same one she always carried, dark gray and encrusted with blue gems around the handle.

Silver hummed an old melody, one that Afton hated, to nudge her sister more. Afton sighed in exasperation, but Silver needed answers. And sometimes pestering her sister as though they were children was the only way.

The thumping of their boots echoed around them, and Afton halted after taking the last step. Silver inched down beside her, the flame of her torch flickering. Afton stood still, seeming to hold her breath, and then she blew out her flame. Silver's torch extinguished at the same time, plunging the two of them into darkness for only a moment before the ones along the walls ignited in bright orange flames, fire bobbing cheerfully atop their metal bodies.

The tunnel reeked of mold and rain from the many times it had flooded. The scurrying of rats, most likely trying to lap up any remains they could find from the skulls and bones piled in the corners, reverberated off the stone. Silver thought of the fresh heads and appendages from their earlier ordeal with Thorin's guards.

As she and Afton traveled farther into the tunnel, more shadows danced across the walls, this time ones of little creatures. Water dripping against stone echoed in the space ahead. With a flick of her wrist, Afton snapped the necks of all the rats, and their bodies collapsed to the ground. Unmoving.

Silence now enveloped Silver, except for the *drip, drip, drip* and the sizzling of the earth's magic flowing through her. Deep below the castle, magic thrummed everywhere around her, synching with the blood pumping through her veins. She wanted to draw it in, spin the energy into something she'd never tried before, then wield it. But she ignored her impulse and instead let it linger inside her.

Silver cocked her head. "Was that really necessary?"

"You know very well all they do is spread disease to our people." Afton rolled her eyes.

"I'm still surprised there are any left to continue breeding."

Afton placed a hand on Silver's shoulder and hauled her back. "You wanted answers? I suppose I'll give them to you now that we're truly alone."

"I'm listening." Silver wiggled out from Afton's grip and set the blown-out torch on the ground. She clasped her palms together, her heart slamming against her rib cage.

"I need your help."

Silver studied her sister's tightened lips. "To pretend to be you."

"Yes, so I can take care of King Thorin. It has to be you. Enare knows we're the only two with eyes like ours. No amount of magic could alter another's to match."

Thorin couldn't be that hard to kill, especially if one was betrothed to him. "I could kill the king just as easily as you." Silver quirked a brow and didn't remove her gaze from Afton. "So what's the point? And who are you pretending to be? Me?"

"Yes. I'm going to be you." Afton's voice lowered. "You're much better at reading people and seeing through their lies. The queen of Ketill can't murder Enare's king. If something goes wrong, well, you will be their queen and would have to continue the charade. I trust you would protect both territories just as I would."

Silver gasped. "Afton, no."

"There's no arguing here. Together, we won't fail."

Silver believed that with her whole heart. Those were the words Afton had always spoken to her, before and after their parents' deaths, to reassure Silver. Together, they were always stronger. But that didn't mean Silver wasn't worried. There was something crucial her sister wasn't considering—the possibility of spies. "No matter how careful you think you've been, someone may still recognize us."

"I've got everything covered if that were to happen. Besides"—Afton smirked—"I don't think you have much experience in seduction."

"You're not wrong about that." Her thoughts turned to Keelen, seeing his naked form—the muscular planes of his chest, and lower, and lower... Maybe her experiences had gone up a notch. Silver wrinkled her nose when she realized something. "You're actually going to tumble Thorin? Does Ragan know about this?" She was completely certain that Ragan would not be all right with any of this, but in the end, it wouldn't be his decision.

"He does not know, and doesn't need to. Neither of us will be required to fuck King Thorin. The engagement will merely serve to get us—me, specifically—close enough to kill him. Out of everyone here, I trust you the most with this."

"I trust you, too."

"Now, I want to see you pretend to be me," Afton said. "Put on a little of your … charm."

"Is that what you think I have?" Silver laughed softly. "Charm? Or a better word might be charisma?"

Afton batted a hand in the air. "Be regal, but not too distant, or else Thorin might know we're setting him up. I'm sure he's heard rumors of the 'Ice Queen.'" The other territories believed that, but Ketill knew Afton was nothing but generous to her people—unless they made an enemy of her. But over the years, not many had caused problems.

"So, what are we to do?" Silver's shoulders relaxed, knowing she wouldn't need to spread her legs for the king. As for Afton, she said she wouldn't tumble him, but that didn't mean she wouldn't get close. Silver imagined having to kiss a king she'd never seen, yet, in that moment, the only face she could see was the one she'd just created—Keelen's.

"You're going to be more like me, unlikable, but a tad more hospitable." Afton gripped the sides of her head.

"I like you." Is that how Afton saw herself? Unlikable? She could seem distant, but that didn't make her any less fierce and respected.

"I like you too." A smirk crossed Afton's face. Grabbing her mace from her back, she handed the weapon to Silver. "Protect this with your life."

"Do you really think I can pull off impersonating you?" Silver inspected the mace, the weight heavy in her grasp.

"If you think like that, then no."

She knew her sister better than anyone, her movements, the way she spoke, the way she carried herself. "So, you're going to woo the king by pretending to be the queen's sister, then let him have an affair on you … with you. It sounds like the perfect tragic tale."

"One that we'll write together." Afton took the other mace from Silver's back.

"We look different." Silver ran a hand over the scar just below her neck. The mark was something she was proud of. It was a reminder that her sister had defeated their parents to save them. She didn't want to hide it, but she would if she must.

"No, we really don't. It will be almost easy. Thorin doesn't know what either one of us looks like anyway." Afton paused. "Switch hair colors. Don't smile."

"That means *you'll* have to smile," Silver pointed out. "Practice that."

Afton didn't smile, only blinked. "Since we have that settled, we need to go visit Willem for herbs and a few other things to prepare ourselves."

"I wonder if he has any love spells that he can conjure up from the earth," Silver teased.

Afton must have thought she was being serious because her face softened as her gaze remained ahead. "Silver, you don't need magic for someone to love you. You could make anyone fall in love with you if you wanted … just by being you."

Silver's heart swelled in her chest. Afton had never spoken words like that to her. "Is that a compliment?"

"You know I love you." Afton waved her off, then spun on her heels and sauntered away.

Silver chuckled and caught up to her sister while shoving the mace into the strap on her back. "I think you need to let Ragan know. He won't be as angry if you warn him beforehand." Especially if he knew Afton was doing it to save and unite both territories. There was a chance the Enarians would rebel after the king was dead, but under Afton's fair rule, most would want to accept.

With an eyeroll, Afton walked faster down the tunnel, past the gray and white spotted bricks, casting a slight sheen. At the end, where the dark iron gate stood, Silver absorbed the magic of the earth. She let out a hard breath, watching as all the flames lighting their way flickered and died. The wind blew the ends of her hair as Afton unlocked the gate for them to head out into the night.

From the stables, the horses neighed when Silver and Afton approached. Midnight was used to nighttime rides, but not the others. As soon as she slipped in, Midnight inched out from his stall toward her, bowing so she could stroke his mane.

Silver led him outside and hopped onto his back while Afton mounted Ivory—a beautiful white mare with sky blue eyes. Together they sped through the darkness, the hooves of the horses pummeling the ground, as they traveled up the steep hill and across the meadow to the old cottage at the edge of the woods. The moon rested high in the sky, the merciless stars brighter than ever as owls hooted in the distance. Silver wondered if the Valgmyr King from the tale studied their world through the stars, or if they whispered to him of what they saw.

Within the windows of the cottage, the lights were already eclipsed, meaning that Willem either wasn't home or was asleep. Silver bet herself that he was sleeping like a babe atop his hay mattress on the floor in the backroom. He was the one who usually supplied them with their remedies to keep the wax boiling—his were the strongest. Since they would be away from home while at Thorin's, they needed a remedy to add to a jar of wax so they could amplify the magic of the land in Enare, the way they could in their castle.

Afton stepped to the crooked door and banged her fist against it. A few seconds later the entrance swung open—not to Willem's wrinkled face, but his grandson, Aris. As he held up a flickering candle, the flame highlighted his shorn black hair and warm brown skin and eyes. Aris's frown vanished when his gaze settled on Afton, taking stock of her.

"Your Highness," he whispered, a blush creeping up his neck. Silver already knew Afton had taken him as a lover in the past. She'd seen her sister bring him to her room on several occasions, though not since Ragan.

"We need supplies," Afton said in a low voice. "If you mention to anyone we came tonight, I shall remove everyone's head you hold dear and save yours for last."

At his sides, Aris's hands trembled. Silver sighed at Afton's failed attempt at jesting.

"I wasn't serious, Aris." Afton brushed past him into the cottage. "Where's Willem?"

Silver stepped inside and followed Afton to the tilted cabinets against the wall. A string of scents enveloped her— lilac, rosemary, and citrus. The entire space was filled with tables, jars and herbs sprawled across them. Two wooden chairs sat beside a window, small stacks of fabric resting in their seats.

"He traveled to my uncle's cottage for the week." Aris tugged open the cabinets for Afton, then shuffled to the side to give her access. "My uncle hasn't been feeling well."

"I'm sure Willem's remedies will help just fine." Afton sifted through the cabinets, grabbing several glass jars of herbs and blessed pebbles to place in her satchel. "Do you have any barley?"

Silver studied Aris as he watched Afton with open longing. She took a deep swallow, feeling for Aris, but knowing that Afton hadn't ever loved him. He'd known that.

"You should give him extra coin. For it being so late." Silver nudged Afton, wanting to at least provide him *something*.

"Of course. I wasn't planning on just taking things for free." Afton straightened her skirts and glanced at Silver. "Give me a few moments alone while I give him payment."

"You're going to tumble him for this?" Silver whisper-shouted, glancing at Aris on the other side of the room.

"No! Am I a pleasure worker?" Afton spat. "But I do need to discuss a few things with him. *Alone*."

With a nod, she stepped outside to give Afton her privacy. Then Silver did what she always did best, she pressed her ear to the now-closed door and listened to what was said.

SIX

SILVER

Silver had been holding her ear to the door for a while now, listening to Afton and Aris. She twiddled her thumbs, growing more bored by the second with the luke-warm conversation, wondering if she should possibly leave. Aris continued to ask Afton the same questions over and over as if there would be a different answer. There wouldn't be—her sister was in love with Ragan.

Why him instead of me?
What did I do wrong?
Just one last kiss.

Afton finally answered, a hint of irritation lacing her words, "You knew from the beginning what my feelings were and would always be. It's been three months since I told you I would only come for remedies from your grandfather—nothing more. If you still can't handle that, then perhaps you should find somewhere else to stay."

Silver was surprised that Afton hadn't threatened to remove parts from him if he didn't stop with his insistence. Before Ragan, when Afton would pull men into her room, she never looked at them like she was in love. It was as if she was in her own world, thinking about something else, and loathing it. More of a vicious and chaotic frenzy instead of a lovely dance.

Aris finally ceased his miserable begging, the conversation taking a turn to the herbs for the amplifier. Silver wasn't invited back in, so she decided to return to the castle to let Afton finish with the supplies. Midnight took a few steps toward her and lowered himself to the damp grass for her to mount his back.

Threading her fingers into his dark mane, she whispered, "Ride as fast as you can."

His ears perked up and he jolted for the castle, causing her to lean forward and grip him tighter. The wind sliced through her hair and caressed her flesh. Silver stopped thinking and stared up at the constellations of stars. She wondered about them, how they still watched. They were always the merciless ones—doing nothing. Supposedly when a loved one was meant to return with unfinished business after leaving this world, the stars would bring them back in a raven form. That was one of the reasons she'd continued to shape Keelen into a raven. Because he still had a life to live here.

Midnight's gallop turned to a slow gait as they approached the stables. Silver thought about having him turn around and ride through the night a while longer, but she needed to mull over what Afton had discussed with her. She would need to pretend to be the queen and parade around as her. Afton would sway King Thorin in her direction, which would be an easy task for her sister. Silver didn't know much about Thorin, but she believed in her sister's abilities.

She hopped down from Midnight. He released heavy snorting breaths through his nostrils as he pranced into the barn. Grabbing the wooden bucket in the corner, Silver scooped clean water from a larger barrel and poured it into Midnight's dwindling trough before making her way to the castle.

Afton would most likely enter back in through the tunnel

to avoid Javan, but Silver had no reason to hide since it was her usual practice to go riding at night.

Walking inside, she considered waiting for Afton in her room, but as she took her first step onto the staircase, a loud *thwack* echoed from the weapons area. She came to an abrupt stop and craned her neck to peer through the cracked door. Two muffled male voices sounded, accompanied by shuffling—Javan wasn't alone. He was always alone in there at this late hour.

Her gaze slid up the staircase then back to the weapons room. Tapping her chin, she had a very good inkling about who might be with Javan.

Silver pushed off the handrail and opened the cracked door wider, finding Javan pristinely put together and seated in a chair with one leg crossed over the other, watching … Keelen. Taking a deep swallow, Silver studied Keelen's back, then the dagger in his fist as he threw it. Her lips parted when the weapon struck the wooden figure directly in the chest.

She'd been right that he would know weapons, but he was better than she could have dreamed.

Trying to appear casual by relaxing her shoulders, even though her heart thundered in her chest, Silver slipped into the room. She peered at Javan, whose eyes were fluttering open and closed. His cane was propped against his leg. "You should go to bed." She smiled at him warmly.

He blinked a few times, straightening in his seat. "I was just resting."

"How did Keelen end up in here?" She sank down in a chair across from Javan.

"I found him out roaming the halls, where he ate a spider..." He shook his head, his lip curling upward.

"Hmm." Not surprised, her smile widened. Even in raven form, he'd scavenged them and other insects over the years.

"Never mind." He wrinkled his nose in disgust. "Can you help him back to his room when he's ready? I'm only doing this for you, putting my trust in your decision.”

“Sure. Thank you, Javan.” If it had been anyone besides her or Afton bringing forth a soul into a new body using dark magic, Javan would have already cut them down. She didn’t tell him she was waiting for Afton to return because then he would remain and ask questions. Afton would want to spring her plan on him when she was ready.

As she twisted in her seat, Silver’s eyes locked on Keelen heaving a hatchet. He then strode across the room, her gaze lowering down his body, and she couldn’t help noticing the way his pants perfectly hugged his backside. Keelen ripped his weapon free from the figure and went to hurl it again. Since she’d been in the weapons room, he hadn’t once glanced back at her, even though she knew he had to have heard her voice. Her heart tightened at that, and she tried to ignore it.

“He’s quite good,” she finally said, turning back to Javan.

“Too good if you ask me.” Javan stood from his chair and let out a yawn, eyeing Keelen. “I still think there’s a chance his soul is tainted.”

“Are you still worried about the dark magic?” Silver asked, gnawing at her lip. “Good souls go to Torlarah, too.”

“I know.” He sighed, leaning on his cane. “I’m only worried about King Thorin.” He would be more worried once he discovered Afton’s plan, a plan he’d find out about in due time.

“It will be fine.” She shrugged, not removing her gaze from Keelen.

“Why do you keep watching him?” Javan asked, a scowl forming on his face.

“Just making sure he’s ready to protect Afton at all costs.” She smiled at him, hoping she looked innocent.

“Afton’s mood was different today.”

“She has a lot to think about. I do believe under that beautiful dark heart of hers she cares about you, Javan.”

“Oh no, she certainly hates me. But not you—she could

never hate you. And possibly … the boy in the kitchens."

Silver wasn't the only one who had noticed the change in Afton around Ragan, the way she seemed freer at times.

"Goodnight, Javan," she said as he stood from his seat.

"Goodnight." He patted the top of her head like he did when she was a child, then lifted his cane and walked out the door, closing it behind him.

Holding her breath, she waited for Keelen to say *something* because he was always the first to speak. Apparently, not anymore. He continued to avoid glancing in her direction. *Fine*. She still had a tongue and could talk first, or shout, which she did. "Remember me yet?"

Keelen tripped over his own feet and caught himself on the wall before he could crash to the floor. He slowly turned his head over his shoulder. "No..."

His violet eyes trailed to the portrait above her. It was one of her and Afton from a few years ago that Javan had requested be painted. Silver sat clothed in a lavender gown and a square neckline, while Afton wore a fitted hunter green dress with sheer lace from shoulders to knuckles, only the tips of her fingers peeking out.

Silver pointed to her sister's painted image. "That's Afton."

Cocking his head, he continued to study the portrait. "You don't look like her."

"Do you wish I looked like her?" Her heart thumped with a loud no, and her brain told it to cease.

"What kind of question is that?" Keelen placed the hatchet on the wall and ran a hand across his bald head.

"What kind of question was that?" Silver threw back at him.

He didn't answer but the edges of his lips twitched.

"So why aren't you in your room?"

"I felt like exploring a bit." His tone sounded distant, so very unlike him.

She sucked in a sharp breath. "All right…"

Darting forward, he gently pushed her legs to the side and swiped at something along the floor with his free hand. Then he placed it into his mouth, chewing. *Crunch. Crunch.*

Her eyes widened and she cupped her hand over her mouth, fighting a smile. "Did you just move me out of the way to eat that spider?"

"Yes." He remained knelt in front of her. Close. Very close. "Perhaps I saved your life from its poison."

"Poor spider." She lowered her hand and grinned. If there weren't the tell-tale signs of who Keelen was, she may have thought she'd collected the wrong soul from Torlarah. But this was very much him.

Keelen furrowed his brow, appearing lost in thought. He still hadn't moved back, and she inhaled a woodsy scent with a hint of jasmine.

She grasped his arm and yanked him from the floor so she wouldn't lean closer into him. "Come on. Let me guide you back to your room." Her gaze connected with the portrait and she tilted her head toward it. "How do you feel about her?"

"*What?*"

"I didn't ask if you were going to marry her." She rolled her eyes. "Guarding her, I mean."

"I don't even know her." Keelen straightened and she released his arm. "But I'll do it, Silver."

"You will? Thank you." She grinned. "You're quite good with weapons. Do you remember anything of your past yet?" *Or me?*

"Not really," he whispered.

With a slow nod while chewing the inside of her cheek, Silver guided Keelen up the staircase toward his room. The silence stretched between them, his gaze fixed straight ahead.

"What's it like to live?" he finally asked as she opened the door to his room.

Silver's eyebrows drew into a caterpillar while she

contemplated his words. Her heart *thump-thumped* within her chest—Keelen had always been inquisitive. "Let me think about it for a moment."

They walked into the bedroom, and he dropped down on the edge of the mattress, lifting his dampened tunic up and over his head in one swift motion. The magic of the earth vibrated all the way to her marrow, along with something else that went straight to her core, as she studied his defined upper torso.

Knowing she was treading on dangerous ground, she still took a seat beside him. "I don't know what everyone in the world lives for, but I live for Afton. She's my queen, my sister, and I would do anything for her."

"Aren't there things *you* want?"

Silver bit her lip, thinking. Two things came to mind. She pushed the one about Keelen remembering her aside. "For Afton to always succeed."

"Hypothetical question—what if Afton didn't exist?" He tilted his head, a mannerism that was already growing familiar to her.

"Yet she does."

His violet gaze locked on hers. "If she didn't?"

"Why would you ask this?"

"I'm wondering what your answer would be. One that doesn't involve Afton." He peered at her for a long moment as if trying to read her.

Fine. She would play the game. Closing her eyes, she thought about being alone, without anyone. Images of the Valgmyr story that she'd read over and over as a child flooded her mind. Images of the king—a male with curled horns and gargoyle leathery wings—and his world filled with imps and magic. The stars that kept watch over the lands he couldn't see. Except in that story, it didn't end well for the people who were swayed into going there. "I'd want to stay here." She opened her eyes and grinned. "And perhaps have a room with never ending strawberry and blueberry tarts. I live for those."

Keelen bit his lip as if he could taste crumbs from it. "I've never had any that I can recall."

She'd given him crumbs of tarts before, but he couldn't ever taste them. "How about I make you some?"

"That would be—"

The door swung open and Afton halted in place, her blonde hair falling perfectly to her waist. "I was looking for you." Her dark gaze fell to Keelen, and she pursed her lips. "He's awake."

Silver was a bit disappointed by the interruption, but she managed to perk up. "Afton, come and meet Keelen. I was about to make tarts."

Afton gripped the handle of her mace. "You will do no such thing right now."

"And why not?" Silver asked, placing her hands on her hips as she stood from the bed.

"Because I need to explain the plans to my new *guard*. He can have tarts another time."

"Alone?" Silver lifted a brow.

"Yes." There was a hint of exhaustion in Afton's gaze, and Silver bet it was from her conversation with Aris. "For now, can you at least go and use magic to color your hair like mine?"

"I'll see what I can do." Silver hesitated before brushing past Afton and murmuring, "Play nice with him. Or as nice as you can muster. Can I have your word you won't hurt him?"

"You have my word as long as he doesn't attack me."

She nodded and gave a quick glance at Keelen who was watching her while she exited the room. It was an expression that seemed as though he'd wanted her to stay, but he hadn't requested it of her, so she left. Silver needed to prepare for Enare anyway.

As children, Silver and Afton's parents had expected their bond to be fragile, but even a fragile one could be stronger than a broken one. Their parents had underestimated what years together might do—their bond had grown into iron.

That iron was what their parents had made Afton burn Silver's chest with. If Afton hadn't obeyed, they would have clipped off Silver's toes and slaughtered Midnight. There'd been no hesitation as Afton brought the hot iron forward.

"You should hate me," Afton said after their parents made her carry Silver to her room.

"I know why you did it." The searing pain from the burn traveled throughout her body. "It wasn't the toes. It was because of my horse. You know how much I love him."

"I know that would have hurt you more than this. It's best you stay away from me," Afton whispered after helping Silver to bed. "You will only ever get hurt."

"Because of them. Not you." She grasped Afton's hand. "No matter what, I'm glad I have you here."

"And I, you," Afton murmured.

Silver walked down the hall and opened the door to her room. Dresses cluttered the floor—notes sprawled across the desk. A complete disarray to Afton's organized space. Stepping over a few velvet gowns, she placed the mace on the bed, then entered her bathroom and slumped on a chair in front of her mirror. Preserved butterfly wings that Silver had attached herself framed the glass.

She gazed in the mirror—her oval face, her pale scar, her upturned nose. Pulling her dark hair over her shoulder, Silver fished out the glass jar of moistened clay from a half-open drawer and added water to it. The magic around her took a moment to rouse before she tugged it from the earth and ran the clay throughout her hair, slathering the sticky texture onto lock after lock.

Silver's hair changed from raven's feathers to the color of yellowed cake, becoming lighter and lighter. Her face appeared nothing like her sister's, though. While Silver looked like her father, Afton was the spitting image of their mother with wide eyes, a plump bottom lip, a pointy nose, and a slender neck.

A thought of Afton having her throat slit by Thorin's hand slipped into her mind. She dropped the glass jar, watching it shatter to pieces.

"She'll be okay," Silver said as she bent to pick up the glass. "She'll be protected."

SEVEN

KEELEN

Silver walked away, her dark hair cascading behind her as she shut the door, and something inside Keelen clenched. Even though he didn't understand it, he almost pleaded for her to stay. But he fucking didn't.

His gaze turned toward her sister—Afton. Her light hair was half coiled in braids atop her head and half hanging freely down her back. Afton's eyebrows mirrored the dark color of Silver's hair. The red dress she wore cinched tight, pushing the cleavage of her breasts up, and one leg peeked from a slit in the skirt. Noticing the unblemished flesh of her chest, Keelen recalled the scars along Silver's skin, delicate crisscrossing marks and light circles that were almost a decoration. He preferred the imperfection.

"So, you're Keelen," she said with a clipped tone and narrowed eyes. Crossing her arms, Afton leaned on the wall, maintaining a healthy distance. Just as quickly as she folded her arms, she unfolded them and clicked her sharp nails against the wall.

Silver had asked him a strange question when they'd been alone together in the weapons room.

Do you wish I looked like her?

As his eyes caught on Afton's coal-colored irises—they matched Silver's but were nothing like hers—he wouldn't wish it of her. While Afton was pretty enough, and appeared as if she could please any man in bed, there was also the feeling that she could rip out their hearts and eat them if she wished. He wasn't one to take it—he would snap back and defend himself.

"Yes," he finally said, smirking at her icy glare.

"You mean, 'yes, Your Highness.'" She paused. "You need to say that when speaking to a queen if you're to be a guard. Regardless of what my sister thinks, I don't need you. But she does. And even though we aren't in Enare yet, you will treat her as such."

The smile dropped from his face.

"If not," she continued, then glided toward him, a second row of sharp teeth sliding down from her gums, "then I can easily send you back to where Silver pulled you from. If I discover that the dark magic she used tarnished her the slightest, I'll make sure you feel every bite and claw mark before I tear your throat out, you hear me?"

Keelen blinked, too stunned at what she'd said, how protective she was of her sister. Perhaps he couldn't snap back when caught off guard.

"You want me to be her guard? Not yours?"

Afton nodded, dark claws sliding out and over her fingernails. "I think we're starting to see eye to eye now." With one swift motion, she pulled something from a hidden pocket of her skirts, then hurled it. The dagger soared in the air and pierced the mattress directly beside his thigh.

Before he could speak, she ran her tongue across her teeth while leaning against the wall with her arms folded once more. "You didn't flinch. Good."

Keelen wasn't going to allow her to stand there with a smirk on her face, thinking she'd gotten the better of him. He yanked the dagger from the mattress and flung the blade toward her.

The weapon hit its mark, landing right above her head. "Looks like we're even."

She hadn't flinched either, only smiled. "Don't mess this up, and don't let my sister down."

"I'll guard her," Keelen said, realizing he'd answered before truly thinking about it. But he didn't believe either one of them were actually in need of a guard. Not when they both could use magic and tear into flesh with their bare hands and teeth.

"And you won't speak of this."

Keelen stayed silent and shrugged. Silver would be easier to be around, so that wouldn't be a problem. What did he care about this queen or territory anyway? He didn't know her and still couldn't remember a damn thing about Silver. Yet that urgency clawing inside him wanted him to protect *her*.

"Good." Afton's sharp claws and razor teeth both receded. "If you want to stay alive, you need to focus now and focus hard. Because if you don't, I won't succeed, which could put Silver's life in jeopardy, which means I will find a way to end you. Do you understand?" She lifted her mace and sauntered toward him.

"I understand, Your Highness." Keelen held back the ire he'd wanted to use on those last two words. And he was proud of himself for it.

"Silver tells me you've been here numerous times in the past. She took your soul from Torlarah and placed it into a wax raven. What do you remember?"

He furrowed his brow, trying to recall his past again. *Anything.* Him in Torlarah. Him alive in human form. Him anywhere but here. Trapped. It all remained somewhere in the hidden depths of his mind.

"Not much," Keelen finally said. "The dying, a few other things that don't hold any significance, but not Silver."

Afton stopped in front of his bed, changing the subject.

"What's your choice of weapon? You'll need something more than a dagger." She twirled the mace in her hand. "This is mine."

"Javan took me to the weapons room earlier."

"And?" She continued to spin the mace while curling her lip.

"It doesn't matter. You can give me a hatchet."

"If you can throw one like you did that dagger, we'll do just fine." She tapped her chin. "There is a problem with hatchets, though. Once it's out of your hand you have to retrieve it."

"Twin swords to wear at my back then."

"Hmm. Fair enough." Afton leaned closer, lowering her body, and she gripped his chin, her fingers digging in. "Now listen, and listen closely. I will be gone for a couple days. In the morning, I'm going to Enare, our enemy territory, where I will accept King Thorin's betrothal. You will stay here, protect my sister at all costs, and if you do anything to her while I'm gone, I'll remove your head and throw it back into the wax. Don't think I didn't notice how she was looking at you."

Keelen frowned. "What do you mean?" Silver hadn't looked at him with any intent. Had she?

Baring her teeth in a smile, Afton released her hand from his face. "Oh nothing, I just know how hearts work, even though my enemies might say I don't have one at all."

"Won't you need a guard if you're going alone? I'm sure Silver will question that."

"Javan will be with me. Besides, I'll be Silver," she said in a voice that mirrored her sister's high-pitched tone, even her expression did so.

He couldn't help being caught off guard, and a sinking feeling washed over him. "I don't understand."

"*You* will constantly be guarding Silver, who will be the queen when we're in Enare, which is why *you* will start now. Silver is going to swap places with me and pretend to be the queen when she goes to meet King Thorin very soon. So Javan and her sister—me—will be bringing the acceptance news of the proposal tomorrow."

"What are you planning to have her do?" Keelen's chest tightened. He shouldn't care, yet something deep within him stirred. He may not remember Silver, but the thought of danger surrounding her put him on edge. Or what Afton could have Silver do...

He didn't know anything about this king or his territory. He needed a better explanation, but more than anything, he *needed* to remember. His memories drifted closer to the surface, bits and pieces of his life while in wax form. Perhaps eventually they would come. Then maybe he would choose to leave Ketill behind, and Silver…

"That's for me to know." She paused and let out a long, exasperated sigh. "You don't have to worry. Silver has shadowed me for years and knows how I work and how I act better than anyone. I already have a plan for her if anything happens to me, and she knows it."

"She's your only weakness." Even though he'd just met Afton, if he could see it, then anyone could. "Don't show it."

Afton pursed her lips and pulled something from another hidden pocket in her dress. She held up a small glass vial containing a dark green liquid swirling inside. "Drink this. It will help you."

"Help with what?" Keelen asked when she tossed him the vial. He easily caught it in his fist.

"Then don't drink it." She shrugged, swishing the skirts of her dress as she turned to leave. Before she exited the room, she glanced over her shoulder. "But you would have wished you had. For Silver."

The door clicked behind her, and Keelen was back to being alone, holding up the glass vial. Thoughts churned in his head, about what was in the glass. Poison? He wouldn't be surprised. Yet she could have instead attempted to slit his throat if she'd wanted.

The feeling from earlier *thump-thumped* inside his chest, yearning to tug on the magic pumping from the earth. But he didn't know how to grasp and draw it forward. What would he do with it if he could? It didn't matter anyway.

He set the vial down beside his bed, deciding against drinking it.

EIGHT

SILVER

Silver sat by the crackling fire, holding the note her sister had slipped into her room beneath the door. The note she had already read ten times. Afton must have left before dawn, not bothering to wake her. Not bothering to tell her anything. Unfolding the paper, Silver read the words from her sister again and again.

Don't do anything stupid. Don't come after me. Shani and Javan are at my side, and we'll be back in a few days from Enare. It will only be to deliver the proposal acceptance. Guard the territory as if you were its queen. I'm only taking Javan with me as my personal guard, so keep a close eye on Keelen. If he betrays you, don't hesitate in killing him.

"She should have taken Keelen with her," Silver grunted. "She shouldn't have left me behind."

The night before had seemed to tick by ever so slowly until Afton had knocked on Silver's door, stopping by once she'd left Keelen's room. Her sister had only mentioned that she'd gotten the herbs from Aris and that she explained the plan to

Keelen.

Afton hadn't appeared different, and there wasn't a reason for Silver to believe her sister would be leaving the next morning.

The blood within her veins pumped with anxiety until she thought the thin canals would burst open. She would give Afton a few days, but if she wasn't back by then, Silver would go after her.

With a heavy sigh, Silver tossed the note into the fire and watched it shrivel to black, then to ash. Pressing a hand to her scarred chest, she ran her fingertips across the raised flesh to her neck. Since their parents' deaths, Silver knew Afton still battled her demons at times.

Silver's gaze drifted to the empty jar on her desk, and she chewed her lip while looking at it. Keelen was still here… Something fluttered in her chest. She reminded herself she was a stranger to him, and perhaps she should do something to help him feel more relaxed.

Scooping up the jar, she headed out of the palace and into the foggy morning. Mist surrounded her as she entered the eastern gardens. White lilies, orange pansies, pink carnations, and red roses were all in full bloom. Thick green vines, covered in thorns and blue and purple flowers, ran the length of the obsidian castle walls, then continued across the curving ivory arches in front of its round windows.

A cool breeze ruffled Silver's hair as she knelt and pressed her hands into the damp soil. The magic rushed through her, causing her to catch her breath before it settled within her, thumping in sync with her heart.

Perfectly spun dew-covered webs draped the thorns of the rose bushes, their silky texture reflecting the sun's morning light. She plucked several beetles, spiders, and grasshoppers, then placed them in the glass jar.

She tightened the lid and stared up at the window to Keelen's room. Closing her eyes, she breathed in, the last time she'd seen him in raven form, months ago, coming to her in a rush.

"What would you do if I was in my true male form?"

Press my lips to yours, *she thought. It wouldn't matter what he looked like either—she would love him regardless.* "Hold your hand. What would you do?"

"That's my little secret." He chuckled. "Maybe you'll find out someday."

She glanced at the window one more time. Or perhaps she would never find out… A frigid wind gusted by her, and she shivered at the change in temperature.

The mist slicked her skin as she dashed back into the castle's warmth. Her skirts swished against her thighs when she came to an abrupt stop in the kitchens. It sat empty. Ragan should have been there. Had Afton confessed to him her plans?

"What did you do to your beautiful hair?" Jeanette gasped from behind Silver, making her jump.

Silver whirled around to find the older woman carrying a bundle of carrots. Jeanette hadn't been working the kitchens as frequently since Ragan started, which left her more time to spend with family.

"I can't discuss it, so talk with no one outside the palace of it." Silver brought her blonde braid over her shoulder and inspected it. She wasn't used to the color yet.

"Of course I won't," Jeanette promised, bowing her head.

Silver knew she would keep her word. "Where's Ragan?"

"He's taking time off to visit his family, so here I am." Her eyes appeared tired with bags beneath them. "I know, I know, you want his tarts. You're lucky—he left a batch for you before he left." With a warm smile, she slipped a plate from beneath the counter and set it on top.

"Perfect." Silver took the plate, a slight ache forming in her chest. Ragan had always been good to her, kind. If Afton left him in the dark about her plans, would it break his heart to learn she didn't trust him enough? "See you later, Jeanette."

"Are those bugs in that jar you're carrying?" she called as Silver started to leave.

"Why yes. Yes, they are." She glanced over her shoulder and winked.

Jeanette's forehead wrinkled and Silver continued to Keelen's room.

As she passed several servants, they kept their eyes down as they did with her sister. It was only the change of her hair, but they didn't seem to recognize her.

When she reached Keelen's door, Silver's palms were clammy with sweat. Blowing out a breath, Silver placed the jar beneath her arm and knocked on the door while tapping her foot.

No answer.

She knocked again. Waiting and waiting. Still the door didn't crack. She hesitated for a moment before turning the knob, possibly even expecting it to be bolted, but the door easily swung open.

"Keelen?" Silver called as her eyes swept across the empty room, lingering on the rumpled sheets.

Taking measured steps into the bedroom, she rapped her knuckles against the bathroom door, then opened it. Empty. A towel rested on the floor, but other than that, it hadn't appeared as if it had been used.

Where was he?

Her heart drummed, mimicking the hasty movements of the bugs in the jar.

The magic of the earth sang within her veins, her emotions tangling into knots. He wouldn't have died again because she would have felt his soul leave as always.

Had he remembered? Had he run away? If he had, it was his choice to make, not hers. He wasn't a prisoner, but he had agreed to be Afton's guard, so why leave now?

As she looked at the disarrayed bed one last time, she wondered if he'd already found a servant to bed. Her heart plummeted at the thought.

Cradling the jar and plate, she bolted from the room and descended the staircase. There was one place he might be. Unless he took a horse and escaped the palace. Did he even know how to ride one?

Thwack. Thwack. The noise of hatchets striking their marks boomed from the weapons room. She exhaled a sigh of relief—she'd been right. Javan was already long gone with Afton, so the only other person who would have the gall to sneak into the weapons room would be Keelen. If anyone else had tried to do such a thing without consulting one of the sisters or Javan, they would be reprimanded by Afton's hands and possibly teeth.

The moment Silver opened the door, her gaze settled on Keelen and his shoulders tensed. He spun around to face her, his gaze scanning her entirety. She took stock of the dark curly hair that had already grown to his eyes, then to where his lashes and brows were filled in.

His surprised expression quickly slipped into something else, masked. "Ah, is it not the dark-haired sister. One of light and one of darkness, but which is which?"

Was he being humorous or an ass? "So … you've seen Afton's hair, too?"

"No." Face hard, as if trying to conjure up a thought, he stepped toward her. Just as close as he'd been with her in this same space the night before.

Ever so slowly, he lifted a lock of her hair and rubbed it between his smooth fingertips. He breathed, she breathed, and they watched one another, his violet irises brightening.

Finally, he spoke, dropping his hand to his side. "I'm not sure the blonde suits you."

"Glad we agree," she said with feigned nonchalance. But she *did* care.

"Afton left this morning. Did she tell you last night she would be leaving?"

"She did." Why would Afton tell a stranger she was leaving but not her own sister who she had always told everything to? *To protect me.* Silver wanted to scream, shatter the glass windows in the castle with her magic. Instead, she inhaled slowly, calming herself.

"I'm not sure if you've eaten yet," Silver finally said, "but I brought you breakfast." She set the jar of bugs on the table and pushed it toward him, while still clutching onto the plate of tarts.

"I prefer to catch my own prey." He cocked his head, yet she watched his throat bob, knowing he was yearning to crack open the jar.

"Is that so?" Silver wanted to smack him as she set down her plate, and she'd never wanted to do that before. But right now, he deserved it. She tilted her head to the side to mirror him—two could play this game. Unscrewing the lid, she dumped the bugs onto the floor and peered down at them as their fragile bodies scattered in different directions. Then she shooed her hands forward. "There. Go on. *Hunt.* And while you do that, I'll eat tarts." Lifting one of the delicacies, drenched in blueberry sauce, she placed it into her mouth and took her time chewing. "Mmm. Mmm. Delicious." The sweetness hit all her senses just right, and she wasn't even faking the euphoria it brought to her mouth. She would certainly miss Ragan's cooking while he was gone.

Keelen's head remained cocked while he stared at her, his gaze fixed on her lips.

"Do you have a favorite weapon?" Keelen asked as he knelt, shooting his hand forward and scooping up two of the grasshoppers. He plopped them onto his tongue, crunches echoing as he chewed.

Just can't help himself. Her hand covered her mouth and she let out a small laugh. She shoved the plate in front of him, relenting. "Eat."

And he did, his eyes rolling with bliss. Crumbs and

strawberry jam stuck to his plump lower lip. She wanted to brush them away, but she controlled her desire and passed him the napkin from the bottom of the plate.

"My favorite weapons are my hands and teeth when I dip into the magic," Silver finally answered once he finished eating. "I like that they are connected to me and I know what each of their movements will be. So I never carry a weapon since I don't prefer one."

"What do you mean you never carry a weapon?" Keelen perked up and scanned her over, as if he didn't quite believe her. "Ever?"

"Sometimes I carry a mace, but I've never used it against an enemy. Just because I don't carry them all the time doesn't mean I don't know how to wield them though."

"If you could pick anything in this room to work with right now, what would it be?" He gestured toward the walls of weapons.

Taking the second to last tart, she observed each one before settling on what called to her. "The war hammer. It has a sharp end and a blunt one, so I could make a choice of how I want my enemy to be defeated. Either end will hurt, punish, and kill."

"Ah, so you have a tender spot for violence. I think you might have a little bit of your sister in you after all." His lips twitched.

Her brow furrowed. "Only when forced." Silver pushed the last dessert toward him then moved for the weapon, running her hand over the smooth metal while letting the coolness absorb into her flesh.

"Anyway," Silver continued, motioning him to follow her, "since you still look hungry, why don't we go to the kitchens. You can tell me what else you and Afton discussed and I'll help prepare you for Enare as best I can."

"Why not?" He shrugged.

On the way to the kitchens, Silver explained how Ketill

and Enare had been separate territories for years and how King Thorin wanted to unite them. About how Enare's clan had fallen harder as each year passed under the old king's rule. Keelen listened intently to all of it.

As they entered the kitchens, Jeanette lifted her head and wiped her hands against her apron. "Back already?" Her gaze settled on Keelen. "Who's this?"

Silver shrugged. "Keelen is Afton's new guard. He'll be shadowing me until she returns."

Her gray eyebrows lifted up her forehead. "Is Javan all right?"

"Javan's fine. He hasn't stepped down yet." Silver skirted around the counter. "We're going to take over the kitchens for a bit, so you're free to leave for a while."

Her brown eyes brightened. "Sure. I'll go help Charly. She hasn't had much time to herself since the babe. But if you need me to come back sooner, I can."

"Thanks, Jeanette." Charly and Shani were both of Jeanette's daughters. Silver had always been surprised that the woman chose to stay after the deaths of the king and queen. This place had to still be a reminder that Silver's parents had cut off Shani's tongue and made her mute.

"You really think you can pretend to be your sister?" Keelen asked once Jeanette left.

Silver's smile vanished, her eyes narrowing in a deadly manner. "Speak like that again and I'll gut you from navel to throat and pull your intestines out through your mouth."

He blinked, his lips parting.

She let out a high-pitched cackle.

A smirk crossed Keelen's lips and he watched her as though he was attempting to figure her out. "From the few moments I've had with her, that wasn't bad. But..." Worry lines creased his forehead.

"If you don't believe in me, then believe in my sister." Silver placed her hands on her hips. "She will accomplish this."

"Oh, I'm certain she can play *her* role, but I'm just not so sure she can play *yours*." He ran the tip of his finger through the specks of pale flour along the counter. "You have to remember that I don't know anything about her or you, besides what I've seen thus far."

"And you?" She drew a line in the flour beneath his, as if it was sizing the other up. "Would you be easily seduced by her?"

"If you're wondering if my cock got hard by the sight of her last night, it didn't."

Silver's eyes widened and she cleared her throat. "Perhaps one of the servants?"

"No." He smirked.

"Hopefully it works then."

"It most definitely works." His voice came out low, deep, as he leaned closer to her.

In that moment, it was very hard to not let her gaze travel lower. Before her hands did things she didn't want them to do, Silver turned to grab the sack of flour and set it beside the eggs. She cracked a few shells on the edge of a bowl.

Keelen scooped up an egg and cracked it over his open mouth, then placed the shell inside, chewing. She was at a loss for words as she studied the pleasurable expression on his face while he consumed the uncooked egg … and shell. While Silver tried to fight a smile, she watched as he picked up another.

She ripped it from his hand. "Do you want to eat raw eggs all day? Or do you want me to make the tarts? Because I need the eggs."

"Raw—"

"Only one more." With a roll of her eyes, she handed him another egg then mixed the water and flour before adding the remainder of the ingredients.

As the tarts cooked for a long while, the silence between

them was growing louder. Screaming. *Screeching*. She focused on the thrum of the magic inside her, the claws beneath her skin pushing in and out over her nails.

"Have you ever heard of Valgmyr?" she asked, when she could take the quiet no longer. "I know I've discussed Torlarah, the territories, but there are so many lands past the seas. Most don't know or believe magic exists. One is a place called Kedaf and its surrounding territories."

Keelen rubbed a hand across his jaw. "I don't know. Maybe?"

"Valgmyr is said to be a secret place connected to Enare. A king of darkness supposedly lives there with his imps. The stars above us are the merciless ones, his watchers."

"Hmm." He arched a brow. "I suppose he likes to stay within his darkness, then?"

She shrugged. "It's just a story to keep our people from going to Enare. For fear of being lured to his world, even though people could be plucked from anywhere. Most don't remember it anymore. But it's an interesting tale."

"Go on."

Silver had told him all of this before, when he was a raven. "The king is said to live in the earth's depths, collecting lovers. It doesn't matter if they are male or female, but it's said they are needed to keep his garden alive."

"What do you mean keep his garden alive? Aren't all gardens alive?"

"Not a regular garden. But something different, darker. One that moves and breathes, with a living heartbeat. It would be interesting to see if it were real."

Keelen frowned. "I can't visualize it."

"Think of a tree." She straightened, slowly lifting her arms, then she moved them in swaying circles. "You see now?"

He cracked a smile. "You're a tree. I see it now." His tone was laced with sarcasm.

She rolled her eyes and dropped her arms. Before she

could discuss any more of the tale, the sweetened scent of the tarts invaded her nose. She grabbed them from the stove, curls of steam rising off their golden crust.

Leaning forward, Silver blew on the edge of one and smothered it in honey. After allowing the tarts to cool a bit, she picked one up and held it to Keelen's face. His eyes almost glazed over as he peered at the dessert. She pushed the pastry into her mouth and relished the savory taste.

"Let me know what you think," she said as he took the treat from her, their fingers brushing in a soft caress, her breathing heavy.

He placed it onto his tongue and chewed slowly. A low groan escaped his throat.

"Good?" She grinned.

"It's damn good." He held her gaze for a moment and licked his bottom lip.

Silver looked away first, wondering what it would have been like if she'd woken into his world instead of him in hers.

NINE

AFTON

The carriage jostled as it traveled out of Ketill and into Enare. Afton sat across from Javan, ignoring his face, and listening to the uneven gallop of the horses' hooves. Shani was outside the carriage, driving it forward. Afton wondered how angry her sister was—they'd never been apart for even a full day. Even when Afton had stayed in her room for days upon days, her sister had always been within the same castle walls. But this was necessary—she needed to see for herself how safe Enare's castle was first, so they could be prepared when arriving later.

Then there'd been Ragan's letter beneath her door that morning, saying he would be taking off for a few days to visit his family and he would see her again soon. She'd wanted to find him and slap him, or kiss him, or perhaps both. But at least she wouldn't have to lie to him about what she was doing.

No other servant would have dared to leave a note under her door over the years, but after Ragan had snuck and done it the first time, Afton had been more impressed than angry. So she'd allowed it to continue.

Afton removed her silk head wrap and relaxed into the seat with a sigh.

"I don't think this is smart, Your Highness," Javan grumbled, his gaze locking on her raven-colored hair. Needless to say, when she'd woken him this morning, he was more annoyed than anything.

"I think it is," she snapped, shifting her long braid over her shoulder so he could catch a better glimpse of her hair. From everything that transpired the night before, exhaustion still lingered, her eyelids hard to keep open. She pinched the soft flesh between her index finger and thumb to push away the fatigue.

"As your guard—"

"I listen to no one—" she interrupted.

"But *yourself*, I know." He sighed, cutting her off right back. "You remind me so much of your mother."

"My mother is *dead*." Afton leaned forward, and in a low voice said, "And I would gladly be the cause of that again." She hadn't needed to draw up dark magic to shatter her parents' hearts into a million pieces, but she had. Her heart had been monstrous enough toward them already—she wanted to feel their hearts in her grasp. That evening, she'd wanted to tear into their chests with her claws, sink her teeth into their throats. But she'd needed to be careful, not get too close. So during the night, the one time she'd ever tapped into dark magic, she let her shadow slide out of her, reaching and stretching with those blackened hands until they pressed against both her parents' chests. Inhaling and exhaling. Afton had made sure their lungs would never pump again. Before their eyes had cracked open, she thrust the extension of herself inside them. Their choked surprises had radiated through the night. She'd squeezed and crushed until the organs exploded beneath her grip.

Beautiful silence had filled the room. Relief had filled her. Not a lingering sense of regret or remorse. Her sister wouldn't have to suffer any longer, and that had mattered most.

"You'll be a much better mother to your children," Javan

murmured finally, staring out the window as though he was conjuring up a past memory.

"I will *never* have children, so you can put an end to that dream." Her parents loved each other deeply, so deeply that they didn't think about anyone else besides each other. Not their people, not their daughters—no one. That was why she'd never wanted to fall in love. Because how could two people love each other so fully yet treat everyone in their territory as if they were nothing? But then, she'd betrayed herself by falling in love anyway. It hadn't come easy, and it hadn't been without struggle for her to accept that she had.

"Why didn't you choose someone else to replace you instead of Silver?" Javan asked, changing the subject to something less arguable. "Or better yet, not swap at all? This seems dangerous and excessive."

"I'm not afraid."

Lie. It was a lie. She liked to believe—desperately wanted to believe—she was afraid of nothing, but really, she was. She was terrified of her sister's fate if Ketill was under Enare's authority. "Silver already knows what to do if something happens to me."

Javan leaned back in his seat, brushing his fingers across the head of his cane. "You haven't even met King Thorin yet. He could be worse than you think."

"Fuck King Thorin." Afton had met his foolish guards and if the rest were like them, they would easily end up the same— dead. She would allow her hatred to surface for her enemy, the way it had for her parents. Except their hearts would be torn out and eaten.

"That is *exactly* why it's dangerous," Javan whispered, his body edging closer toward hers. His scowl softened, and he appeared as if he wanted to comfort her. "You're going to have to watch that tongue of yours. You are a great queen, you treat our people fairly, and *I* don't want us to lose you."

Something in Afton's chest tightened, and then like

always, she remembered their past. Javan standing against the wall, watching, watching, and *watching*, doing nothing as she burned her sister.

"As a guard, and *only* a guard, you will obey me," she said slowly. "Do not think because you are blood that it means anything to me. You have no right to tell me what to do. And if I recall, you're lucky I didn't remove your head for not once protecting Silver." Her voice was low, serious, so he would understand that she wouldn't allow him to question her like he had in the past. Afton rarely let herself think of him as her grandfather—he was her mother's father, and it meant *nothing*.

"It would have only made things worse."

"For who? *You*?" she spat, finally getting this off her chest after all these years.

"You wouldn't understand." He peered down at his hands, studying his clean nails. As though those nails were more important to look at than her. Just as he would do when her parents had requested her to do something vicious to her sister. At that time, he'd been their parents' guard, not hers.

Until afterward.

Javan had been one of the most skilled guards, even without magic. Why had he done nothing? She hadn't discovered he was their grandfather until after murdering her parents, and she'd left Silver in the dark about it because she hadn't wanted to see the defeat on her sister's face when she learned another family member had made her suffer.

Even though Silver resembled their father, it didn't matter—she still looked like Silver. Afton loved her deeply, fiercely. She'd left Keelen with Silver because her sister had wanted Afton to trust her about him, and if he was as good of a friend as she said he was, then he would be a perfect guard for her. However, she was still furious that Silver had used dark magic to bring his soul there.

Afton remained quiet, as did Javan, yet her nostrils continued to flare. What she needed in that moment was

Ragan's warm body against her, inside her, to soothe her, take the stress away for a few stolen moments. But that wouldn't happen until the journey was over.

Before the tense silence could snap, Afton glanced toward Javan, his eyes closed, but she knew he wasn't sleeping. "We're going to stay the night. I need to get a feel of what lies within the castle walls."

His lids flicked open, his spine straightening. "Too risky. Accept the betrothal and return."

"No"—she shook her head—"my way."

"You're going to be the death of me," Javan groaned, clenching his jaw. Afton was surprised none of his teeth had broken over the years from repeating that motion so often.

"One way or another, that will be true." Finished talking, she shut her lids and let the carriage jostle her as it continued its journey along the barren countryside, nothing but brown hills as far as the eye could see.

"Afton."

Her eyes jerked open to a deep voice. She swung her hand forward, aiming for the throat of the possible danger.

"Nightmare?" A cane lifted just in time to block her arm. Javan's brow was arched as he eyed her pointed fingernails. "We're here."

He was right—there had been a nightmare. The same one of her burning her sister's flesh over and over again while Silver screamed. Taking a deep swallow, Afton's body relaxed, but she didn't drop her hand as she peered out the tiny glass window of the carriage.

A looming castle of gray and cream stone sat before her, with rows of dead rose bushes in the gardens. Sinewy trees, empty of leaves, swept across the area and a small pond, where ravens perched on its shore, was across from the dead bushes. Tall pyramid-shaped towers steepled the top of the palace, iron bars surrounding several of them.

Fury gripped her heart as she gazed up at the castle. This bastard king would surely trap her there if she'd planned on actually marrying him.

"Most of Enare is like this. All the plant life seems to be dead or withering," Javan said.

"I'm sure the king is the cause of it as well."

Shani opened the carriage door, her dark hair disheveled from the journey. Afton started to step out when a hand pulled her back.

"Wrong move. I'm still your guard," Javan said as he pushed in front of her and hopped down.

Afton pursed her lips, but walked beside him toward the palace doors. Shani remained silent at her other side. Afton clearly remembered her parents forcing Shani to be silenced forever by removing her tongue and stripping her vocal cords away. Shani had done nothing wrong, only arrived at the palace late because her father had died. If Afton could conjure Shani's voice and tongue up from the earth and give them back to her, she would.

The *tick-ticking* she normally felt pulsing inside her in Ketill wasn't thrumming the least bit here. There wasn't the slightest movement or pinch of energy, as if the earth itself was dead. There was nothing. Worry stormed through her— she couldn't extract her claws or teeth. She could do nothing but use her mace if needed. Relief washed over her once more—she'd done the right thing by leaving Silver at home.

Realizing she was tilting her chin too high, Afton lowered it at a downward angle, then proceeded to carry herself the way Silver would have. A bit willowier, her feet lighter, her chin leveled.

Outside the castle stood two guards dressed in black tunics and pants, both of them quiet, their eyes watching them in a way that didn't seem human. *Strange.* She tightened her grip on her mace.

Javan puffed his chest forward. "We have come on behalf of Queen Afton to speak with King Thorin regarding the betrothal request."

A tall guard with her red hair pulled into a long braid stepped forward and opened the door. She didn't say a single word as she guided them inside the castle walls. Empty vases and withered plants filled the wide-open room, and a faint smoky and grassy scent greeted her. Massive quilts with unique, colorful designs hung across the tall walls that connected to a dome-shaped ceiling. Javan gripped his cane and eyed the guards with suspicion while Shani pressed a hand to the dagger at her waist. He'd only been using the cane for a month, but Javan still managed to have quick reflexes. Besides for his sword, he could easily release the blade hidden within his walking stick.

The guard guided them down a long hallway—decorated with ornate metal flowers—to the first door. She, Javan, and Shani stepped inside a large oval sitting room. In the middle of the space was a grand circular table, surrounded by iron chairs with blue velvet cushioning. The sound of the door closing caused her to glance back and notice the guard was now missing.

No one took a seat. They each held their weapons, and Afton peered up at the paintings lining the walls. They were pitiful. All portraits with misshapen faces, too long noses, drooping eyes. It was odd… Everything about being here seemed out of place. Afton tried again to tap into the magic, deeper into the earth where any ounce of it could be hidden. Not even a drop was there.

"I can't feel anything," she whispered so low that she wasn't sure if Javan could hear her.

"Hmm?" He removed his gaze from a portrait and studied Afton. Javan wouldn't have known anyway because he'd never been able to feel it.

"No magic."

"I knew this was an awful idea." His throat bobbed as he looked from her to their exit, then turned to Shani. "And you?"

Shani shook her head. The woman had always felt the magic but couldn't draw it in to use. Perhaps if she could, she would have stopped Afton's parents from silencing her.

Is it possible magic can be used up?

The door swung open, interrupting her thoughts. In walked the same female guard and the other man who had been outside the castle with her. He appeared close to her age with darker red hair tied back in a low ponytail.

As she gazed back up at the paintings, she couldn't hold her tongue and apparently needed to be the first to speak. "The portraits are … awful." Afton could feel Javan's heated stare. She wasn't pretending to be a servant, so she could still say things as they were.

"I would have to agree." The voice was familiar. It was a voice Afton would remember anywhere. A voice that whispered to her in the dark, lips on her throat, his heart beating beneath her hand. It was a voice she had loved—loved until this moment.

Afton spun to face Ragan as he stepped into the room, dressed all in black.

"Ragan?" she inhaled sharply. "What are you doing here?"

"This is my home." He rubbed the back of his neck, his piercing brown eyes meeting hers. "I couldn't tell you before, Afton."

Afton… What a fool she was. She was here trying to impersonate Silver, and this bastard, who cracked open her heart, was standing in her enemy's castle. A traitorous spy. She exchanged a glance with Javan and Shani who appeared to be as stunned as she was.

She would feign as though it didn't affect her, as if she didn't love him. "Has His Majesty chosen not to grace us with his presence today?"

"He's standing right here before you," he said, his fingers tapping against his legs as though he was nervous.

Afton couldn't breathe. Couldn't *think*. Ragan—King Thorin? Her heart felt like it would burst in her chest, but she was determined not to show him her anguish. Had *everything* been a lie? How could she have been so stupid? Her teeth and claws were itching to be released, but the magic here was dead.

She knew Thorin's father had died before he was crowned as king. But from the way he continued to take care of his people, then recently sending guards to snatch her, he was just as deceitful as his father. Ragan had been at her castle when the guards—*his* guards—had come. She was *always* careful about who she allowed to work in the palace. What a fantastic imposter he was.

"What do you want with Queen Afton?" Javan asked, removing the sword at his waist. Shani mirrored his movements with her own blade.

"Yes, *Your Highness*. What do you want with me?" Afton seethed. "Do you want this betrothal? Because it's not happening, so you can fuck right off."

Thorin's brow furrowed as he glanced between the three of them. "I'm not going to harm any of you. There is something you don't know about Enare."

"Is that why you sent messengers to capture and bring me back here? Because they were ready to haul me off to be your bride before I tore them to pieces." Afton growled, her lips pressing in to a thin line.

He sighed, his expression unreadable. "They weren't meant to do it in that way."

She lifted her mace, ready to use it, despite everything she'd felt for him in the past.

"In what way were they supposed to do it, then?" Javan asked, his voice sharp, his teeth gritted. He stepped closer to Afton. "Bring you shackled to her territory instead, then have a proper wedding?" She'd never seen Javan so furious, and she rather liked seeing his feathers ruffled.

Thorin blew out a breath and rubbed at his temple. "They were supposed to give you a letter. That was all." He paused, his brown gaze locking on hers. "If I had known what they were doing, I would have slaughtered them myself."

Afton dug her fingernails into her palms, her eyes narrowing. She couldn't take her stare off him, her heart feeling too exposed, and that only made her hate him.

"I guess we won't be needing this anymore." Afton fished out the sealed envelope from her satchel and tore it in half before dropping the betrothal document on the floor. She gave a wide grin, laced with venom, stretching her cheeks. "Javan, Shani, I think we're done here."

"Wait!" Thorin shouted, his face desperate.

"No waiting," Afton said. "We're going back to Ketill."

"Please stay," he rushed the words out, moving toward her.

She swung her mace, barely missing his neck as he shifted back.

Thorin held up a hand, his eyes pleading. "Wait until the evening, to see what happens at night, and you'll understand. That's why I needed you to come here."

Afton took a step back, shaking her head. Was he mad? What was he asking? "You have been lying like a coward in my castle for months. Why didn't you tell me there? On any number of occasions?" she said between clenched teeth.

"Would you have come?"

"No." Not after being betrayed by him. Not after his gentle caresses against her naked skin, or his soft words spoken in her ear.

"Let my guards show you a room, and tonight, come to me in the garden alone, and I'll explain everything. You won't believe anything I say until you see it for yourself."

Javan shook his head no. Afton wanted to say no, too, but something in that gaze, his pleading expression, made the part of her that still wanted to give all of herself to him, cave. "For one night, we'll stay, and this reason better be a good one." She held up a finger. "But try anything, and I'll tear open your rib cage, understand?"

"Of course." He gave her a small smile, his shoulders relaxing. "I'd like to keep my rib cage where it is."

She didn't smile in return.

"For now," Thorin continued when he must have realized Afton was done talking to him, "one of the guards will take you to the guest rooms."

Afton nodded and watched as Thorin held her gaze for a few seconds then backed out of the room, his shoulders now stiff.

"He should be dead for what he's done," Javan said.

Shani rubbed her lower lip and pointed to her face. She'd read something truthful in Thorin's eyes that Afton had seen too.

"Let's find out what these miracle reasons are for his treachery." Afton frowned, lowering her mace only a fraction.

After a moment, the male guard motioned them to follow and led them down several hallways with elegant carpet and pale green walls. Javan and Shani were shown to two rooms across from Afton's own before the guard left them without a word.

Shaking her head, Afton went into her room and shut the door. A musty smell struck her nose. Pushed up against the far wall was a dresser and desk—across from them rested a canopy-covered bed. Cobwebs dangled in almost every corner. She glided her finger down the top of the dresser and came away with dust. *Someone needs to clean here.*

Before she could sink down onto the bed, a knock sounded at her door. Her heart beat wildly, a part of her hoping it was Thorin. She shoved that blasted thought down and tugged open the door, coming face to face with Javan instead.

Brushing past her, he mumbled, "I don't think we should

stay the night here.”

“You’re right across the hall.” Afton lifted her mace. “You and I both know that the three of us are able to protect ourselves.”

“You wouldn’t have lasted playing Silver’s role anyway.” He tilted his head. “She smiles. You don’t.”

She bared her teeth for him.

He pinched the bridge of his nose. “You’re not going alone to meet him tonight.”

“It depends on my mood. If I do go, I’ll bring Shani. Either way, I don’t want to see you until morning.” Afton wouldn’t bring either one. She would go alone, then decide if what Thorin had hidden was worth his treachery.

TEN

KEELEN

The sun blazed above Keelen, burning his eyes as he glanced at it. He looked away and studied Silver as she rode her horse around him, its hooves pounding along the grass that surrounded the boulder he sat on. His ass was numb from the stone, and his memories remained locked away.

Silver's pale cheeks flushed pink from the heat. Since Keelen had agreed to be her guard, he wasn't going to let her out of his sight. On her chest, her scar stood more prominent than ever. A raised jagged design that looked more like a painting. The way she must have received it couldn't have been beautiful at all, but ugly, harrowing.

Blood coursed through Keelen, running straight to his cock, while he watched her. His pants were becoming more and more uncomfortable as each moment passed. He didn't even know how many lovers he'd had before. None? One? Hundreds? Thousands?

Silver's guard, her weapon, that was what he was supposed to be. Besides, he was sure Afton would rip his cock off if he brought Silver to his bed … or her bed. But why did he care? He imagined his hand running up her bare breast, in between her thighs, the wetness of her core pooling around his fingertips.

Fuck, he needed to stop watching her.

Rising from the ground, he adjusted his pants and turned to head toward the palace. Anywhere but out here. He needed to throw a few hatchets and daggers to take the edge off, the lust.

"Where are you going?" Silver asked, her horse whinnying when it came to a stop in front of him. She pulled on the reins as the horse stomped its feet on the moistened grass.

"Weapons room." He was supposed to be watching her… *Damn it.* "Care to join me?"

Keelen met her gaze and she stared down at him, her lips parted. He missed her dark locks of hair already, but even with the white-blonde strands, she still looked like herself, only closer to a bright star than an alluring shadow.

"You're asking me?" She grinned.

"I suppose you would have just followed me in, correct?" The edges of his lips tilted upward.

Silver hopped from her horse with swift grace and planted her feet onto the earth. "All right, but I want you to practice riding Midnight first. Since you're going to be Afton's guard, you at least need to know the basics." She reached forward and swept his hair out of his eyes. "I can trim your hair if you want."

That morning, he'd noticed himself in the mirror and had frozen when his gaze fell to the lashes, the dark brows, the matching hair that had almost fallen in his eyes.

"You don't have to." His heart kicked up a notch, a strong sensation pulling at his chest from the tapping of the magic. Keelen still couldn't grasp it, and he wondered if perhaps he wasn't ever meant to. He tried not to think about what he might do with its power if he could.

"It will be easier for you to see."

"I suppose, Your Highness." He gave her a mock bow.

"Ah, you know just what to say."

Fighting back a smile, he shifted his attention to the horse. The thing looked unstable, and he wasn't sure if he could even last two seconds on its back. He honestly just wanted to throw the horse into its barn.

"Have a steady hand and hold on tight." Silver nudged him forward. "Do you need help up?"

"Are you being serious?" He glanced back at her with a brow lifted. "I'd crush you to death."

"We're practically the same height."

"If there was another half of you, then yes."

She rolled her eyes and brushed her palm across the horse's throat. "His name's Midnight."

"I'm not sure he's naughty enough to have a name like that." As soon as he gripped the reins and was halfway on Midnight, the horse reared its legs and body, tossing Keelen to the grass, flat on his back. A sharp pain radiated up his spine while the blue sky above stared down at him. A deep chuckle escaped his lips.

Above him, a shadow slid forward, blocking the sun and eclipsing his view of the sky—Silver. "You should have taken my offer," she sang.

She held out a hand, wiggling her fingers. Grunting, chest heaving, he gripped it and stood. Her skin was soft, her hand small and delicate in his grip. He imagined slowly scaling his own fingers up the length of her bare arm, and quickly released her hand, his heart racing again.

"So," Keelen drawled, peering at the stallion. "How should I get on him then?"

Silver ran a palm beneath Midnight's throat like before, gently stroking the area, then brought her hand up and weaved her fingertips through the horse's mane. "Just show him you're his friend and aren't only using him for the ride."

A crease formed between Keelen's brows as he studied Midnight's dark eyes. "Isn't that what they're used for? To go places?"

Smiling, Silver took a step back. "Well, I like to make it an even trade. Feed him, brush his hair, and anything else he needs." She paused and gave Keelen a wink, one that made him hard once more. What was wrong with him? "Afton's horse, Ivory, keeps him company in the barn. I think he likes her a bit more than she likes him though. Remember that time when we— Never mind." Her tone came out rushed as she shook her head.

That time when we what? Keelen wanted her to finish her sentence, but she wasn't looking at him anymore.

"I think it would be easier to walk," he finally said to splinter the quiet.

"Try crossing the territory and see if you can get there faster than me on Midnight's back," she challenged.

Keelen imagined trying to keep the pace with the horse's quick strides and giving up sooner than he would have liked. "I see your point." He moved closer to Silver, her rosy scent enveloping him, and he was tempted to shift even closer. But he didn't.

Lifting his hand, he repeated the same motions she'd done to Midnight by gliding his hand up the horse's throat, then ran it through its mane. With his shoulder at the horse's neck, Keelen gripped a handful of Midnight's mane down at the withers. Drawing in a deep breath, he mirrored Silver by taking a skip and a jump and swinging his right leg over the animal. He blinked in surprise when Midnight merely stood in place, only releasing a low neigh.

"Good," Silver said, sounding impressed. She gestured with her hands while lightly kicking at the air with her foot. "Now ride."

Keelen flicked the reins and pressed his boots into the horse's belly. Midnight jolted forward across the field, as if he were flying through the clouds.

"Pull the reins back toward you!" Silver yelled, barreling after him.

The stables were approaching, and Keelen realized he was getting too close, so he listened to Silver. Midnight slowed to a canter, then a trot before halting. A horse was as much of a weapon as the ones he'd used inside the castle.

Silver caught up to them, her loose hair disheveled from the wind. "That was good. You're almost a natural."

"Almost?" Keelen chuckled and hopped down from Midnight. He gave the horse a rub between the ears before Midnight trotted into the stables.

"I mean, you *did* need my help." She laughed.

The sweet, musical sound hit his eardrums, and he had to get out of there. "Weapons room now?"

"Sure." Silver shrugged and walked beside him at a leisurely pace as they headed indoors. Once again, he puzzled over the strange skeleton paintings hanging on the wall.

"It's said the paintings represent a place in Torlarah that used to be known as the Bone Valley," Silver said softly. "For a time, the people there were cursed as bones before the land was returned to its former glory."

"Why keep the memory alive then?"

"So we remember never to take anything for granted." Silver smiled.

Keelen nodded, thinking about what she said, wondering if he'd taken things for granted in his past. He continued to observe Silver until they entered the weapons room. As if on instinct, he removed the hatchet from the wall, the weight just right in his hand. He hurled it forward, aiming true. While he went to collect it from the creature's chest, he found Silver skimming her fingers across the weapons on the other wall.

"Are you going to keep *touching* them or use them?" he asked with a smirk.

"I'll have the mace in Enare, so the war hammer would be pointless to practice with today." By the way her fingers twitched as she studied the weapon, she desperately wanted to curl her hand around its handle.

"Get the war hammer."

Without a word, she lifted the weapon and stopped beside him. Closing her eyes, she breathed steadily for several moments, focusing. Opening her lids, she let the hammer fly. The sharp end buried itself deeply into the wooden beast's chest.

Damn.

"Even if I wasn't able to throw it, I could use the magic to help me." She shrugged. "But that would feel like cheating right now."

"I can feel the magic here, but I can't draw it forward," he said.

"You may never be able to." Silver plucked a mace from the wall, the spiked ball a glistening gold. She twirled it in her hand. "Let's grab something to eat first?"

He took a deep swallow, watching as she exited the room. To distract himself from her movements, he grabbed a jeweled dagger and tossed it forward.

For the first time, he missed.

That night, after practicing long hours with Silver in the weapons room, Keelen lay in bed, inspecting the vial Afton had given him. The green liquid practically glowed within the glass. He'd almost forgotten all about his *gift*. It seemed to stare back at him, urging him to drink it down, and see what Afton had meant when she'd said, *For Silver.*

"Damn the temptation," Keelen grumbled as he reached for the glass and uncorked it. He'd expected the smell to be unpleasant, but a rosy scent—like Silver—caressed his nostrils. With a flick of the wrist, he tossed the contents back into his mouth. The liquid was cold like ice as it slid down his throat. He waited for the rush of something to burst through him, or even the magic of the earth to sing harder. But he, the room, and everything in it, remained the same.

A glimpse of Silver flashed through his mind. Her beside him, wielding the mace, him wanting her pressed against him, clothing off. *Fuck.* His hair fell forward into his eye and he shoved it out of the way. Silver had mentioned cutting his hair, but after the long day, he'd forgotten. Perhaps he could go to her and let that lead to something more—their naked skin flushed with one another—so he could stop this lusting.

Fine. Keelen pushed up from the bed, placed the swords at his back, and headed out into the hallway. He passed several servants who watched him questioningly, perhaps a bit flirtatiously, while he made his way to Silver's room. She'd pointed it out to him earlier before taking him to his. As soon as he stood outside her door, he rapped his knuckles against the wood.

She didn't answer.

A few violet and white flowers rested in vases on the wall. Keelen was tempted to grab them and bring them to her as a … what? Gift? Flowers in exchange for a fuck? He didn't take them.

Keelen cradled the sides of his head, trying to remember how he was before. Remember *anything*. At that moment he wanted to shred his skull apart and piece everything back together to see if that would help.

Cradling the knob, he turned it and the door pushed open. She'd left it *unlocked*. He could see why Afton would want a guard for her sister if Silver couldn't even manage to lock a door. Someone could easily walk in. Like him…

As Keelen slipped inside, he peered around her room. The walls were painted a pink and black with a matching canopied bed. Everything looked … messy. Clothing strewn across the floor, bedside table with papers scattered. Her bed was rumpled, pillows thrown on the floor, as if she'd fought someone… He froze. *Had* she been attacked? Taken? When he was supposed to be guarding her.

A rustling echoed just ahead. He pulled a sword from the sheathe at his back and rounded the bed, where he found another door with candlelight spilling out from the bottom. Fumbling sounds stirred from inside.

Keelen rushed to the door and wiggled the handle. Locked. A crash reverberated on the other side. As he was about to ram his shoulder against the door, it flew open. Silver surged out, barreling him to the ground.

Silver was on top of him, her razor teeth released, her claws digging into his shoulders, her hair wet. The blacks of her irises eclipsing the white and blazing with a glittery sheen.

"It's just me," Keelen rasped, his sword still in his hand against the floor. "Your door was unlocked."

Silver's eyes cleared, her teeth and claws retracting. "Sorry, I didn't know it was you. And I didn't know I had left the door unlocked. Sometimes I leave it like that for Afton." She quickly released him and stood.

Keelen already missed her soft body pressed against him. Pushing up from the floor, he tucked the sword at his back. He studied her reddened cheeks, then his gaze dropped to a silky robe wrapped around her. The upper swells of her breasts greeted him, and he yearned to push the cloth back, to expose everything so he could explore with his tongue, teeth, and hands.

"You should still always keep it locked," he said, struggling to keep his voice even.

"I'll remember that next time."

With her wet hair swept back, Keelen could see every single curve and feature of her face. The scar on her chest stood out even more than when they'd been outside. But not more than her red lips. He wondered what it would be like to kiss them now … had wondered it for years. *What*? Why was he thinking about years? He'd meant *day*…

"Did you need something?" Silver asked, fiddling with the

tie at her waist.

"You were going to cut my hair earlier." Keelen didn't know what else to say. He was still busy thinking about the *years*.

"Oh, follow me." She walked back into the bathroom, with him trailing behind her, and motioned for him to sit at a stool in front of an oval mirror. Preserved butterfly wings of different colors circled the glass.

He slipped inside the room and watched as she picked up a comb, running it through her locks. Sinking down onto the stool, he straightened his spine while Silver took the same comb to him.

"I'm not the best at cutting, but I can trim a little." She bit her lip and grabbed the scissors, her eyes settling on his in the mirror.

Magic hummed harder within him as she cut chunks off at his brow, his loose curls bouncing. Then she clipped a few areas at his nape before setting the scissors down. She pushed her own hair behind her shoulders, and he imagined the strands were back to the color of a night sky. The way it always was, when he'd been nestled in her hair.

Keelen stilled, swallowing deeply. Nothing else came to him. Brushing off whatever was going on, he placed his hands around her wrists and gently pulled her toward him, to where he was level with her. "I wanted to tell you something."

His hands started to shake, perspiration coating his palms. Why was he getting nervous?

Silver blinked, her dark eyes dancing with amusement. "You look as though you're about to propose."

"What? No, I..." *Fuck.* He slid his hand to her cheek as he'd rehearsed in his head earlier, dragging it slowly down to her neck, across the scar on her chest, letting his palm linger. She sucked in a breath but didn't move away. The texture of her chest was uneven but still so soft, more delicate than he'd imagined. *For years.* His fingers trembled at that.

Keelen couldn't read her thoughts but badly yearned to. "I want to kiss you."

Her eyes widened. "We shouldn't." But then she edged closer, her warm breath brushing his mouth. "We should."

Licking his bottom lip, he leaned forward and closed the distance. His hand slid up the back of her neck until his fingers entwined in her damp hair.

Keelen's lips caressed hers while hers mirrored his. He parted them with his tongue and something inside him seemed to be fracturing. A low moan escaped her throat when his tongue flicked hers, tasting all that he could. She shifted closer until she was in his lap. He drew her nearer, allowing her legs to wrap around his waist. The kiss deepened, while his hands cradled her face, claiming her mouth for as long as he could. He then scaled his fingers to the open slit of her robe.

Keelen's hands wanted to feel every inch of her skin, as did his mouth, desperately. His finger trailed down to the valley between her breasts, then he teased Silver, as well as himself, by drifting it up to her scar. "Tell me what happened."

Her gaze caught his, her white pupils dilated. "My parents made Afton do it."

He froze. "Couldn't she have made another choice?"

She shook her head. "No. They would have taken something worse from me if she hadn't done it. So my sister made the decision I would have wanted her to make."

"What happened to your chest?" Keelen asked as he sat nestled against her neck, wishing he could feel her warmth.

Silver took a spider out from the jar and pushed it into his beak. "Let me start from the beginning. My sister isn't the villain, she's the hero."

Keelen blinked, unable to catch his breath. He couldn't… He couldn't do this. Biting the inside of his cheek, he lifted Silver off him.

"I need to go. I shouldn't have come." His chest thrummed and hummed and sang. Blood coursed through his veins as if going straight to his heart, his head. Silver in various ages stood before him—a younger girl, a woman he found to be more beautiful than the most perfect rose. And he *remembered.*

"Wait!" she called after him as he hurried out the door.

His chest heaved when he stumbled and rounded the corner, not giving her a chance to catch up while he continued down the halls.

Throwing open the door to his room, he sank to his knees on the plush carpet. He'd always wondered what it would be like to have Silver's lips pressed to his, their tongues intertwining. But he'd always been in a wax raven form while with her. The bits and pieces unfolded, wrapping around his mind, squeezing tightly. More and more and *more*. He remembered … *loving* her. *Always* loving her.

Keelen loved her so much that it had hurt at times because the form he'd been in wasn't that of a man. He may not have remembered where he'd come from, but he always knew what he was, a male hidden inside a shape that wasn't meant to align with her body. Loving her was a secret he'd always meant to keep. And he'd just fucked that up.

How did he suddenly remember? His gaze drifted to the empty vial beside his bed. Afton. She'd known what she was giving him and hadn't said outright what the glass contained. What if he'd never chosen to drink it? Would Afton have even told him? He bet she wouldn't have.

All he could feel and think about now were those brief moments of Silver's lips on his, her legs spread around him. He'd told her just yesterday that he never wanted to come back if he died, but the truth was, he would gladly die over and over to see her again. Even though Silver had brought him here to be Afton's weapon, he was never meant to be hers. He was always meant to be Silver's. Afton had gotten that part right when choosing him to be her sister's guard.

Something else nagged at him, growing stronger with each

passing moment. Something dark, attempting to rise to the surface, but it was still too far away to grasp.

ELEVEN

AFTON

Afton bathed, cleansing her body of the journey, and struggling to wash the memories of Ragan ... *Thorin* ... into oblivion. As she scrubbed and scrubbed, she only became more irritable at the thought of Thorin, of his deception.

Too soon the water was cold, and Afton left it with a sigh. After drying herself, she dressed in a simple nightgown and sat on the edge of the bed. She combed the tangles from her wet hair, wondering how her sister was faring back at home, when a knock at the door interrupted her thoughts.

She grabbed her mace and opened the door to find a tray of fruit and wine in the deserted hallway. Afton snorted. If Thorin thought she would eat a mystery dinner, then he didn't know her at all.

Shutting the door on the food, Afton pulled out her own apple and jerky from her trunk. She wasn't hungry, but she shoved down as much as she could and let time pass.

No one else came to her door. Not Javan, not Shani, not any of the guards or servants, nor Thorin. He hadn't even slipped a letter under the door like he used to. She didn't know how to feel about any of this.

The castle remained quiet, too quiet for her liking. Afton

had expected to at least hear the pitter-patter sounds of servants passing through the hallway. Without a drop of magic at her disposal, Afton felt naked, exposed, so she clutched her mace like a lifeline.

She leaned against the headboard, watching the candle flame lick its way down the wax—only a little light remained before the room would be bathed in darkness. Afton wondered if Keelen had drunk from the vial she'd given him. The tonic had come from Willem's collection and was one of the reasons she'd asked Silver to step outside. Afton had waited until she'd heard Midnight's hooves stomping away, then she'd asked Aris for a vial of the tonic.

She knew Keelen had to have memories buried somewhere within himself. At first, she thought he could be lying about not remembering who he was, but then she saw him, studied how he watched Silver. A sort of protectiveness in those few moments, even if he hadn't realized it, and that was why he would make the perfect guard for her sister. With the friendship they'd shared in their past, he could be a better guard for Silver if his memories returned. Besides, if he ended up not being trustworthy, Silver was strong enough to rip him apart. If she didn't, Afton would. But if he hadn't taken the tonic by the time she got back, she would just have to force the liquid down his throat.

A dull throb drummed inside her. Or she thought it had… For a brief moment, she could have sworn there was the familiarity, that stirring of magic. The grassy, smoky scent of the castle permeated the air, stronger than before.

But then the brush of what she imagined to be tiny fingers poking at her insides roused again. She pushed herself from the bed and stood. A slow hammering through her veins traveled upward, connecting to every inch of her before ceasing under her rib cage.

Her heartbeat quickened its pace, and she pressed one hand to her chest. She then grabbed her mace and patted the dagger hidden in the pocket of her nightgown. Whatever this was—this touching, stroking, squeezing—it wasn't like the gentle hum of magic from Ketill. It was more sensual, ferocious. And as the energy swelled, it was nothing like the dark magic she'd tapped into when she'd killed her parents—it was worse. She'd traveled across Enare when she was younger, and the magic throughout the lands had always been the same as Ketill's.

Was this what Thorin wanted her to wait for? This pit of tarnished energy?

A thrashing of wings sounded from outside. Afton rushed to the window and yanked the heavy curtains to the side. Dust swirled as Afton peered out the grime-covered glass and into the night.

Silvery moonlight illuminated a lone figure standing in the garden. *Thorin.* He was waiting for her, just as he said he would.

Afton narrowed her eyes and released the curtains. Why hadn't he just asked her to meet him somewhere in the castle instead? She plucked up her mace and tugged on her boots before leaving the room.

Candles lit the empty hallway, their waxy smell filling the dusty space. A door opened, startling Afton, and she raised her mace. Her shoulders relaxed as she met Shani's gaze.

Afton pressed her finger to her lips for Shani to keep her movements quiet. She didn't want to have to deal with Javan hearing and trying to intervene.

Shani blinked, her eyelids heavy as she mouthed, *Do you feel this strange energy?*

Afton pushed past Shani and entered her room, finding it still lit with two candles. It was a mirror image of the space where she was staying—the same style of bed, wooden nightstands, and one mahogany wardrobe.

She whirled around to face Shani, keeping her voice low. "I feel it. And I don't know what it is."

Shani bit her lip as though concentrating, then straightened, her eyes wide. *I can't draw in this magic here either, but it's nothing like back in Ketill.*

"Was it like this for you when we traveled with my parents?" Afton asked, the energy squeezing all the way down to her bones.

Placing a hand to her heart, Shani shook her head.

A dagger rested on the nightstand beside Shani's bed. Afton grabbed it and placed it into the woman's hands. "Keep this on you and stay here. I'm going to meet Thorin in the garden and discuss this with the bastard." She knew exactly why he hadn't tried to tell her about this earlier—she wouldn't have believed him. Not until she truly felt it.

Inhaling sharply, Shani frantically waved her hands back and forth. She pointed at herself to go with Afton.

"This isn't a request for you to remain here—it's a command."

Shani tightened her lips together, as if she didn't want to listen, but she nodded.

Without another word, Afton grabbed the skirt of her nightgown and slipped out of the room. Down the halls, not a single human silhouette stood or passed. Candles, in curving bronze holders, flickered along the walls, guiding her to the front of the castle.

Gently, Afton opened the door with a low creak. A shiver raced down her spine from the chilly breeze as she ventured out into the night. Even though it wasn't winter yet, she could already see her breath in the air.

Despite the breeze, the limbs of the trees didn't rustle, the dead bushes didn't shake. She squinted her eyes. Was this a trick of her mind? It wasn't.

Afton crept behind the trees as she made her way to the garden. She wanted to catch a glimpse of Thorin, to see what he was doing, before making herself known. Peering around a wide trunk, Afton's gaze latched onto his tall, broad frame. He stood as frozen as the trees within the dead rose garden. But then he folded his arms at his chest and stared up at the star-lit sky. He was as beautiful as he always was—his sculpted face, his plump lips, his strong jaw—and she hated herself for thinking that.

The energy matched the palpitation of her heart, swelling with a certain *wrongness*. An ugliness, rawness, as though a dark smoke was enveloping the entire world. It was like her heart was beating along with a cacophonous tune of music. And even though she'd never had a problem ignoring dark magic, something inside her yearned to relish this.

"What did you want, *Thorin*?" she hissed, stepping out from behind the tree.

His head jerked toward her. "You came." He sighed, his face full of relief.

She ignored the rush of wanting to go to him, to fold her arms around him. "Why did you have me meet you here?"

"Please listen to me," he rasped. "This decaying energy is because of Valgmyr. It's why I need to unite with you. Why I *lied*."

Valgmyr… Valgmyr… *That old tale Silver used to worship*? The one that Afton had told her repeatedly was only a story like all the other fairytales.

"Valgmyr?" she spat. "That world doesn't exist. Barely anyone in our territory even knows the tale anymore."

"It does." He pursed his lips. "That's why there are only two guards remaining here—there were five. More before. The servants are all gone. Some have been lured to Valgmyr, but most I sent away. They vowed not to say a word while I worked on the situation here. The ones you've met were silenced by the unrestful energy, their minds in a fog."

"You're lying again."

"Did the guards speak to you when they tried to force you to come here?"

Afton thought back to before she'd torn into the guards'

flesh. They'd come in with the letter, then tried to take her. Not a word had been exchanged from them. Did it matter though?

She couldn't let herself fall into that hole this soon, be gullible enough to trust Enare's king. "And you? Why are you still here? Able to speak freely? Your mind clear?"

"Perhaps I'm cursed." He paused, clenching his jaw. "Don't you feel it, Afton? This is why I wanted you to stay the night. So you would understand why I did what I did to get you to come."

To admit anything would be pure ignorance, especially to an enemy. "No, I don't feel anything." Afton narrowed her eyes at him. "You fucked me for months. You could have told me who you were."

"You ignored every single one of my letters for the first month!" His voice rose an octave. "That's why I came. Even then, I still had letters sent to you which you chose to ignore."

"You came as a servant named Ragan! That isn't the same thing."

"I hadn't planned on becoming a servant there. I don't know! Things changed when I met you."

"If your territory was in such danger, then you wasted another three months by being in Ketill." She never would have left her own lands at risk.

"There was still time. It wasn't as bad as it is now," he whispered. "But to have gotten to know you was worth everything."

She scowled. For once in her life, she couldn't think of anything to say, couldn't come up with a way to hurt him.

"You have to know that the guards who tried to take you, I never would have allowed that. They were desperate."

If she hadn't met this man before, she would have pretended as though she cared, as if she believed him. Then later she would have brought him down to his knees before burying her mace in his chest.

She took a step closer, inhaling the comforting musky scent that was all him. "I'll listen to what you have to say, and that's the best I can offer."

"I'll take whatever you wish to give." That hopeful look on his face was the same one he'd worn when she'd met him back in Ketill. She wanted to scream at herself for being weak with him still. He was a liar… But what if he wasn't lying about this?

"I need tea," she finally demanded, wanting to find somewhere to sit and think.

"I'll make you some." Thorin's face softened. "I know you still don't know how."

Afton caught herself almost smiling before ripping the expression away. It was true, though. She had never made tea in her damn life, but she'd seen Silver do it. "Perhaps I do know how."

"Hmm. Then you can show me." He grinned, motioning her with a finger. Even though it wasn't a seductive movement, her body heated on its own accord, the energy thrumming harder.

The smile stayed planted on his mouth when she moved to follow him. She didn't know if she was being a heroine, hell-bent on securing Ketill, or a fool.

Afton studied Thorin's movements, how he carried himself. He was assured, same as he was back in her castle—the type of man she had always chosen to bring to her bed. Yet there had been something different about him, something that had made her fall in love with him. His kindness was one of the reasons. It was a trait she didn't know she could want, *need*. That, paired with his humor, the way his naked body aligned with hers—it had all lured her in.

They turned into the kitchens, both coming to a stop. Black pans hung across the walls and a cutting table sat in the middle with knives atop it. Dust covered a stove that looked as if it hadn't been used in ages.

Thorin followed her gaze to the unclean area. "I need to tidy up a bit. That's why I brought you fruit and wine earlier instead. With only two guards left and no servants…"

So he had been by her room… A swarm of blasted butterflies fluttered in her stomach at the thought. Afton was falling, falling, falling into the trap again. She bit the inside of her cheek, drawing blood, to pull herself out of the hole. Picking up a tea kettle on top of the stove, she gritted her teeth. "Where's the water, Your Highness?"

A hint of a smile played on his lips. "It's right behind you." He gestured to a bucket full of water.

As she poured in the liquid, her brow furrowed and water splashed everywhere.

"Hmm, I would say you still don't know how to make tea." He covered his mouth with a fist, seeming to fight back a laugh, and took the kettle from her. He then placed it on the stove to heat.

"How do you think I can help your situation?" Afton asked, keeping her gaze trained on him, hoping to read any lie he should mutter.

"Because you saved your own territory before," he said softly. "Remember what you told me about you and your parents?"

She gritted her teeth and nodded. Thorin knew, like everyone, that she'd murdered her parents when she was younger. But he also knew why she had … for Silver.

"I would have done the same." A serious expression crossed his face. "For my sibling."

"You don't have any."

His gazed focused on her. "Even though I don't have a sister, I understand. I would have done the same. Perhaps worse."

Afton frowned, at a loss for words. If Ketill had known exactly *how* she'd murdered her parents, they would have believed her to be a true monster. Thorin knew she'd tapped into dark magic, burst their hearts with her shadow. However, she couldn't let herself be swayed by him after less than a day of finding out who he was—it would be too dangerous.

The tea kettle screeched and Afton backed away from him to pour the water into two cups. She thought about poison once more, but if Thorin had wanted to poison her, he could have easily performed the task back at his cottage. Besides, she knew enough about herbs to determine what was safe. It took her only a moment to find a basket of chamomile, sage, and mint in one of the cabinets. She stirred in the chamomile and took in the fresh aroma.

"Thanks," he said when she handed him a steaming cup. "So, will you help me? The land is dying. You've seen the trees, the bushes."

Afton blew on her tea, considering his question. Even if what he said was true, what could she do? There wasn't a way for her to tap into any of the magic here. "No, we're leaving in the morning."

"I think you'll change your mind when you hear the rest." He held up his cup and took a long swig of the tea. A haunted look appeared within his eyes.

"And why's that?"

"Because it's already spreading into your territory."

Afton froze, taking his words in. Yet she had to remember who she was talking to, not the man from her castle kitchens, but the King of Enare, who she truly didn't know. "You've lied to me before, and you could be lying now." Rising from the chair, she stepped away from him.

"I wouldn't lie to you about this." He stood from his seat. "I know how much you care about Ketill, which is why I'm asking this of you. It isn't only me who's been deceitful, you know. You came here dressed as your sister. To what? Murder me? And I forgive you anyway."

Closing her eyes for a brief moment, she turned away from him before she could give into the urge to do whatever he wished. "Goodnight and goodbye."

The taunting energy continued to thrum, yelling at her that she'd made a mistake, as she hurried down the hallways and into her room. Yet she ignored it, wishing she could thrash it to pieces instead.

Removing her boots, Afton slipped into bed but didn't shut her eyes. She would explain everything in the morning to Javan and Shani once they were in the carriage. All she could think about was Valgmyr. Nagging thoughts knocked at her. What if Thorin wasn't lying about her territory? What if this haunting energy was spreading into Ketill? What if the King of Valgmyr was real? Because if Valgmyr did exist, for the first time in her life, Afton wouldn't have an answer on how to undo what was being done.

TWELVE

SILVER

All day Silver had thought about the night before—Keelen's lips on hers, his hand trailing her scar, then sliding between her breasts. She'd still been covered by her robe, but she'd never been exposed like that to anyone, and in that moment, she'd wanted to give him everything.

That was, until he didn't want anything she had to offer.

Silver pressed her fingers to her mouth, still missing his warm lips on hers. It wouldn't happen again—she'd seen the regret on Keelen's face. Perhaps it was meant to happen this way, fate's way of telling her to keep her attention on Afton and Ketill. She'd loved him for so long, and as she told herself before, it wouldn't have mattered what he looked like because he was still hers.

But he wasn't hers…

For most of the day, she'd stayed locked inside her room, attempting to clean. Yet, somehow, more gowns ended up on the floor as she tried to rearrange her wardrobe. She scanned over a yellow dress, stitched with black flowers at the hem and metal skulls resting at the shoulders, debating where to put it. A knock came at the door and she shoved it between two other garments.

Silver hurried to the door, expecting Afton. Her sister was overdue, and if she didn't return today, Silver was going to track her down. As she pulled the door open, Keelen stood there, his curled locks rumpled in different directions. In his hands was a plate filled with tarts covered in strawberry and grape jam.

Keelen's fingers tapped the bottom of the plate, his expression unreadable while he watched her. Then his throat bobbed as he swallowed. "I brought you something since you haven't come downstairs."

Blinking, Silver peered down at the plate, her stomach twitching for the desserts. A peace offering?

She couldn't deny such a glorious thing. "Ah, I'll owe you some next." With a smile, she took the plate, the bottom warming her hands.

"You don't owe me, Silver." He smiled back.

She tilted her head, studying his teeth, her heart singing at the sight. His smile was the most beautiful one she'd ever seen, and he was only just now showing it. "You seem different today?"

Pressing a fist to his mouth, he cleared his throat. "I wanted to apologize for last night. Fuck, I'm truly sorry."

His hot mouth against hers, the tender stroke of his fingertips…

"Don't worry. It meant nothing." Silver winced on the inside—it wasn't the truth. But she didn't want Keelen to know how much she'd enjoyed it when he obviously hadn't.

"Sometimes we do things we shouldn't," he said, his brows lowering. "I'm headed to the weapons room if you care to join."

Silver glanced back at her mess of a room and figured she could procrastinate a little longer—or forever. It would only get messy again anyway. Nodding, she picked up a tart, bit into its magical sweetness, and walked beside him down the hall.

His eyes continued to flick back and forth at the tarts.

She released a small laugh and gestured at the plate. "Eat some."

"Jeanette gave me several already."

Keelen was still eyeing the tarts, so she took one and handed it to him. "Here. You need another."

His long lashes fluttered as he pushed it into his mouth. A spot of grape jam stuck to his lower lip.

"You have some right there." She pointed to the speck.

He slowly swiped his tongue across the area, catching the lingering jam. "There?"

"Yes, right there," she said, a bit breathless.

Over something as small as that, her chest cracked, her heart bursting free, and she didn't know how to contain it. She glanced away to stop the heat from spreading through her. No more distractions.

They spent the next several hours silently practicing the art of killing—Keelen throwing dagger after dagger and Silver swinging, thrusting, and circling her familiar mace—until sweat drenched them. Silver was about to tell him to just remove his shirt already when the echo of footsteps interrupted her thoughts.

A servant brought them steaming bowls of potato soup, and as Silver sank into the chair at the table, her stomach growled. She hadn't realized how famished the exercise had made her. Neither of them spoke as they hungrily ate their portions before returning to training.

Silver again worried about her sister when practicing, but she swung the mace without pause to divert her thoughts. And yet, that distraction led her to continuously sneak glances at Keelen's muscular form while he used his twin blades.

The clatter of approaching horse hooves and the screech of wagon wheels from outside drew their attention to the door. Silver and Keelen exchanged a heavy glance as she clutched her mace.

Afton.

"I'll be right back," she said, setting her mace on the table. "I think Afton's carriage is here."

"All right," he replied, hurling a dagger forward.

Lifting her skirts, Silver raced out of the weapons room, passing a servant carrying a basket of laundry. She threw open the door and flew outside, her claws extending. Normally she wouldn't have rushed, but she wanted to make sure Afton was in one piece.

Shani sat at the front of the carriage, prepared to return it to the stables. She gave a wave but was without her usual smile. Javan stood outside the carriage, leaning on his cane as Afton stepped down onto the pebbled ground. A sapphire dress, with a sweetheart neckline, showed off her curves, and a dark ribbon laced up the front. The sunlight caressed Afton's hair, the black making her skin appear paler than before. For only a moment, Silver had thought she was looking at her reflection, the image that always quietly stared back.

"You're safe," Silver called, withdrawing her claws and striding up to her.

Afton's dark eyes met Silver's and something in them didn't seem right.

"I need to speak with you." Afton grabbed Silver's wrist and pulled her toward the castle. Silver glanced back at Javan and Shani, but both wore the same distant expression as her sister. What had happened in Enare?

"What's going on, Afton?" Silver said hurriedly, worry bubbling. "Are you all right?"

"I'm fine, but I need us to sit down and talk."

Now that she knew her sister was home safe, her worry turned to something else. "You shouldn't have left me here like that!"

"Sometimes we have to make tough decisions."

Silver twisted out from Afton's grip and glared at her sister's back as she followed her into the weapons room.

Keelen turned to face them, and his hand clenching the dagger dropped to his side.

Afton remained silent as she twirled her mace in between her fingers. Silver knew these motions—Afton was wound up and trying to find a release so she could hold whatever she was feeling inside.

A few moments later, Javan came in and shut the door. Perspiration dotted his forehead, his demeanor stiffer than usual.

"Are you going to tell me what's going on?" Silver asked.

Afton stopped twirling the weapon, her chest heaving as she scanned Silver's face. "You got the hair color right. But, it doesn't matter anymore."

"Something happened in Enare, didn't it?" Silver balled her hands into tight fists, wanting to scream at her sister because Afton was never like this, toying around and avoiding the point. "What is it?" she shouted, unable to hold it back any longer. "How was Thorin? Did he hurt you? You shouldn't have left me with only a note. What if you'd *died*?"

Afton laughed. *Laughed.* "I'm fine, Silver. But things are *wholly* different than I expected. Thorin isn't who we thought he was, and Enare will need to take care of their own issues."

"He doesn't need to die anymore?" Silver arched a brow. "After his guards tried to take you against your will?" Afton was never one to be swayed, let alone by a stranger, so there had to be something else that brought her to this decision.

"There's something strange at the castle in Enare." Javan cleared his throat. "When we arrived, Afton and Shani couldn't sense any magic from the land, but then in the middle of the night, I awoke to a darkness I've never felt. Energy I've never experienced. I went to Afton to tell her we needed to leave, but she'd already had a discussion with *the king* and decided to remain until morning." His gaze flicked to Afton, a scowl on his face.

"I don't understand?" Silver's mouth parted as she turned

to her sister. "And what does he mean by strange?"

"It was as if the magic there was dead during the day. I couldn't even set my claws or teeth free. The two guards there didn't speak, like the other three who came here. Only Thorin. He pleaded with us to stay the night and for me to meet him in the garden. I hadn't expected anything, but then during the night, I felt this energy and decided to meet with Thorin. He explained that his guards have been silenced by the energy, and the others have either vanished because of it or he sent them away. We left before anyone stirred in the morning, including the king."

"Vanished?" No one just vanished unless they were murdered. Even with the magic here, Silver couldn't will people to appear and disappear. She may have drawn Keelen's soul out from Torlarah, but she couldn't make him physically disappear.

"So he says." Afton shrugged. "You remember the Valgmyr story?"

"I remember. You were the one who told me it wasn't real when I believed it." She still did, especially on nights when the stars were shining at their brightest. The mysterious king who lured others to his kingdom, never to be seen again.

"Thorin claims the King of Valgmyr is the cause of his problems." Afton shrugged.

"Why would he not take Thorin then?" Keelen asked. Silver startled. She hadn't even heard him come up beside her.

"I don't know. That's a good question." Afton arched a brow, her gaze shifting to Keelen. "And aren't you becoming the perfect guard? I assume you used my gift while I was gone."

A rush of confusion flowed through Silver. "What gift?"

"The weapons of course." Afton sank down into a chair. Silver didn't believe that was the whole answer, but as she went to speak, her sister continued, "In the morning, the new energy I'd felt was gone. Thorin mentioned this darkness is now seeping into our territory, that it will continue spreading unless we find a way to stop it."

Silver's chest tightened. How could they stop this energy if her sister didn't understand it? "Perhaps we could figure it out together and work alongside Thorin?"

"I told him we wouldn't be returning."

"We have to!" she shouted.

"No, we don't."

Afton would always protect Ketill, regardless if an enemy had relayed the message. It was still a possible threat. To her Kingdom. To her *people*. Something was different. Something was off about Afton. It was as if a part of her had been sucked away then unleashed elsewhere. "What is it? What's truly bothering you?"

"Ragan's the king," Javan said. "He's Thorin."

"What!" Silver gasped, darting her gaze between her sister and Javan. "He can't be."

"I told you to keep quiet about that," Afton snapped. Her expression softened as she looked back at Silver. "Thorin came here in disguise to figure out a way to get me there to help. He claimed if he'd told me everything early on, then I wouldn't have gone, that I already hadn't answered any of his letters." She paused and took a breath. "But he also doesn't know I felt the energy there—he doesn't need to know either."

Ragan was Thorin. Silver let it spin in her mind. He'd lied. Lied to all of them. But perhaps there was a reason … Valgmyr. If the same thing was happening to Ketill, Afton would lie to anyone to make sure her territory was saved. Despite what he'd done to her sister, what if he truly wasn't lying about a darkness spreading here? It wasn't as if he'd lied about the strange energy in Enare if Afton, Javan, and Shani had all felt it.

"I want to go, Afton," Silver said. "You felt it yourself. Let me do the same, and if what he says is true, then it has to be stopped."

"No." Afton gripped the mace.

"This is because Ragan is Thorin, isn't it?" Silver asked. "If Thorin hadn't been Ragan, would you be returning? There are innocents in Enare too—you wanted to help them."

Afton narrowed her eyes at her sister, and Silver cocked her head in return.

They held each other's stares for what felt like days when Afton finally relented. "Three nights. Only because I know you would run off in the middle of the night to seek it out yourself."

That was true—she would have. "And if Thorin is good and on our side, then what?"

"Then our territories will remain separate, and he'll be lucky I let him live." Afton rose out of her seat and stepped toward Keelen. "We'll be leaving tomorrow morning. Are you prepared to guard?"

He nodded. "With my life."

"I see you now have hair. You look almost human." Afton gave a feral smirk and studied him for a moment too long before grabbing Silver by the wrist. "I need to talk to my sister. *Alone*." Motioning Silver to follow her out of the weapons room, Afton closed the door behind them.

They stopped in front of the stairs and Afton leaned forward. "Did Keelen do anything to you while I was gone?"

"What?" Silver's voice squeaked. She thought about his tongue tasting her, his warm fingers traveling across her flesh.

"Did he try to hurt you at all?"

"Oh." A rush of relief flowed through her. "No, he's the perfect guard."

"Good. Don't argue, but he will continue guarding you in Enare while Javan will be with me. I guess it's pointless to pretend to be me anymore. But show me what you can do to defend yourself there if the magic is still gone." Afton tossed her the mace.

"Fine." Silver easily caught the weapon, twirled it in

between her fingers and swung it forward. She stopped just before it struck Afton's cheek—her sister didn't even flinch. "Do you dare to defy me? If you open your mouth once more, I will remove your head and pull your entire skeleton out from within the gaping hole."

Afton rubbed at her chin.

"It was quite good, wasn't it?" Silver grinned, tugging the weapon to her chest. "Very you."

"Enough of that." Afton craned her neck and rotated her shoulders. "Be ready early, so we arrive before nightfall, otherwise we're not leaving. I'm going to find something to eat, preferably bloody to suit my mood." She rolled her eyes and headed to the kitchens, but Silver could have sworn there was a twitch of her lips before she'd turned around.

THIRTEEN

AFTON

A new feeling washed over Afton as she headed toward the kitchens. Disappointment? If Ragan hadn't been Thorin, she would have been searching for him, anxious to take him to her bedroom, the lake behind the palace, or one of the walls in the kitchens. Then she and Silver would have prepared for their swapped roles in Enare, in which her sister would have excelled perfectly. But no need for that now, even though she'd agreed for them to travel to Enare. Part of her should have said no, and not because Thorin was there, but because Silver wouldn't be able to use any magic. Then at night… That strange energy…

Afton should have lied about everything to Silver, but she couldn't. She had planned on concealing Ragan's true identity, yet that wouldn't have lasted long—Silver would have questioned why he hadn't returned to working the kitchens. Despite all that, Silver could be stubborn and would have left for Enare alone.

Thorin's face came to her then, how she would kiss him awake in places that would make him groan, how he would surprise her with new things he'd cooked.

Afton shrugged it off—she needed to forget seeing him

like that and find a distraction, another body to stop her from thinking or feeling, like she used to do. The village's monthly full moon celebration began at nightfall, so for now, she would comfort herself with eating, then later she'd get lost in warm skin.

As for Keelen, she was certain he'd taken the tonic—his expression was different, knowing, softer. Whatever memories of Silver he'd had before blossomed back. Silver didn't know yet either—perhaps it was better that way. Silver wouldn't have to focus on him when there were more important things at hand.

The scent of roasted lamb drifted through the air, and Afton inhaled the delicious aroma. As she entered the kitchens, Jeanette was drizzling gravy onto the meat. Her graying hair was pulled back in a disarrayed bun, and brown stains spotted her apron.

Jeanette's gaze met Afton's, and the woman offered her a soft smile. "Ragan hasn't returned yet."

Afton frowned, picking up a knife to cut into the browned meat, her tone clipped. "He won't be back. We'll have to find someone else to cover his shifts."

"I see." Jeanette plucked a potato from a basket and started slicing it into thin slivers.

"You can take leave for the rest of the day."

"Thank you, Your Highness." Jeanette's smile remained gentle. "I never thought you and your sister looked alike, but with that hair, you're the spitting image of her and your—" She winced, stopping herself.

Father. That was what Jeanette was going to say. If she had finished that sentence, Afton would have said something that wouldn't have easily been forgotten. When Jeanette had found out what Afton's parents had done to Shani, the woman hadn't stood up to them either. But how could she? Afton's parents would have done worse than silence her daughter, they would have slaughtered Shani in front of Jeanette.

"Shani's bringing the carriage around to the back." Afton knew Jeanette was desperate to see her daughter by the way she kept gnawing on her lip.

With a nod, Jeanette untied her apron and left Afton standing alone in the kitchens. Peering at the steaming meat and setting down the knife, Afton extended her claws and sliced into its tenderness. Even though she tried not to think about Thorin when he pretended to be a servant named Ragan, her mind wouldn't listen.

"I like the feel of your body on mine." Ragan smirked.

Afton straddled his hips and leaned in closer to him, yearning to press her lips to his. She desperately wanted her first kiss to be given to him, even if she believed she deserved no one. Biting the inside of her cheek, she forced herself to nip at his collarbone instead. "I prefer when you're inside me," she purred.

"Mmm." He lifted her chin. "I never want to share you with anyone." He wrapped his arms around her waist and nuzzled her neck.

"I'm yours." Since meeting Ragan, she'd only wanted her body given to him, had only wanted his words whispered in her ear.

She lifted her body then lowered it, taking all of him in—he groaned—she moaned—as he filled her with pleasure and something far, far richer.

Afton ripped the lamb with her claws as hard as she could. She was glad she hadn't given him her kisses because the bastard had already taken everything else. Thorin was just another lover to add to her past. That was all. One who could easily be replaced.

"Afton, no one will ever truly love you. It will always be that way because you're queen, and even then, you will always wonder if that's the only reason they love you," her mother cooed.

Perhaps her mother had been right about one thing. She

wasn't meant to be loved.

Afton shut her bedroom door and stepped into the hallway. She'd wrapped her hair in a low bun at the nape of her neck and wore a simple dress and cloak so no one at the celebration would notice her. She brought the cloak's hood over her head, concealing her eyes until she found another warm body. When she returned, she would change her hair back to white-blonde. For now, the black would do.

As Afton descended the stairs, sounds of banging metal echoed in the weapons room. She peered through the open door. Keelen held two blades, striking them against each other.

"Where is everyone?" Afton called as she hovered at the door with her arms crossed. "Aren't you supposed to be watching over my sister?"

"She's with Javan in his office," he said, setting down the blades. His hand fell to a glass jar with spiders crawling inside as he looked at her. "Why are you dressed like you're in hiding?"

Afton leaned forward, lips parting, and ignored his question about her clothing. "Why do you have a jar of spiders?"

"Silver brought them to me." He straightened his tunic, something flickering in his gaze. She could see through his act. It was as if he *knew* something.

"Release the spiders outside."

"I was planning on it. It seems I no longer have an appetite for them."

He ate them before? *Ate* them? And her sister was *fine* with that?

Dropping her arms to her sides, she ignored anything else on that matter and stepped toward him. "You drank the tonic."

It wasn't a question.

Keelen's eyes shifted away from hers and he shook his head. "I'm not going to drink it."

She clicked her nails against the table. "You're lying. Tell me what you remember."

He clenched his jaw, but after a few moments he caved. With a sigh, Keelen shut the door. "Nothing from outside of Ketill. But I remember Silver. I remember being the raven she created. I remember Silver's stories about you and seeing you when she carried me in her pocket. I remember everything about when I was here before. Every time."

Her eyes narrowed. "You were around me in the past?"

"Sometimes." He shrugged.

The thought of being spied on made her blood boil. It cooled quickly, though, because it had been Silver's doing.

His face strained as if he was somewhere else instead of in this room.

"What else is bothering you?" she asked.

"I don't fucking know yet. It's all still muddled." His aggravated tone softened with the next three words. "Everything but her."

This was worse than she'd imagined. The fool really was in love with her sister. And she'd known it even before he could remember. "Does she know?"

"Know what?" Keelen's violet gaze caught hers. The face Silver had created for him was pleasant to look at, yet it wasn't what had gotten her sister's attention. It must have been from how he'd treated her when he was a raven, but from what Afton had seen thus far from him, he was all angles and edges, and she didn't like broken glass.

"Does Silver know you're in love with her?" Afton hissed.

His eyes widened and shot toward the closed door. "No…" He exhaled. "And she won't."

Afton reeled in the magic, her heart thrumming as she released her claws and sharpened teeth. "You're supposed to be her guard. Nothing more. Hear me?" Caring for someone as a friend was one thing, but lusting after someone would only distract him.

He glared at her and changed the subject. "There's another thing."

"What is it?" It couldn't be worse than finding out that the softness she knew he'd felt for Silver went far deeper.

"Silver and Javan know I can feel the magic here. I always could, but I can't wield it."

Afton relaxed, her shoulders loosening. "Plenty of people in Ketill can. It could be from when Silver brought you here, her magic entangling with you."

"Maybe."

"Guard her. Keep her safe. That's all you have to do."

"With my life," he repeated his earlier words.

He'd better fucking do that.

Afton turned on her heels and headed outside. A gust of cool wind blew past her. She wasn't one to go to these celebrations, only a few times with Silver in the past when she'd begged her to, then recently with Thorin. Afton had always pretended not to care about it, but when the moon rose high into the sky at its fullest, there was something fascinating about that.

She ventured down several curved paths and around leafless trees preparing for winter. Afton would have taken one of the horses, but they were almost as recognizable as she was. Her gaze trained on the trees once more and she squinted at them. They weren't only without leaves—they looked like they were ... *dying*.

With a gasp, she took the pebbled path to the stream and followed it to the celebration, studying each tree along the path. Most appeared fine, but some sprinkled in with sickly shades. Afton brushed the thoughts away. She was choosing to believe something was wrong, but it wasn't. Thorin had planted these seeds in her mind.

As she slipped closer to the festivities, the savory aromas of cooking meat filled the air, mingling with laughter and music. The beats of drums and the sounds of flutes soared through the woods. Between the trees, people in the distance danced and stared up at the darkening sky, the moon already rising. The last two full moon celebrations, she'd danced with Thorin. Before that, she'd never danced with anyone. Dancing with him had filled her with a different kind of rush, more than lust, like she was falling and flying all at once, the sensation leaving her body humming its own harmonious song. Light and dark. Entwined.

Thorin's cottage nestled the riverside, and she half expected him to be sitting on his porch steps, waiting for her as always. But of course, he wasn't.

She'd always met him there, then he would lead her inside. Make her *tea*. That only reminded her of making Thorin's tea in Enare. She was about to turn away, find a body to make her forget all that had happened when something in her veins pulsed, like a whisper. A feather soft caress that wasn't innocent at all. A breeze blew past her and a light scent, grassy and smoky, tickled her nose. Peering around, she didn't see anyone else, but she knew that strange pull of energy. Then it stopped.

Afton hadn't brought her mace, so she slipped two daggers from her cloak as she headed to Thorin's cottage. From experience, she knew it was easy to stab and lose a single weapon, which was why she always carried a spare. Usually, it was her mace and a hidden dagger. Her sister still chose not to arm herself, even when Afton reprimanded her.

Extending her claws and teeth, she went up the steps and turned the knob. Locked. The magic of Ketill thrummed its regular heartbeat, and she tapped into it, reeling it forward. Using invisible fingertips, she reached through the door and unbolted the lock.

As the door opened, the sensation hit her again—this time,

the strange energy thrumming stronger. Thorin's musky aroma lingered. Narrowing her eyes, she scanned the room. Two candles rested on the middle of a table in front of the two chairs. She picked up one of the candles and lit the wick with her fingertips.

Holding it in front of her, she walked into the small dining area. Pots and pans littered the top of the stove, and in front of the cabinets … something curled on the floor. The creature's skeleton peeked through its dark gray skin, and paper-thin wings were tucked at its back.

Afton inhaled sharply—she'd never seen anything like it. A sensation tickled her palms, then spread. Darkness. That familiar draw tugged at her like it had in Enare.

Afton shook her arms to make it stop, pretend she'd imagined it, but it was still there.

As she stepped closer to the creature, the thing lurched forward. Blackened lips, eyes wholly white, and small pointed horns protruding from its head—it was an *imp* like the ones described in the Valgmyr story. How? She stumbled back, baring her teeth, lifting her claws, and growled. The imp appeared even more skeletal now that it was on its feet, its gray wings expanding. The creature stood to her mid-thigh.

The same energy that she'd felt in Enare hammered within her again, growing stronger. Here. In *Ketill*.

With a lunge, Afton struck, her claws poised to disembowel the creature. But faster still, the imp was gone, disappearing through the ceiling.

Not possible…

Afton wouldn't let the bastard get away. She ran out the door to dip into the earth's magic. She would kill it from the inside out like she'd done to the rats in the tunnel. But as she threw her head back toward the night sky, there was nothing there. Not any sign of a creature flying. She hurried to inspect the roof, only to find it bare.

The energy was no longer roaring—only the comforting

magic of her home remained.

Afton's heart caught in her throat. Even though she wished Thorin had been lying about this, her territory, she knew now he hadn't.

Anger coursed through her veins as she stared up at the darkness, freckled with bright, glistening diamonds surrounding the full moon. The Valgmyr tale wasn't only a story after all. She would find the Valgmyr King and his imps, then gut them before they could destroy Ketill.

From above, she knew the merciless stars were watching her. *Let them*. She would find a way to pluck them from the sky and dim them for all eternity.

FOURTEEN

SILVER

A soft tapping came from somewhere… Silver lazily opened her eyes, the world still blurry. When she didn't hear it again, she rolled to her side and shut her lids, wanting to crawl back inside her dream where a hand was feeding her tarts.

The noise sounded again, louder than before, and Silver jolted up in her bed with a start. Morning light trickled in through the window. Her eyes widened as she kicked the blanket from her body—she'd overslept!

Tripping over her own two feet, then a pile of gowns on the floor, she rushed to the door and yanked it open. Keelen stood outside, wearing a light brown tunic, tight pants, dark boots, his twin swords at his back, daggers at his hips.

"Come in!" she whisper-shouted, tugging him into her space.

He scanned her up and down, his bright eyes sweeping from her hair that she'd changed back to black, then to the thin material of her nightgown, where they lingered. "You aren't dressed yet?" His voice bounced off the walls and echoed everywhere around her. "Afton's waiting downstairs."

"Shh!" Silver pressed a finger to her lips as if that would make a magical dress appear on her body. "Sorry, I couldn't sleep last night." She'd contemplated several times about going to Keelen to see if he would want to go with her to celebrate the full moon. But instead, she'd denied herself and celebrated from her balcony, alone.

"I know." The edges of his lips turned up a fraction.

"You do?" Silver arched a brow.

"I couldn't sleep either, so I went for a walk around the castle. You were standing on the balcony, peering up at the night sky."

Curiosity nudged at her … what part of the evening was it? She'd been staring at the stars and the moon for most of the night. "And why didn't you say anything?"

He shrugged. "I didn't want to interrupt. You looked at peace."

Perhaps if he could read her thoughts, he would have known that she'd been anything but. For a moment, she wondered what might have happened if he'd called out to her. But there was no use in dwelling on something that hadn't occurred.

The light spilling into her room shimmered in the mirror, reminding her she needed to hurry. No more chit-chat.

"Quick," she breathed, "grab a dress from the wardrobe … or floor. I don't care which, as long as it's fancier than usual."

Before he could answer, Silver whirled around and tore off her nightgown, leaving her wearing only a thin slip. It was too late for her to call up a servant to help lace up a corset. She generally avoided wearing them, and preferred lighter and freer dresses that were a one-person task. But she wanted to look presentable when she confronted Thorin for not only deceiving Afton but her as well.

She would be bringing several weapons with her. Tugging free the drawer at her bedside, she pulled out two sheathed daggers. Normally she wouldn't carry them, but without magic in Enare, she needed to be safe.

As she rolled up her slip, exposing her thigh, Silver

glanced up and found Keelen standing there, watching. "Don't just stand there, help me!"

Biting his lip, he turned from her and picked through the pile of gowns on the floor. "I don't know what the fuck is the difference between any of these. A dress is a dress."

She rolled her eyes. "A dress most certainly is not just a dress. Pick something dark, lacy." With fumbling fingers, she strapped one of the daggers to her thigh, and the other she would place in the pocket of her dress. Even after her late-night rides through the moonlit hills, she'd never been late for anything. And, of course, the one time Afton demanded her presence at a given hour, she would be behind schedule.

The shuffling of fabric came to an end as Keelen plucked up a blue dress that was so dark it almost appeared black. There was a throat collar that connected to the front, leaving a diamond opening at the chest. *Perfect.*

"Wait." She scooped up a corset beside her bed, that she believed was clean, and slipped it on. "Help me tie the back of this first."

Tossing the dress on the bed, Keelen stood behind her as she faced the wall. So close, she could feel his warm breath tickling her neck.

"I don't know what to do with this." His fingers skimmed the corset, dangerously close to her skin, and she suppressed a shiver.

"Pull as tight as you can, then tie it."

"Sure, just pull it, she says." He gave a sharp tug and she sucked in a breath. "Just tie it, she says. I don't know what's going on here!"

"Just do something!" Silver wiggled her hands in a crisscross motion. She could feel him rolling his eyes behind her, but he must have figured out what to do because he didn't ask any questions.

With one firm yank from his strong hands, performing some sort of miracle, he made her back straighten and her chest push upward.

"Thank you," Silver said, collecting the dress from the bed and drawing it over her head.

"Ugh," she continued. "Can you help me with this too? You chose one of the more complicated dresses. I can button the collar." The sleeves were tight all the way down to her wrists, and the skirt flowed from waist to ankles.

Keelen huffed as he buttoned up the back and tied the sash behind her. "There."

Spinning around, she peered down at herself and tucked her other dagger into the secret pocket inside her skirts. "Do I look all right?"

He took a step back and folded his arms, his eyes blazing. "Like Silver."

She wrinkled her nose, not understanding if that was a good or bad thing.

"I mean," he hurried on, "you look like you're about to confront a king."

"Good enough." Silver straightened, her heart striking her sternum. It wasn't that she was nervous about Enare or Thorin, but it was the longing for Keelen that never evaporated.

Taking her gaze from him, Silver slipped on her boots and collected the mace from the corner of the room. Shani had already taken her trunks to the carriage the night before— Silver had packed them with dresses, herbs, candles, and other tinctures she may require. She shouldn't need anything else.

As Keelen walked beside her down the hall to the stairs, her hand grew clammy while gripping the mace. She switched it to her other hand and wiped her sweaty palm against her skirts.

Afton stood at the bottom of the stairs, her blonde hair hanging freely, except for a few braids in various places. A yellow satin dress, stitched with diamond shapes along the hem, covered her body. Golden skulls decorated her shoulders. Afton blinked as Silver stopped beside her.

"You're late." Afton glanced toward Keelen. "And why did it take so long for you to retrieve her?" Something about Afton was different today, distant. She couldn't detect exactly what it was, but purple bags hung beneath her eyes.

"Are you all right?" Silver leaned in and whispered.

"It's nothing," Afton snapped, her razor-sharp teeth sliding out. She paused, softening her gaze. "I'm just ready to leave is all." Then she looked at Keelen. "Grab her a couple muffins from the kitchens. Jeanette has a batch ready." She turned on her heels and headed toward the front door.

Something was truly bothering Afton, and Silver chalked it up to her having to see Thorin again. She waited for Keelen to return, and he came back carrying a small basket of muffins.

He took one out and passed it to Silver. "Is Afton already outside?"

She nodded as they walked out the door to numerous clouds dotting the bright sky. The hair on her arms rose from the cool air of the morning.

At the front of the carriage, Shani held the door open for Afton. The queen spoke a few words, then lifted her skirts to climb inside.

Silver would miss Midnight over the next few days, but he and Afton's horse would be safer at the castle anyway. Curling a smidge of magic from the earth, she shot it in Midnight's direction and hoped he would feel her temporary goodbye.

Stepping into the carriage, Silver's gaze fell to Javan seated across from Afton. She sank down beside her sister as Keelen unstrapped the swords at his back and settled next to Javan.

The carriage rocked when Shani took her seat at the reins, and a moment later they jolted into motion, the sound of hooves against cobblestones filling the air. Silver bit into her still-warm muffin and peered over at her sister, who was staring out the window with her face drawn into a scowl. She wouldn't have thought anything about it, but normally Afton would have said a few exchanges before looking out at the scenery she'd seen a thousand times over. Silver glanced at Keelen who was studying Afton, too, as if he could tell something wasn't right.

Silver poked Afton and held up the muffin. "Eat."

"I'm not hungry."

"Did you even have breakfast?"

"I had tea." She waved her off. "I'll eat something later."

Javan didn't seem to be paying attention as he cracked open a tattered book and started to pore over its yellowed pages.

Perhaps it's nothing. Silver leaned back in her seat and watched the scenery that she had seen time and time again as well.

The carriage ride seemed to last months upon months, though it was less than half a day. They had stopped only to relieve themselves and had eaten jerky inside the carriage. The closer they'd gotten to the castle, the more the scenery appeared to be withering or dead. Silver hadn't been able to feel any magic in Enare just like her sister had said.

Silver was moments from shutting her eyes as exhaustion washed over her, but then out the window, in the distance, a structure loomed through the trees. King Thorin's castle.

She straightened in her seat and turned to Afton, about to speak, when she noticed her sister was asleep.

"We're here," Silver whispered, nudging her.

Afton jerked forward, a high-pitched scream tearing from her throat. "Where did it fly off to?"

Keelen was in front of Silver just as Afton's nails slashed forward, striking his arm instead of her face. Silver gasped. If Afton's claws had been extended, Keelen's arm would have been torn to shreds.

Afton's eyes were wide as she peered around at the three of them. Javan even looked taken aback. She'd woken like this with Javan plenty of times in the past when they'd journeyed but never toward Silver.

"What flew off?" Silver asked, her brow furrowed.

Afton reclined back in her seat, her body shaking for a brief moment before she straightened. "It was a nightmare. I'm sorry, Silver. I didn't mean it."

"It's okay." But the haunted look lingering in Afton's eyes told her otherwise.

Only a few hours of light remained before the sun scurried away for the evening, allowing the mystery energy Afton had experienced to fall across the land. When she'd been younger, Silver had traveled through the areas of Enare, but never near the castle. Even then, she'd been able to feel the magic thrumming in those parts.

Silver concentrated, tightening her fists, attempting to draw up any energy. Nothing here either.

"It really isn't here," she whispered. "There isn't a speck of magic at all."

"Only the energy that comes at night," Afton said. "Promise me you'll keep your guard up the entire time. No matter what you feel or see."

"Of course. We will all protect each other."

"I know you thought you trusted Thorin before. Keep the walls of your own safety stronger than that trust tonight. For me."

If what Thorin had said was true, then he had a reason for being deceitful. But what of Afton? Did he truly love her?

As the carriage pulled up to the castle and slowed to a stop, Silver surveyed her surroundings. Thorin's home wasn't as pristine as theirs. Thick twisting brown vines covered the walls, and in between them, long cracks ran up the bricks. A few of the barred windows on the pyramid towers reminded

Silver of how her parents used to keep their enemies—mostly innocent—trapped in cages. Around the castle, the dead bushes and shriveled trees were nothing like the blooming foliage in Ketill.

Shani opened the door, pulling Silver from her staring spell. Keelen picked up his blades and placed them at his back. Javan stepped out first, then Afton followed behind him.

"We'll take it from here, Shani," Afton said as Keelen and Silver exited. "Bring the carriage around the back, take one of the horses, and go home. Help protect the castle with the other guards while we're gone, and Javan will drive the carriage home when we're ready."

Shani shook her head no.

"It's not a request." Afton's tone made it known that it was the end of that discussion. Silver silently agreed with this—it would be for the best. For Shani's protection.

Frowning, Shani nodded and retrieved their trunks from the back of the carriage. Javan and Keelen took them from her before she retreated to her seat.

Silver gripped her mace and tried once more to conjure any magic that could be rooted deep down, even dark energy. Only emptiness. A hollowness.

Keelen's fists clenched around the trunks' handles, and he glanced back at Silver, shaking his head. He couldn't feel any magic either.

Up ahead, two red-headed guards stood outside the castle in front of the closed doors. A female, her hair in a braid over her shoulder, and a man with short locks. Silver padded toward them, and they remained still, silent. When Javan stepped ahead, the female tugged open the door, motioning them in. She then followed behind them.

It was just as Afton had said.

Inside the castle, a mild scent hit her nose, grass mixed with smoke, but the candles flickering on the walls weren't giving off the smell.

"Where is the king?" Afton asked as they walked past vases of various shapes and sizes, a set of velvet chaises, and large quilts on the walls covered in a variety of different animals—elk by a waterfall, lions hunting their prey, deer bowing to tree spirits.

No answer. It was truly like the guard was under a spell. The Valgmyr King's spell… She shuddered inwardly.

Dust tickled Silver's nose, and she sneezed, the sound echoing.

"Bless you," Keelen said.

She smiled at him in thanks, but something, all the way to her marrow, felt *wrong* here.

The guard led them up a flight of navy-carpeted stairs to an area filled with golden suns and moons hanging on the walls. In front of two doors, the guard flicked her hand for Afton and Javan to stay, then gestured for Silver and Keelen to follow her, a few feet down from the rooms, to the next set of stairs.

Javan stayed behind while Afton came with them up the staircase. It was a tight squeeze as the stairs curved upward, the bricked walls feeling like they would close in on her.

Once they reached the top, the guard waved at the two doors before turning around. She then went back down the staircase, leaving the three of them alone.

"I'm going to find out where Thorin is." Afton lifted her chin. "Stay here until Javan and I return."

"Be careful," Silver said, but her sister was already disappearing down the stairs.

Silver picked a random door and pushed it open. A room with a large bed draped in ivory silk sheets greeted her. The walls were painted a deep blue and an ornate rug was spread out in the middle of the stone floor. Three wardrobes rested against the far wall, and on the opposite side stood a chair and a circular table.

Holding the handle, she looked at Keelen. "Do you want

to come in?"

"I'll stand guard out here," Keelen said, inspecting every inch of the small area. "Just in case."

She nodded. "Night should be falling soon." Her heart beat to the rhythm of hummingbird wings, while she waited for what was to come.

FIFTEEN

AFTON

Afton sat in the empty porcelain bathtub, dress and all, folding and unfolding the letter the female guard had given to her before she could thoroughly search for Thorin. The letter read that the king was out hunting but would return soon for dinner and they could meet him then. Thorin hadn't known that she would return, but something in her had still hoped he'd spent the time since her departure merely waiting for her, yearning for her presence. The realization that he hadn't didn't sit well with her.

She'd gone upstairs to let Silver know the details of the letter. Silver had wanted her to stay with her, but Afton said she wanted to rest when all she really wanted was to be alone, sitting in the empty porcelain bathtub in her dress.

Setting the letter beside her, Afton cradled her face with her hands. She'd managed to pull herself together—mostly—but here alone, with only her thoughts, Afton's body trembled as she thought about everything.

The withering trees.

The imp.

Its white eyes.

The way it flew through the ceiling.

She'd gone back and forth with herself about the choice to not tell Silver, but finally decided her sister didn't need the added worry. Afton would shoulder that.

In that moment, she wanted her claws and her viciously sharp teeth so she could tear apart any enemy who got in her way, the same way she'd shredded Enare's guards when they'd tried to take her.

Once she got a hold of whoever was behind the tarnished energy seeping into her territory—be it the Valgmyr King or his imps—she swore to herself that she would bask in a bath of their blood while eating their hearts.

A knocking came at her door—Afton jerked her chin up and quickly stood. She stepped out of the tub and straightened her dress. Grabbing her mace, she padded toward the door.

Another tap sounded and she wedged it open to find Javan with his hand in mid-knock, the other resting on his cane.

"I think we should see if the king has returned. Do you need more time?" Javan asked.

"No." Afton frowned. She looked at Javan who leaned harder on his cane than usual, his face worn and wrinkled. Secretly, she hated seeing him that way, deteriorating. She preferred him as the guard he was before, where she could hate and seethe at him all she wanted to. His frailer state made her want to regret it at times. "Wait here, while I go and get Silver."

Lifting her dress, she ascended the steps, the bare walls unbearably tight around her. Empty cobwebs lingered in corners of the ceiling.

At the top of the stairs, in the small square space, Keelen, eyes closed, sat at Silver's door, his head pressed against it.

Useless.

"I know it's you," he said, not opening his eyes. "Just as I would have been able to tell if it was Javan or Silver."

Afton frowned.

Keelen opened his lids and stood from the floor, popping

his neck. "She's napping."

"How is it she can fall asleep at a time like this?" Afton bet her sister could even drift off on a bed of broken glass or sharp daggers. She moved toward the door and brushed past him to go inside.

Silver was on the bed, wearing only a thin slip, sleeping on her stomach on top of the covers.

"Are you ready?" Afton asked, her voice booming.

Silver's eyes flew open and she quickly sat up with a yawn. "I was about to put another dress on. That one got too unbearable, so I cut it and the corset off with the dagger."

"A bit dramatic?" Afton rolled her eyes and grabbed her sister's hand, helping her up. "You still should have gotten ready before taking a nap."

"I unpacked the dresses." Silver pointed to a pile of gowns crumpled on the floor.

Afton sighed and plucked up a gray dress with a rounded neckline. The entire skirt was decorated in tiny white pearls, and crisscrossing ivory lace trailed up the sides of the bodice. She tossed the dress to Silver, who easily caught it, then tugged the fabric over her head. After Silver shoved her arms through the sleeves, she struggled with the ties at the back of the dress.

"Let me show you how to do it," Afton groaned and turned her sister around. "Suck in."

Silver took in a deep breath, and Afton pressed her foot against Silver's lower back, then yanked the strings. Silver squeaked, and her body straightened while Afton tied the ends off into a knot.

"Thank you, but now I can't breathe. This feels worse than a corset. How do you do this every day?" Silver asked, placing a black collared necklace at her throat before collecting the mace from the floor.

"You'll manage. And it won't unravel." Afton smirked and opened the door.

Keelen glanced up as they both stepped out of the room. He peered straight past Afton toward Silver. "It's a little off center."

Afton looked to where his gaze was now lingering—Silver's breasts. "Eyes up here." She pointed at her face.

Keelen rubbed at his jaw, crimson creeping up his neck. "Not *that*. The collar around her throat. The sword piece in the middle is dangling too far over."

"Oh!" Silver shifted the cloth until it was centered.

At that moment, pride washed over Afton. Her sister looked like a true warrior—confident, strong, and capable of slicing an enemy into two without a second thought.

Her gut tightened when she settled her gaze on her sister's scar. Like always, she had to remind herself that if she hadn't burned Silver, her parents would have done much worse.

"I think we're ready now," Silver said.

Afton led the way down the winding staircase, finding Javan no longer alone but waiting with the female guard.

Neither spoke to the other. Not surprising.

"What's going on?" Afton asked, her skirts swishing, as she came up beside Javan.

He handed her a note on a small sheet of paper.

Afton,
I'm sorry I wasn't here. Meet me in the dining room.
Yours,
Thorin

Perhaps Thorin should have come and sought her out as soon as he arrived instead of serving a note to her like a coward. Even though she'd loved the notes he would sneak under her door in the past… Taking a deep swallow, she had to remember where she was, and who he was.

The female guard motioned them forward, her blank expression only making Afton grow more curious. It seemed as if the guard had sampled too many wines, but, in reality, it was more than that.

The guard guided them down several more hallways, silent except for the sound of their feet against carpet, then marble. They passed the kitchens, which drew up the memory of Afton drinking tea with Thorin, when she'd told him she wouldn't help Enare. He would have her sister to thank for this, not her—she hadn't wanted to come back. But deep down she knew that was a lie. The truth was she wanted to see him, to be near him, to touch him, in spite of his treachery. And after the imp and the withering trees appeared in her own kingdom, Afton couldn't stay away, no matter what she was or wasn't feeling for him.

They walked through an arched hallway with vaulted ceilings, covered in evenly-dispersed iron chandeliers, into a spacious dining area. Ornate silver and gold flowers hung on the walls, and a large rectangular table, suited to fit at least twenty people, stretched across the room. The chairs' rounded tops featured sharp points, like thorns, at each end.

Wine-filled glasses, bowls of fresh fruit, and dried meat sprawled across the table. Afton wished instead for steaming platters of buttered rolls, vegetables, and meat slathered in gravy. But she supposed this was the most he could do after being left with no servants.

"You came back," a deep voice said from behind her, driving a rush of lust straight to her center.

But she hardened her heart again as she whirled to find Thorin entering the room, wearing a crimson tunic and dark breeches that cradled his strong thighs deliciously. Mud covered the heels of his boots, and several tendrils of hair hung loose from the leather tie. It looked as if he'd just come in from hunting and hadn't changed. His simple appearance, the familiarity, calmed her. Numerous times, she'd unfastened those pants, gripped him in her hand, and pumped him until he shouted her name.

He smiled warmly as he glanced from her to Silver, but his eyes returned to Afton. She didn't smile back, even though she was tempted.

Before Afton could answer, Silver moved forward and brought a hand across Thorin's cheek. His head slammed to the side, the sound echoing. Afton's eyes widened—she hadn't even done that when he'd revealed his true identity on her last visit. For whatever reason, she hadn't been able to unleash true fury on him. Her heart swelled with pride that her caring, loving sister had done it for her.

"I deserve that," Thorin said softly, pressing a palm to the reddened area.

"You should have told us sooner," Silver replied in a low tone.

"I had my reasons, but I'm sorry." Sincerity rang true in his voice as he kept his eyes trained on Silver.

Sorry? *Sorry?* The bastard hadn't even told her that. Afton squared her shoulders, her jaw clenched. No, she refused to give him the satisfaction by pouting like a child about it.

"Don't lie to me or my sister again," Silver growled.

Thorin lowered his hand. "How about we discuss what's been happening here? I'm sure you've heard everything from Afton." His gaze fell to Keelen. "It seems you brought a different guard to replace Shani this time? He's new?"

Silver nodded. "His name is Keelen."

Keelen didn't say anything, only watched Thorin with a hard stare.

"Very well." Thorin pulled out a chair for Silver then drew out another, his eyes meeting Afton's. "I really didn't think you were coming back."

"I didn't either."

"Maybe I can make you some tea?" Thorin gave her a small, almost boyish, smile.

Afton glared but couldn't control the twitch of her lips as she took a seat.

Thorin moved to the head of the table, while Javan and Keelen both remained standing. Running a finger across his lower lip, Javan observed the dried meat as if it was doused in poison. He focused on Afton with an annoyed expression.

As she studied an apple, a rush of energy stormed through her, like a gust of winter wind accompanied by hail. Not white but dark, darker than any starless night. It was there, like last time. The smoky, grassy scent bloomed, but she didn't let it show, didn't even fidget.

The king blinked. "Do you feel it?"

"The magic you last spoke of?" She squinted, pretending to concentrate. "No."

Thorin lifted his head and peered around the table, his eyes wide. "Do any of you? It can't only be me."

They all shook their heads. She could tell by Silver's expression that she wanted to speak the truth, but she held back for Afton.

Keelen stood closer to Silver than he had been, maybe too close for her liking.

Thorin reached for a peach, exchanging a glance with the three of them. "Are you willing to stay and help?"

Afton tipped her glass of wine back, taking a slow sip of its sweetness. "For now." She would speak to him alone later, to discuss what she saw in Ketill.

"Then we're united." The way he'd said united made it seem as if he didn't want only Enare safe, but her territory as well. He brought the glass to his lips, and drank it down. His eyes lingered on her, and she liked that they did.

A loud screech sounded, horrid, reverberating around them. But it was only the five of them in the room. Stomping pounded down the hallway, and the red-headed male guard charged forward, his mouth open, skin cracking.

Afton reached for her dagger and was about to make the killing blow, when a weapon flew through the air, striking the male in the throat. Another dagger shot forward, puncturing the guard's chest, driving into his heart.

Keelen had done it, his nostrils flaring.

Thorin stood, sword in hand. He didn't go to seek vengeance on Keelen though, but toward the guard.

"What is this?" Afton seethed, unable to hold back her temper.

"It's starting." Thorin said as he knelt beside the guard who was wriggling, taking choking gasps, before lapsing into eternal silence. "I didn't know it would be like this tonight, but it now means things are going to get worse. Go to your rooms and lock the doors. I promise you will be safe there. Let me keep watch for now."

Afton pursed her lips, not knowing whether to believe him. She stared at the guard's cracked flesh. "What's wrong with his skin?"

Above them, the sound of something crawling on the other side of the ceiling stirred—something with long claws and impatient wings.

"Go! Now!" Thorin shouted.

Silver opened her mouth to speak when Keelen lifted her from the chair. "I'm taking her to her room."

As he rushed Silver through the hallway, Afton was relieved he'd known what to do.

Turning to Thorin, she kept her voice steady. "I will see my sister safely to her room, then you will meet me in the garden later." She didn't wait for Thorin's answer and hurried beside Javan to catch up with Keelen. The sounds continued to follow them until they made it up the stairs to the room where Silver was staying.

Keelen placed Silver on the floor, and she glanced up at him. "You killed the guard."

"And I would again."

"Thorin's telling the truth." Silver pressed her hands down her dress. "Whatever it is, I feel the sinister energy. He may have been a skilled liar in Ketill, but he isn't lying about this."

"I don't trust any of it one bit," Javan said, gripping his chest as he leaned heavily on the wall. He'd still managed to keep his pace with her the whole way.

"You're staying in this room tonight, unless what happened downstairs occurs up here," Afton demanded. It would be the final decision. "Promise me."

"An order?"

"A direct one. And Keelen is staying inside your room." Afton spun on her heels, gesturing for Javan to follow her. She was going to meet Thorin out in the gardens, then find a way to connect with this energy so she could put an end to it.

SIXTEEN

KEELEN

The first blow wounded. Then the second made the kill.

Keelen could have murdered the guard easily, but he'd wanted him to suffer first because he had been a threat to Silver and her sister.

He was remembering things. Ugly things. Things he'd done in his past. A slit of the throat, a stab of a heart, a choking until there was nothing left. But it had been things he'd had to do when they were no longer themselves, when there was no turning back.

But Keelen still couldn't recall who he was, what he was. He only knew himself as Keelen, and that was how he wanted it to remain.

He'd held Silver in his arms, her soft curves against him, while running her up the stairs, the dark energy of Valgmyr thrumming through him, hammering and pulsing. And he knew that was exactly what it was. He didn't know how, but he agreed with Silver—Thorin wasn't lying. The king may have lied about his identity, but he seemed to want to save his territory from this decaying threat. Whatever Keelen had in him was dark, a midnight gathering of things. Perhaps the world needed protecting from *him*.

No.

Pushing his fingers against his temples, Keelen stared up at the ceiling and tried to forget it all.

"I don't know what to make of this." Silver bit her lip.

"Everything will be all right." But he didn't know if that was the truth.

Two hands pressed against his cheeks, tilting his face down. Two obsidian irises with ivory centers studied him. Silver's brow furrowed as he and she continued the staring dance, then a gasp escaped her pretty mouth. "It's you," she whispered.

Keelen took a deep swallow, his hands quivering at his sides. "Yes? I've been here since you put my soul in this new body," he deadpanned, trying hard not to shift his gaze to the side.

She leaned forward, her face inching closer to his while craning her neck. "You remember me, don't you? You're *looking* at me like you used to when you were the raven." Her warm fingers hadn't left his cheeks, but then they skimmed lightly across the planes of his face, each angle, each curve, each slope. And he held back a shiver, his body wanting to melt against her, sink into her. Do everything he damn well could with her if their clothing was anywhere but on their bodies.

"No." Keelen didn't want her to know, not as he was learning destructive things about himself that he couldn't explain. He didn't know what the fuck they were. Afton hadn't wanted him to confess the truth either, but she wasn't his queen. Silver was.

"You're lying!" She released his face, and took a step back, her dark eyes boring into him. "How long have you remembered?" If she could have dipped into magic now, he knew her claws would have been extended, even though she wouldn't have used them on him. But perhaps she should, perhaps he deserved it.

"I don't remember." He turned away from her, hoping she would put an end to the questioning, go away from him so he didn't have to inhale her intoxicating rosy scent. Damn those merciless stars. And damn himself.

And what if this thing stirring inside him had the potential to hurt her, what if… He shook off the thought. No. It couldn't be. *He* wouldn't.

But things were becoming different, confusing—he was starting to recall more this time than any others. He was beginning to remember everything, everything, *everything*. And he wished he wouldn't because he didn't want to lie to her. He didn't want to do to her what Thorin had done to Afton, but he already was, already had been.

Silver grabbed Keelen's shoulder and whirled him around to face her, narrowing her eyes, teeth bared. "I can be just as vicious as my sister if I need to be. Especially when lied to." Truth. She'd shown it when she'd slapped Thorin across his cheek. The way she stood before him now mirrored the way Afton had in his room, and in that moment, he could very well tell they were sisters. However, even when she was angry, even when deadly or murderous, he *wanted* her.

This time, Keelen was the one to take a step away from her. In one swift movement, he removed his tunic over his head, exposing his naked chest. "Rip my heart out, then. Eat it if you wish." If she knew what darkness was whirling inside him, she would want to destroy it, destroy him.

There wasn't anger in her expression any longer as her eyes grew glassy. "Just tell me the truth, please. When?"

Keelen caved—she would keep pressing, and he didn't have the energy to continue denying her anything. "Since the night after I entered your room," he said softly.

"Oh." She covered her mouth, seeming to come to a realization. "That's why you left, isn't it?"

"Afton gave me a tonic to remember."

"*What?*" Silver hissed, her eyes wide. "She didn't tell me

this. I'm assuming this was really the gift she mentioned in the weapons room."

"She wanted to protect you. That's all," he murmured. "And I can understand why. I believed it would be better this way too. You would care less if I wasn't the same as before. Remain focused here."

"I cared for you either way, you, you, you—"

"You, you, you, what? Can't think of the word?" He cut her off and smirked. "Bastard? Idiot? Fool? Ass? I'm perhaps all of them."

"None of those!" she shouted, her anger returning. "*You* are none of those."

He was *something*.

Keelen did the only thing he could, since he wouldn't leave her unguarded in the room—he turned away from her.

"Stop doing that!" Silver seethed, skirting around him and placing a hand on his bare chest. Her palm was directly over his heart, and she had to have been able to feel the savage beats coming from it. Because he could hear it, deafening in his ears.

She stood there. He stood there. Both looking at each other, chests heaving, neither seeming to know how to collect words and let them spill from their lips.

"Come on," Silver finally said, motioning him to follow her.

He watched her sit on top of the bed, the mattress dipping when she scooted back to lay down. Her boots remained on her feet as she patted the spot beside her. Keelen couldn't deny the need to be closer to her warmth, no matter how much he wanted to fight it.

Not removing his boots either, Keelen slid his tunic back on and sank down beside her, like he used to. Only now he wasn't in raven form—they were the same.

"I'm trying to ignore the energy," she whispered, "but it's like it's growing louder, though I don't hear anything. I can't even touch or dip into it if I wanted to."

"I feel it too." Yet, Keelen suspected it was worse for him. "Try and stay calm. I'm guarding you."

"You're Afton's."

He wasn't. He was hers.

"Not for tonight, not while we're here."

When her head dropped to his shoulder, his body stiffened. He waited for her to speak and when she didn't, he tilted his head so he could see her face. Silver's eyes were shut, and her lips were slightly parted, her breathing quiet. But he knew she wasn't sleeping.

Another memory flashed through his head. A garden enveloped him, pale white edelweiss and ivory roses growing across thorned branches that enclosed a kingdom. Circled around him were topiaries, shaped into different creatures. Stallions, stags, *ravens…*

He blinked, and the scene changed to where he was no longer alone—he stood at the edge of a sparkling lake, surrounded by frozen women and men. Not of stone, not of glass, not of metal, but in their human state. Unable to move.

The breath in his lungs halted.

There could only be one reason he knew this.

Valgmyr. King.

A king who lured people to his kingdom, hoping to find his perfect mate. But instead, he tossed each one aside and used them to keep his garden alive.

The magic clawed at Keelen and he just … *knew* he was the Valgmyr King. It had to be him. Nothing else explained this feeling, this drowning in darkness.

He squeezed his eyes shut and tore at his hair, trying to remember, but his mind refused to allow any more. *Fuck*!

Silver couldn't know.

No one could.

SEVENTEEN

AFTON

Silence settled over the room as Javan paced back and forth while Afton stared out her window. Her patience ran thin as she waited for Thorin to appear in the garden below. Shadows of branches danced across the ceiling as the energy sang through her veins, calling for her. How could something so strong be untouchable?

She told herself she didn't want to harness it, but that was a lie—she did want to, wanted desperately to caress the darkened flames. What could she even do with it? *Everything.* That was what she could do. The night was all around her, inside her.

"I'm going out to the garden now," Afton said. "He's taking too long. I want you outside Silver's room, so she has protection both inside and out."

"No."

"I know you are like this because you're my grandfather, but as a guard you're going to obey." Her voice, low and serious, left no doubt that she would no longer allow him to question her like he had in the past. She chose to push their blood connection to the back of her mind where she could temporarily forget who he truly was.

"On all of Ketill, if something happens to you..." Javan scowled.

"I'm not afraid." Whirling around, she opened the door and entered the hallway. She was about to leave Javan when a loud scratch reverberated from the wall in front of her, then another and another. Something was clawing from the other side like it had in the dining room. Nothing appeared. No one. Was it the imps? Or something else? Gripping her mace, she held it up.

"Check on your sister, and I'll meet you up there." Javan took off down the hallway.

Afton was already on her way, darting up the spiral staircase—she needed to know Silver was safe. With rapid motions, she rapped her knuckles against the door. It took a moment before it opened, and she met Keelen's face instead of her sister's.

Pushing the door the remainder of the way open, Afton brushed past him without saying a word.

"Are you all right?" Silver shot forward from the edge of the bed, her dark hair spilling around her shoulders.

"I was going to meet Thorin when Javan and I stepped into the hall from my room. Loud, scratching sounds emanated from the walls, like the ones from earlier." The noises stirred again, echoing below them. Afton was about to go back down and check on Javan when he entered the room.

"I didn't see anything," Javan said, perspiration lining his brow. "There was only the scratching as I cleared the hallways."

"How is the energy? Is it making you feel anything?" Afton asked her sister, trying to ignore the sensation flowing through her.

"I want to tap into it, but I can't." Silver rubbed her hand over her scarred chest.

"Same." Afton sighed.

"I think it's best for you all to go home," Keelen said.

Afton stood, rubbing her temple. "I didn't ask you."

"Maybe we should for now." Silver got up from the bed and folded her arms. "We can't use the magic here, and this isn't just some dark energy. Now there's something inside the walls, and who knows what else. We can bring Thorin with us while we think of a new plan."

Afton shook her head, knowing that wouldn't solve a damn thing. "We can't go back home."

"Why not?" Silver's brows knitted together.

"Because it's already spread to our territory." Afton paused. "I felt this energy there."

"Are you sure?" Silver asked, her shoulders stiffening.

"And you failed to mention this to anyone?" Javan scowled.

"Yes. I wasn't going to tell any of you until we returned to Ketill, but on the way to the celebration, I noticed some of the trees were withering like they are here. I could *feel* the tainted energy, while catching whiffs of the same smoky and grassy scent that we smell now. Then I discovered a creature, not of this world, at the cottage where Thorin was staying. An imp, like from the Valgmyr story." Afton's eyes didn't leave her sister's. "It flew and vanished through the ceiling."

Silver's lips parted, her body trembling. "And you don't know where it went?"

"No." Afton couldn't stop seeing the gnarled creature, its white eyes, its skeletal body, its dark wings.

"You should have told me," Silver said with a sigh, disappointment crossing her face.

"I was only protecting you," Afton bit back.

"Just as you were *protecting* me from Keelen?" Silver pressed a finger at Afton's chest. "When you gave him a memory tonic and didn't tell me what your real *gift* was? I didn't even know you could do that."

Afton turned to Keelen. "Do you have a death wish?"

"It wasn't him who told me." Silver removed her finger

from Afton and pointed at herself. "I could tell the difference in him."

She should have known Silver would be able to realize it sooner or later—her sister read people better than anyone. Afton hadn't known him at all and could see the change when she'd returned from Enare.

The clawing stopped and a flicker of light shone at the window. She moved toward it. Peering through the glass, her eyes swept over the tops of the trees to a figure standing in the garden holding a lantern—Thorin. Alone. Afton wondered what he was thinking. She had to go to him, demand answers.

As it never had before, her heart beat rapidly with fear. Because for once in her life, she didn't know how to control things or find a solution. Even with her parents, she had never felt this helpless. And whatever was happening here—whatever was spreading to her territory—wasn't in her hands.

"We can go to him," Silver said, studying Thorin's form.

"No," Afton replied. "You and Keelen will stay here. Javan will guard outside your door."

Silver started to argue when Afton held up her hand. "Remain here. You can easily see me from the window." Without another word and ignoring Javan's heavy stare, she clenched her mace and left the room.

Afton headed down the stairs to the main entry where she inspected the walls, listening for the scratching. But all that lingered there were the silent decorations on the walls of different golden shapes of the sun and the moon, like lovers who could never quite stay for each other. If something did appear from the wall, she may not have had her claws and sharpened teeth, but she still could use the ones she did have to do damage.

As she continued through the castle and out into the night's darkness, the energy, though still present, was no longer thrashing at her. A cold gust of wind swept around her, so chilly that her teeth chattered.

Afton searched the dead garden, and found it empty, only Thorin's glowing lantern on the ground. Scowling, she glanced up at Silver's window where she could see the flicker of candle flames and the silhouettes of her and Keelen. Blowing out a breath, Afton was about to return to the castle when a hand pressed down on her shoulder.

Spinning from the grasp, Afton brought her mace down in a swift movement, but the figure ducked out of the way. As she swung it again, Thorin's voice sounded. "Stop. I know you hate me at the moment, but I do appreciate staying intact."

With a glare, she didn't lower the mace. "What the fuck are you doing? Where did you go, and why did you leave your lantern behind? Especially now when there are scratching sounds in the castle. Not only that, but then you sneak up on someone and expect not to lose a limb? Are you really that much of a fool?"

She expected him to shout in return, but he didn't—his lips pulled back into a grin. "I had to relieve myself, so I left the lantern out here in case you showed up while I was gone."

Oh. She pushed the warm feeling spreading through her away. "You didn't warn us that things lived in the walls."

"You know the Valgmyr story." Thorin ran a hand through his hair. "I told you how some of the guards and servants were lured there. Did you think they vanished on their own?" He held up a finger. "But things have become even more unstable since I've been back here. This is nothing like before, when I left for Ketill."

That was exactly what she thought, but she didn't let him know that. "I want to go over some things with you tonight. Then I want us to have dinner tomorrow night with the others and see if these same incidents occur."

"Whatever you want," he said, his voice soft.

Afton was forming a new plan. After tomorrow, she would send everyone home the following morning. She would stay and work with Thorin alone, while Silver watched over Ketill.

At least for now, her territory wasn't as unstable as Enare.

"Tell me what's on the other side of the walls." It was time for her to confess some things. "Back in your old cottage in Ketill, I stumbled upon a creature. Pure white eyes, wings, its body skeletal."

"You saw an imp…" He sighed. "On the other side of the walls are the imps."

"And you brought this to my land?" she gritted out. "It was in *your* cottage."

"Nothing was there when I left, and as you know, I haven't been back since." He paused and glanced up at her. "Will you come with me to the library? I want to show you something."

Afton mulled it over for a moment, but curiosity won the war. "I suppose it's better than shivering out here in the cold." She looked up toward her sister and held up her hand, letting her know she was going with the king.

Thorin started walking and Afton followed beside him toward the castle. It had only been a few days since she found out who he was, but she missed this, missed him, missed the way they would stroll in the woods near his cottage.

The king led her through the entryway, then down a hall on the other side of the castle that she hadn't traveled through. He took a candle from the wall and opened a door into a pitch-black room. Grabbing another candle from inside, he lit it and passed it to her. She then helped him light the other wicks around the room, wishing she had her magic so she could have easily done it in one swift movement. Around her, endless shelves of books became illuminated as light filled the darkness. Like the other rooms, a layer of dust coated the tomes and furniture. In the center of the space was a round table holding a stack of books. Four high-backed velvet chairs were pushed into the wood.

"Over here." Thorin motioned to a seat at a table and took a tome from the top of the stack. On the cover was an engraved drawing of a male, otherworldly. His back was turned to her, and his dark beautiful wings took up a large portion of the cover. Surrounding him were creatures, like the one she'd seen at Thorin's cottage. She recognized this book because she had a similar tome back in her castle library, the one Silver would read repeatedly. As he cracked open the spine, several loose pages almost fell out, revealing sketches of the imps.

"I've always believed these were just stories." She sat beside him and slid the book so it was between them both. "In the tale, he was bound to an underground garden."

"Maybe he is? Maybe he's not? That's part of what I need you to help me with." Thorin chewed his lip—that perfectly formed mouth that she'd wanted to kiss day after day.

Afton flicked her gaze away from his lips and to a page written in thick cursive. If she was going to stay and help him, she needed to be honest. "I do feel it," she said, knowing she should have told him as soon as she'd arrived, instead of withholding the information out of spite.

"Hmm?" He continued to pore over the words.

"The magic. I lied before, but I do feel the energy. It's dark and it's vicious." She paused, finally meeting his eyes. "Tomorrow after dinner I'm going to send everyone home. It was a mistake bringing them here. But I will stay, and I will help your territory in order to protect mine."

"Then what?" He sucked in a breath, leaning closer, closer, his full lips dangerously close to touching hers.

Then perhaps we can see what will happen next… She left those words unspoken as his mouth softly lowered to her neck, brushing her skin tenderly. He knew not to kiss her on the lips and did this for her, but she ached to feel that hot mouth on hers.

"You want to know why I haven't apologized for lying to you?" he whispered in her ear. "It's because … how can I be sorry for anything that happened between us? I only did these things for my kingdom, and I'd been lonely for so long. That is, until I met you."

Her chest tightened. How could she be angry at that? She knew that feeling all too well. Despite wanting to shift closer so she could straddle his hips, get lost in him, she had to pull back. At least for the night. "Let's focus on reading for now." She kissed him on his cheek, right at the edge of his mouth, the nearest she'd ever been to touching his lips. "Maybe we can find a portal to the Valgmyr King's world."

Thorin groaned and lifted the book. "This story says Valgmyr's kingdom is below Enare's castle. Those who are drawn to the darkness are brought there or destroyed. But those that do go never last because of their mortality. It is said that eventually there will be one meant to stand by the king's side for all eternity."

"I wonder if any of the people tried to murder him," Afton muttered.

"Maybe they did, but failed." He shrugged.

"Or perhaps some fell in love with him? Don't they all do that in stories?" She flipped through a few more pages. "Love can be a weakness." It had been for her. The two times she'd felt it. Once for her sister, and the other for Thorin. Her sister was always worth it, and perhaps Thorin was too.

While scanning page after page of the book, Afton's eyes grew heavy, the words blurring. She turned to Thorin to tell him she was going to go stay with her sister, but his head was against the back of the chair, his eyes shut, his breathing soft.

The scratching in the walls had ceased, the energy was there but only a low drumbeat, and a part of her didn't want to leave Thorin here by himself. Closing the book, she stood from the chair and curled up in his lap. His arms wrapped around her, and his groggy voice murmured, "I'm glad you lightened your hair color back. The shade of midnight is beautiful, but yours is like the color of the stars."

Afton didn't say anything as his breathing grew even once more. She nestled into his warmth, and shut her eyes, pretending they were back in his cottage for the night.

A clearing of a throat sounded and Afton jerked her eyes open. Her gaze settled on Javan who glowered at her near the library door.

Thorin's arms slipped away as Afton stood from the chair. The warmth his enveloping arms had given her faded, and she already missed it.

"I need to speak with you," Javan said.

Thorin rose from his seat. "You two can stay here. I need to run into town and collect some herbs from one of the local witches and see if they know anything about portals." He turned to Afton. "I'll meet you for dinner tonight."

She nodded, her heart fluttering as he walked out of the room. If Valgmyr was looking to collect another, then perhaps it truly was Thorin who was wanted. And he just hadn't given into the darkness yet. Afton could fight, she could kill, she could do almost anything to win, but she didn't know anything about curses or how to break them.

Javan's heavy breathing caught her attention. "What is it?" she asked, focusing on his flaring nostrils. "How long were you standing here and just watching? Again?"

"After all these years, you still don't understand that it was the only way?" Javan pinched the bridge of his nose. "Do you really think I fear for my life that much? I didn't intervene because that was the only way I could watch over the two of you. If I had tried to put a stop to your parents, then I would have been dead."

"What good is another person watching if they can't help?"

"I've cared. I've *always* cared." His hand came to his heart, gripping his shirt.

Something in his tone struck her hard in the chest. Maybe

she did too. And maybe that was why she kept him around, which was one of the reasons she was sending him home.

"Tomorrow morning, you are to take Silver and Keelen home."

His eyebrows furrowed. "And you?" He seemed to know better than to question why she was sleeping in the King of Enare's lap.

"I'm staying." She held up her finger. "It's for the better."

"I don't think Silver will go easily."

"I don't think she will either, but she'll have to." All she could think about if her sister remained here was Silver's body being slashed by creatures like the one Afton had seen in Ketill. Her eyes missing, her jaw open wide, her words silenced forever.

Afton shrugged off the horrid thought. Her sister would go home.

EIGHTEEN

KEELEN

A knock pounded at the door, and Keelen peeled his eyes open, his arm draped tightly around Silver's waist. After Afton had left, he'd stayed with Silver, watching her sister in the garden with the king before the two of them returned inside the castle. Silver had seen Afton's hand signal, one that told her not to search her out until the morning. But that hadn't meant she couldn't send someone else to check on her sister, so she'd sent Javan to keep a close eye on her.

Keelen hadn't fallen asleep until late. Not after what he'd realized the night before about himself, about *Valgmyr*.

Taking his arm from around Silver, he rolled from the bed while she continued to sleep. He shuffled to the door and pulled it open, expecting to see Javan.

Afton stood there, mace in one hand and a book under her arm, dressed in the same gown she'd worn the previous night. Her disheveled hair spilled down her back. She looked as if she'd done more than *talk* with the king.

Holding a finger over her lips, she motioned him toward the stairs before he could wake Silver. With a scowl, he pulled the door shut behind him and met her near the top of the steps.

He leaned against the wall, crossed one foot over the other, and folded his arms. "What is it? Are you going to run off with the king again and leave your sister behind?"

Her chin remained lifted, her eyes narrowed. "Silver can defend herself, and I left her with both you and Javan. I should have known one of you would disobey." She paused, staring at the closed door. "I need to ask you to do something else for me."

He furrowed his brow. *What is she trying to do now?*

"We will all dine with Thorin, and then you, Silver, and Javan will immediately return to Ketill. Javan knows," Afton whispered. "Thorin knows. I would tell you all to leave now, but Silver must stay long enough to discover if there are any changes in this energy. She needs to understand as much as possible in order for her to watch over Ketill. Both times I've experienced this dark energy, the results were different."

"Silver will never agree to it." Keelen straightened. "And to be honest, I don't think it's a good idea for you to stay here alone either." As he thought about it, she'd felt the energy in Ketill and hadn't before, not until after his soul had been placed in his current form. He could be the true reason the energy was seeping into their territory. *Fuck.*

She took the book from under her arm and tossed it at him. He easily caught the tome, the coloring a faded silver and gold. Flipping it over to inspect the cover, his gaze locked on gangly creatures with white eyes. His heart kicked up in his chest as he stared not at the creatures, but what rested in the center of them. A tall male with his back turned, broad shoulders, large leathery wings like that of a gargoyle. The Valgmyr King.

Keelen inhaled deeply as he looked at the book. He lifted his gaze to Afton. "What are you trying to do?"

"I'm going to help Thorin find a way to crack open a portal to Valgmyr so we can seek out that bastard of a king."

Keelen closed his eyes for a brief moment and swallowed, his words trapped in his throat. *I'm right here.* "The energy here seems unstable, and I'm not sure how many creatures there are. Silver wouldn't want to sacrifice you for her safety." A flash of something blurred his vision, the creatures flying over a lake, soaring above bodies that stood like statues, the corpses' faces frozen in serene expressions forever.

"Do it," Afton demanded, but something like fear was hidden deep down in those two words. "Get out of here and be my sister's guard. That's why you're here, to protect her. Now do the same for her back in Ketill."

"It's one thing to try and stop the tainted energy from spreading while here. But to go to Valgmyr? You know the stories. Once you go there, you can't ever come back."

"It's a risk I'm willing to take." Afton studied him, her eyes training on his, digging down into his soul, seeing his darkness, as if she knew all that lay hidden within him. "There's something even more different about you today. It's because of my sister, isn't it? Protect her. Not fuck her. Understand?"

"I promise." Keelen would do it. He would take Silver home, then leave so she would be protected from him. He'd find a way to go home. Back to Valgmyr. Then he would find his own way to stop the energy.

"Now, this is the plan." She wiggled a finger for him to lean closer and whispered the rest into his ear.

As she spoke, the book in his hand seemed to thrum, as if it had its own heartbeat, calling him to come home.

Keelen placed his swords at his back—dusk would start to fall soon. He knew the plan. It was simple enough. Get Silver out of the castle and to the carriage, letting her think Afton was coming. The one challenging part of it would be Silver remaining in Ketill and not trying to return for Afton. Even if he could draw up the magic and place a barrier around Silver in her castle, she was strong enough to use her own energy to break through it if she wished. But Afton knew her sister better than anyone and if it was the only way to protect Ketill, then Silver would stand guard there.

He'd flipped through the Valgmyr book before he'd given it back to Afton. All the way down to his bones, he knew it held truths, but not everything about Valgmyr would fit into a single book, and not everything would be accurate. However, he knew the enclosed kingdom surrounded by branches, the topiaries, the victims' blank eyes when their life ended were all truths. His mind was becoming clearer with each passing second. He closed his eyes and shut out the memories.

For most of the day, Keelen had stayed outside Silver's room to bathe, to breathe, to not want her, to protect her.

Lifting his fist, Keelen knocked on Silver's door. It swung open, revealing her in a flowing ivory gown with gold stitching and golden metal flowers on each shoulder. She seemed to be alone, and he wasn't sure when Afton had decided to leave and get ready.

Silver offered him a warm smile. "You've been avoiding me." She pressed a hand to his chest and his heart accelerated beneath her touch.

"I'm sorry." He bit his lip. As her face fell, he hurried on, "I didn't want to, but I needed to think."

"I did too." She leaned forward and murmured, "Afton told me we're leaving tonight, but we'll return soon."

"Mm-hmm." He gnawed on his lip harder, trying not to let her rosy scent entice him into telling her the truth yet.

"Let's go downstairs so we can see if the energy will be the same as last night."

They descended the two flights of stairs while Silver chatted about Midnight. He couldn't bring himself to truly absorb the words when his mind was spinning too much. Fuck, he wished he could go back and forget his past that was becoming clearer, but not his past with her.

As soon as Silver took the last step, she paused.

"What?" he asked as she flicked her gaze up the stairs, then toward the ceiling.

She released a huff. "I knew I should have relieved myself before putting on this gown, and I forgot the damn mace."

He scanned the thick layers of her dress, the laces running up the front between her breasts. "Do you need help with the ties?"

"I don't need to untie the front of my dress to relieve myself." She leaned in and whispered with a grin. "Maneuvering these dresses only takes a bit of practice, which I can do."

"Ah, I'm glad I haven't had to deal with that myself." Keelen chuckled.

He started to turn to head back up the steps with her, when she held his arm. "It won't take too dreadfully long. Go check on Afton in the dining room."

"I'll wait for you here." He didn't trust the night that was inching nearer, and he wasn't about to put more physical distance between them until they returned to Ketill. But it was only her going upstairs, so he would allow it.

"Fine. Stubborn." She laughed softly before ascending the stairs. She glanced one more time over her shoulder and grinned—his heart struck his sternum at that look. Keelen couldn't fight a smile this time and held it until she disappeared from his view. His thoughts then turned to meeting her for the first time.

Bright light filled his eyes. He couldn't remember his name. Who was he? He was ten years old. A boy. But that was all he knew.

"Hello," a high-pitched voice said.

His eyes cleared and he met irises of midnight and pupils of ivory. A girl. Long black hair framed her oval face, and a raised scar was at her chest.

"Hello," he said in return. Lips didn't move when he'd

spoken though. It was something else. A beak?

"I drew your soul here from the afterlife. I needed someone to talk to besides my sister. She has a lot going on at the moment since becoming queen. I hope that's all right?"

Peering down at himself, he studied his waxy skin. He lifted his arm. No, not an arm—a wing. He should have been frightened about why he was a damn bird, but the girl's gaze held him steady.

"You're a raven. For now." She smiled hesitantly. "I'm Silver. What's your name?"

He thought about it. But no answer was coming to him. "I don't know." He then told her everything he did know, which wasn't much at all.

"You need a name." She tilted her head to the side. "How about Keelen?"

As he mulled over the name, while looking at her wide eyes, he knew he never wanted to leave her again. "I like it. Now tell me about you."

And she had. She'd confided in him about her deepest secrets, her past, how she liked spending every day out in her edelweiss meadow with Midnight.

Keelen glanced up the stairs. Silver had been gone a while. His veins expanded when the energy of the night filled the room, the coursing of his blood attuned with it, as though it was tasting the new guest.

Familiar. Familiar. And he knew just what that darkness could do to the world.

NINETEEN

SILVER

Perhaps Silver did need help with her dress after relieving herself. The skirts somehow became a twisted mess and she pressed the fabric down several times, trying to smooth them out. She should have gone for simple, but sometimes she just wasn't in a simple mood. And after the evening before, she at least wanted to have on a beautiful gown if she needed to murder something in the night.

"There." She sighed. The dress finally didn't look like she'd been ravished by a beast in the woods. However, her hair still did. She wasn't going to worry about that now—her sister would most likely try and break down the door soon if she didn't hurry up. Not to mention that Keelen probably didn't know what in all the spirits she was doing.

As she collected her mace from the bed, the same energy as the previous night jolted through her, the odor of the castle more potent. Black, the blackest of blacks. The darkest of darks. It was as if her veins were attempting to escape her body. Then, the energy twisted and shifted, turning rotten.

Outside her window, the night was painted obsidian. A gust of wind extinguished every candle, plunging her into darkness. Only a spot on the floor, where the stars' light filtered in through the glass, shone.

Scratching and shuffling echoed within the room. Above. Below. All around her. From *everywhere*.

Squinting her eyes, she raised her mace and attempted to see where the noises were coming from, but she couldn't tell. Her heart raced, and she tried to tap into the energy, no matter what may come, to release her claws and sharp teeth. But she couldn't penetrate the invisible barrier.

A swishing sounded, followed by a soft padding. Shadows moved across the walls. With a deep breath, Silver rushed for the door, prepared to throw it open. She needed more light in the room if she hoped to fight and murder each creature with her mace. But the door wouldn't open. It was sealed shut.

"Damn it!" Silver growled.

She should have had Keelen with her, but she'd never needed anyone before, especially with something as mundane as relieving herself.

Whirling around, nostrils flaring, Silver kept her voice low, deadly. "Show yourselves, cowards." She'd never been afraid of the magic she drew from the earth, not once, but whatever lurked in these hidden depths wasn't of this world. Fear pulsed in her veins.

A shadow scuttled below her in the darkness. Silver kicked her foot forward—the thing squished beneath her boot, and she recoiled. Gurgling, the creature scampered away, its claws clicking the stone floor. Something sharp brushed her waist, and she spun, kicking her foot out again. Baring her teeth, Silver tried once more to tap into the energy. But she still couldn't.

More claws scraped the floor, the walls, the ceiling, louder this time. She swung her mace, connecting only with air. Her gaze landed on the window. Scaling down the castle would be her only chance for escape.

She rushed toward the window, but before her fingers could find the latch, several rough hands grasped her ankle, claws digging in. With a hard yank, they pulled her back. Her body, falling face first, collided with the floor.

Pain radiated through Silver, and her head felt as if it had been cracked open, the blackened room spinning around her.

She held firm onto her mace, not willing to relinquish her weapon. A sound like the beating of wings echoed all around her. As her body jerked, back arching, something scaly wrapped around her mouth with a tight grip. She tried opening her mouth to bite and draw blood, but the hand was clamped, keeping her lips firmly shut.

Silver lifted her arms, struggling with the creature on her back. Two more grips tightened at her wrists, forcing her arms down, preventing her from doing anything.

Around the room, one by one, the candles relit. Shadows swayed along the walls behind the bobbing flames, then bodies pushed forward, sliding out from their hiding spots. Skeletal frames, hunched backs, ivory eyes, dark horns, leathery wings, and blackened lips. *Imps*. She shifted her gaze upward and glimpsed a head leaning over her.

The creature with its hand around her mouth was just as hideous as the others. Silver twisted and jerked. She wished Afton was there to rip them from her back and wrists, that Keelen was there to bring down his swords, and that she was free so she could tear the bastards' hearts out to give to her sister.

The familiar scent of smoke and grass enveloped her, growing stronger. As if she'd been struck by a sleeping aid, her eyelids grew heavy, her body limp, her fingers slackening on the mace. Numbness spread all the way down to the marrow in her bones.

Silver attempted to scream as loud as she could to warn the others, but even her voice was too numb to escape.

Her eyes closed. Dark.

Darker.

Complete Darkness.

TWENTY

AFTON

The *thump, thump* of Javan's cane sounded as Afton walked beside him down the stairs and entered the main room. Neither had said a word to each other since their short conversation that morning, but he'd been hovering all day. She'd stayed with Silver for a long while, then wandered around the garden alone, to collect her thoughts before getting ready for dinner. Afton hadn't seen anyone, not even the one remaining guard who must have left to go into town with Thorin. She'd thought about the night before, when she was in his lap, kissed his cheek...

Together, Afton and Javan continued toward the dining room's open doors. Thorin was seated alone at the head of the table, his hair down, free of his leather strap. The dead guard's body from the night before was gone, the blood on the floor cleaned. A paltry selection of dried meat, glasses of water, and fruit that didn't appear as fresh as the last time scattered across the table.

"I know, it's not much of a dinner." Thorin winced, rising from his seat. "The hunt yesterday didn't go as planned, and I didn't find much fruit at the market. I also left my last guard with one of the witches to see if there was a temporary spell or something else that could cure her.”

“It’s fine.” Afton took in the rest of the room, finding Silver and Keelen hadn’t arrived yet. “I’m going to go and retrieve my sister.”

“Your Highness, I believe your sister is more than capable of taking care of herself,” Javan said. “You know she takes longer getting ready than you. And sometimes you need to worry about yourself too.”

She sighed. But he was right. Silver hadn’t come after her last night when Afton had used her hand signal, asking for her trust. She needed to do the same. At least this one time. Once the strength of the night’s energy could be determined, the plan would commence with the exit of Javan, Keelen, and Silver from Enare.

Afton’s gaze found Thorin’s once more, and he bowed before walking toward her, a small smile on his face.

“I have something I need to tell you,” Afton said, when he stopped in front of her. She wanted to tell him what would be happening before Silver came inside. Javan remained silent, but she could feel his eyes burning holes into her back.

Thorin watched her, carefully, a line forming between his brows. “What is it?”

“Silver is the only one who doesn’t know the plan.” She kept her voice low. “So you need to stay silent about it.”

“That won’t be a problem.” As Thorin opened his mouth to say something else, the energy of the night fully awakened—a river of darkness rushed through her, its magic tickling every inch of her skin.

She glanced again at the door, wishing her sister would hurry.

Thorin touched Afton’s shoulder, drawing her attention back to him. “I need to confess something.” He closed his eyes, his breathing heavy.

The energy roared even louder within her. “What?” she asked. “What is it?”

"I'm not sorry for finding you," Thorin whispered, "but after all this time, I knew you could be the one."

Afton's brows drew together. "The one?"

"Yes," he said, opening his lids and not meeting her gaze. "The one who could possibly stay." And then he did look at her.

Afton inhaled, recoiling from his touch, her chest tightening. His eyes were no longer warm brown but black as her own, their pupils like twin moons in the night sky. The energy thumping the walls, the ground, the ceiling, increased, circling her.

It was him. It was him all along. The Valgmyr King. "You!" she shouted, swinging her mace, but he was faster, dodging out of the way.

Her gaze darted to Javan who had inexplicably still done *nothing*. But then she noticed his hand clutching his chest, his face flushed purple beneath his gray hair. He fell to his knees, his weapon slipping from his grasp with a clang.

As Afton watched in horror, he reached hopelessly for his sword even as he pitched sideways, where he lay still against the stone. His eyes closed.

Dead.

Warring emotions flooded through Afton, and she gasped, realizing only too late that she didn't hate her grandfather as she believed she always had. That she never had. He had always been there for her. *Always*, even when she thought he hadn't. And now he was gone. He would never feel her gratitude. Her mind whirled with regret—her heart broke for the years lost. But her grief would have to come later. After she made the Valgmyr King pay for his treachery.

"His heart is still beating, but not for much longer," he whispered. "A heart that has grown old and tired can't be saved."

Afton screamed in rage, hurling herself at him. Thorin grabbed her wrists, backing her against the wall, and pressed his forehead to hers. "Please do as I say tonight," he said in a soft voice. "I'll explain it all later."

A fire lit within her, burning and spreading. "No," Afton seethed, her anger intensifying. "You want me to do as you say after you revealed who you are? *Him*? The Valgmyr King." She brought up her leg to his stomach, and he groaned as she shoved him away.

Tightening her grip on her mace, she swung her weapon, and she easily would have struck him, but he ducked and moved out of the way, faster than any human could. Two hands grabbed her wrists once more, pressing her back against his chest. The Valgmyr King somehow ended up behind her and he was more monstrous than she or her sister had ever been. Yelling as loud as she could, she bucked and wriggled to escape his grip, but he held firm.

"Afton—"

She snapped her teeth, yet she still couldn't reach any part of his flesh. Her body heated at the thought of ripping him apart right there, for giving him her trust a second time to only be betrayed. *Again.*

The energy pulsed around her, harder, as she tried to sink into it. If she could get to the Valgmyr King, he would be dead. But there was something else stirring in her body as the energy twisted, as if it was so close to being connected to her. A hair's breadth away.

"What do you want, Valgmyr King?" she growled, her heart slamming against her ribs.

"Stop fighting me. Their music is about to start. Just pretend for a few moments you don't want me dead," he murmured, releasing her as though he hadn't held her twice against her will. He was foolish.

"Stop? *Stop*? I don't think so!" Her hands shook as she whirled and lunged at him, yet he was too quick again when he twisted out of the way.

"For your sister's safety, *stop*." His voice was pleading.

And that did it. Her body stilled. Her heart doing practically the same. "What about her?"

"When I said you could be the one," he said, holding her gaze, "I didn't say you could be the only one. Your eyes hold the same Valgmyr energy as Silver's, and the imps will gladly choose her, even if I refuse."

Then the sounds started, not instruments, not singing, but the scratching and clawing within the walls. The imps own form of music, seeming to string together a song, an alluring and dangerous one.

The doors were still open, and Afton needed to get to her sister. *Now.* She rushed forward to escape the room but something yanked her back, lifting her feet from the floor. Yet no one was holding onto her, not Thorin, not whatever was behind the walls. It was as if the energy itself was halting her from leaving.

"I don't think you want to go," Thorin murmured. "If you did, the energy couldn't hold you back."

"Get me *the fuck* down." Afton shook and wriggled, slashing her nails into the air. But a part of herself knew he wasn't lying because she could feel the energy burying itself within her blood, her bones. However, she roared past that, "Tell me what's happening!"

"You chose to trust me before—"

"I don't anymore!" She should have killed this male when she'd first seen him at the Enare castle. Slit his neck open and reached down his throat to rip his heart out. Or perhaps, she should have done it when he'd been living in Ketill.

From the walls, the sounds picked up, the musical pitch charging around her as grayish creatures with dark wings pushed themselves through. Beastly things with skin wrapped so tight around their skeletons that she thought it may crack. She looked at their features—the all-white eyes, blackened lips, long pointy noses, horns protruding from their foreheads. Imps. Like the one she'd seen in Ketill.

They drew closer to her in synchronized steps. Afton swiped at their faces, but they weren't close enough for her to claw their thin flesh.

Afton had one weapon left and she tucked her fingers into the secret opening of her dress, ripping the dagger free from its sheath at her thigh. With quick precision, she hurled it, watching the blade surge forward, piercing Thorin's throat.

The energy pulsed and she dropped from the ground. A searing pain blasted through her knees as she landed on them. Afton ignored the aches and pushed up from the floor, then ran to the open door. A figure already stood there, blocking her path, blood spilling down his neck. He should be *dead*. Or at least wriggling on the floor and gasping for air.

The Valgmyr King yanked the blade from his throat, the wound closing. A crestfallen expression crossed his face, like what she'd done hurt him more emotionally instead of physically. "You need to stop fighting and listen to me."

Listen to a monster whose heart was darker than hers?

Feet pounded outside the dining room. Keelen's tall frame appeared as he neared, his face pale, eyes wide. "Silver's gone," he panted and stopped behind the Valgmyr King. His wild gaze cleared as it flicked from the imps to the male, then to Afton.

"They're tired of waiting for me." The Valgmyr King raked a hand fiercely through his hair.

Afton scowled just as the creatures flew down and plucked her from the floor. They drew her higher and higher toward the ceiling. Her heart pounded in fear for her sister.

Jerking her right arm out of a beast's grasp, Afton grabbed the head of the one holding her by the shoulder. She jammed her teeth into the side of the creature's neck. A shriek ripped from the beast, but it hadn't been enough to do any damage. Above her, a booming sound reverberated, and from the ceiling, more creatures poured through. Not alone, but with her *sister*. Silver's body was limp, her head lolling to the side, eyes shut.

Afton's horrified gaze fell to Thorin, and she completely froze. He was still there—beautiful, pale, his brown hair sweeping his shoulders. But black horns, like that of a ram, curled out from his temples. Leather wings splayed wide open at his back. His dark eyes stared up at her.

The Valgmyr King in all his menacing glory.

"Give her to me!" Keelen shouted at the Valgmyr King. But imps were holding Keelen back too.

"I can't. It's up to her." His piercing eyes turned to Afton. "If you want to save her, then you have to come with me. Otherwise, they will take her."

"I'll come," Afton said hurriedly. She didn't even need a second to think about it. For her sister, she would do anything. Silver would hate her for it, but she would have chosen the same. And Afton wouldn't give her the opportunity to do so.

The Valgmyr King slowly nodded and the imps lowered Silver to the floor.

Keelen was released and he tore toward Silver, scooping her up in his arms. His eyes met Afton's, and she gave him a look that told him to let this be. Before she could tell him to watch over Silver with his life, two strong arms wrapped around her waist, taking her away from the creatures and straight toward the wall in front of her. Not closing her eyes, she prepared for impact, for pain, but neither came.

Just as the imps had earlier, she and the king passed through the wall, his wings beating fiercer and harder while he cradled her to his chest, as though he *cared* about her. The world around her was a muted gray for only a moment, but then a blue sky surrounded them. He flew down and she noticed different shades of brown weaving over one another. Branches and limbs blooming with white roses and edelweiss. And in between the slivers were bright greens, but she couldn't see what else rested inside.

The limbs slowly unraveled as they inched closer, creating

a space large enough for them to fly into. Behind them, the beats of the imps' wings drew nearer.

"What do I call you, *Your Majesty*?" Afton growled, keeping her gaze trained on his *perfect* face.

"Ragan. I didn't lie about that. I wanted you to have my name as soon as I met you. Now sleep," he whispered against her temple. Though she tried to fight it, Valgmyr's energy became a part of her then, forcing her eyes closed.

TWENTY-ONE

SILVER

Something gentle tapped Silver's cheek. Then it was there again, the pads of soft fingers. Someone was holding her as a hand brushed hair from her face. Silver peeled open her eyes, and they flickered before locking on two violet irises.

Keelen.

She started to smile, then noticed his worried expression. Suddenly, the memories flooded back: her bedroom, the creatures, the hands around her mouth. How she'd been knocked out by their energy.

Silver bolted from Keelen's arms, finding that she was no longer in her room but in the dining area. Dried meat, fruit, and water rested on the table, waiting to be consumed, but the chairs sat empty. Her gaze flicked to the walls, and her already wide eyes opened even wider as she stared at the green patterned paper, waiting for the same creatures to push themselves out like they had in her room. The imps from the Valgmyr story—they were real.

The space remained quiet—too quiet—except for her heavy breathing. She stiffened, realizing the tarnished energy was no longer pulsing within her, yet something else was. Familiar but good. The same magical energy that she felt every day in Ketill.

Silver dove into it, pulling on the magic, and extended her claws and razor teeth. She could protect herself now, defend the others.

"She's all right," a voice rasped from behind her.

Silver whirled around to find Javan across the room, his palms pressed to his chest, but there wasn't a sign of blood anywhere. Along his forehead were beads of sweat, his hair damp, his breathing ragged.

"What happened?" Silver screeched, racing toward him, then placed her own palms against his chest, searching for a hidden gaping wound. There wasn't even a scratch on him. "I was knocked out in my room by imps."

"Javan woke up just before you did. But…" Keelen closed his eyes and shook his head, kneeling beside her.

"What is it?" Silver breathed. "It never does any good to keep silent more than is necessary."

"He took Afton."

"Who?"

"The Valgmyr King," Keelen finally murmured, biting his lip.

Silver's heart plummeted to her toes—he'd come, taken her sister.

Javan lifted his head and an anguished moan escaped his lips.

"Don't move," Silver cried, drawing back her claws and teeth while clasping his clammy hands.

His breaths came out even more ragged as he looked at Silver. "There's so much I want to say, and I never deserved to be called Grandfather by you or your sister, but you two mean everything to me. If anyone can save Afton, you can."

Grandfather… She'd never once said that word because Javan had felt more true, meaningful to her.

"Do you think me that naïve, Javan?" She placed a hand to his cool cheek. "Of course I knew you were my grandfather, probably even before Afton." It had been the way he'd looked at their mother, even though he was her guard, disappointed but still loving her, as if he wanted to turn back time to when she was a child and fix her so she wouldn't become what she was.

He nodded, smiling sadly. "My heart won't last much longer. Finish it."

Silver stared at her grandfather, his determined hazel eyes, knowing what he meant—she wouldn't let him suffer any longer. Afton may not have believed him courageous, but Silver did. He'd only been so quietly, and because of that, he'd allowed Afton to kill their parents and save their kingdom. Javan could have stopped Afton when he was supposed to be guarding them, yet he'd left the opportunity wide open.

"I love you," Silver said softly, gently placing a hand at each side of Javan's skull. Keelen scooted back and left her space. With a deep breath then a sharp twist to the right of his head, Javan's bones inside his neck cracked and snapped, the sounds echoing. Silence trickled into the room again, his body completely limp.

Hot tears spilled down her cheeks as she lowered Javan's head carefully to the floor, thinking of their times together over the years. Javan helping her learn to ride Midnight, him shifting closer to her when her parents' tempers would rise, him sneaking her and Afton tarts, even though she was the only one who would accept them. Silver studied his lined face for a few minutes before collecting his sword and cane. She placed them in both his hands in case he would need them in Torlarah. But she was certain he wouldn't, and maybe some of his inner demons would be healed so he could forgive himself.

Later there would need to be a pyre for him, but for now, she wiped her tears and rose from the floor, putting her emotions away like Afton would have done. "How did he take her? What happened?"

Keelen ran a hand along his jaw, a resigned expression on

his face. "Ragan was pretending to be Thorin—his horns, eye color, and wings were hidden."

"Ragan? I don't understand." Silver placed a hand over her mouth. "Thorin was pretending to be Ragan, you mean."

"No." His throat bobbed, his tongue swiping at his lower lip before he finally spoke. "The Valgmyr King's true name is Ragan. He's been here for the past four months, and he was the one working in your kitchens. After Thorin's father died, the newly-crowned king went to Valgmyr willingly, to try and save Enare, when the dark energy had started to seep into his land. It was only a temporary solution for the energy because he didn't survive, just as the others never do."

Keelen's manner was different, like he knew this without being told, like he knew even more that hadn't spilled from his lips yet. No one had known the Valgmyr King's true name before, even in the stories.

Silver slowly stood, taking a step back. She released her claws, lowered her teeth, and snatched up Afton's mace from the floor. "How do you know this?"

"Because I remember everything, Silver." He sighed, not grabbing a weapon of his own. "While we were here, I started to remember more and more. These images would flash through my mind, and the only conclusion I could draw from it was that I was indeed the Valgmyr King. But I'm not."

Silver furrowed her brow, her voice coming out low and dangerous. "Then how do you know all of this? Did he tell you a *bedtime story* before taking my sister?"

"Because I'm his brother."

It felt as if he'd just taken out his sword and struck her with the blade. "Brother?" Taking a deep swallow, her eyes widening, Silver stepped toward him. *"Brother?"* Was he going to try to take her to Valgmyr too? Each take a bride to their wicked lair? She held her mace up, ready to swing it at him.

Keelen still didn't reach for a weapon, nor did he budge as

she drew closer with the mace.

"I think if I continue, you'll kill me," he said. "And if I'm being honest, if that's what you want, then do it. I won't fight back."

Lunging forward, Silver shoved him by his chest against the nearest wall, her heart on fire, her claws curving, her sharp teeth ready to tear into his flesh. She pressed her claws—not steady, but shaking—at his throat. Then her hands trembled even more. Silver should have slit his throat without hesitation, yet as she stared at his face, the one she'd created, she couldn't. She wished she could, but she just … couldn't. She hadn't created his soul, though, and that soul she still loved regardless. Yet that didn't mean she would let him or his brother bring any more harm to her world.

She drew her claws and teeth back, but didn't drop her mace or move away from him. "What else do you have to say?"

His gaze didn't leave hers, not for a second. "In Ketill, Afton had me promise to be your guard and not hers. And tonight, I failed when I let you go to your room alone. She wanted me to take you home tonight instead of in the morning while she stayed behind to help Enare. I agreed because I thought I was the Valgmyr King, and I was planning on taking you back to Ketill before leaving.

"I don't know everything because Ragan had been gone from Valgmyr for months. He was always meant to have someone at his side, dividing and controlling the energy there. I killed some of the ones whose minds were too unstable, who would continue to suffer. Others went out to the lake with their last breath, then stood there still for all eternity. But even the bodies of the lives I ended appeared around the water too.

"After Ragan was released, I learned from the imps that he was to choose between two sisters who had eyes of darkness and starlight, like ours. Then I knew, and there was nothing I could do. Not even warn Ragan…"

"How are our eyes the same?" A part of her wanted to see the violet shade flickering in his gaze gone, and replaced with his natural hue.

"Because of the dark magic your parents used," Keelen continued, "the imps believed that perhaps one of you could survive since Valgmyr energy was born with you. That's when, for the first time, Ragan was allowed to leave and choose one of you. Tonight marked the end of his four-month trial, and he had to make a decision. If he didn't, they would choose you. But Ragan let Afton decide, and she took your place in order to save you."

Silver's body trembled. Even though her parents were dead, it was as though their spirits were still haunting them, causing this. "And what about you? Each time I brought you here from *that place*, did you know? Ever?" How could she not have known it wasn't Torlarah she was drawing his soul from? How could she have been so foolish?

"Every time I came here, I didn't know." Keelen closed his eyes, then opened them. "Yet each time I went back, I did. I never told Ragan or any of the imps because I feared if I did, they would put an end to it. Just as you feared with Afton. I was created by the imps to possibly stand by Ragan's side, as brothers, to divide the energy, but it still remained unstable. So I was worthless, useless."

Silver didn't know what to say. He hadn't been deceitful with her when she'd drawn his soul out—he truly hadn't known what he was. Yet there was always a chance he could be lying, but maybe he wasn't. The way he was looking at her now, that hollowed expression—screamed at her that he was truthful.

"I want you to take me to Afton so I can bring her back," Silver finally said.

Keelen shook his head, a look of pity forming on his face. "I would do anything you asked of me, Silver, but I don't feel Valgmyr's energy here anymore. The earth's magic has returned because Ragan has another body at his side. While someone is with him, the magic here will continue to thrive and keep the land alive. If the magic isn't alive, then Valgmyr's energy seeps out, killing everything, which is why it had started to not only sweep across Enare but trickle into Ketill." He then placed his hand on the wall and splayed his fingers. "Without Valgmyr's energy, you can't slide into the walls to reach my home."

His home…

"My brother isn't evil," Keelen continued when she stayed quiet. "He only does what the imps require him to do."

"He wasn't required to deceive and tumble my sister." She frowned, knowing that Ragan wasn't like Keelen in the sense where he hadn't remembered. Ragan *had*.

"No, I suppose not that. But the imps would have taken one of you, anyhow. Ragan may be king, but they still overrule him."

Silver needed to find a way to slip through the portal leading to Valgmyr. She would break open the land to reach Afton if needed. "There has to be a way to get to her."

"There is one way, but it will require magic like you've never used before." His violet eyes burned into hers. "You'll have to dip into the dark magic that you used to bring me here."

Regardless of the repercussions, she would try anything. "Just show me what I need to do."

He nodded, his lips forming a tight line, like he wanted to fight her on it.

If Keelen remembered everything, including the fact that he was Ragan's brother, then he would know who he truly was. "What's your name?"

"Keelen."

"No, your real name," she said, biting her inner cheek.

He sighed, seeming not to want to tell her at first. "Rory."

TWENTY-TWO

AFTON

Afton cracked open her eyes and blinked several times to clear the blurriness. Above her was a gold ceiling with a large ivory lantern hanging from its center. Her head lolled to the side to a glass door where bright light spilled inside.

Her pupils focused on the glass and what was hovering outside of it. A female imp stood on the ledge, peering into the room with its white eyes fixed on her. Afton hissed, flinging the blankets back, and got into a crouched position to retrieve her dagger. It wasn't where it should have been, and she remembered hurling the blade and it piercing Thorin's—the Valgmyr King's—neck. The Valgmyr King … *Ragan*. The name by which she'd known him for months.

She flicked her gaze to the glass door again, but the skeletal creature was no longer there. Leaping from the bed, Afton threw the gold curtains shut, bathing the room in a light orange. She moved back toward the bed and halted in her place. The imps could crawl, *fly*, through walls. And there hadn't just been one, there'd been *many*.

Ragan had flown her from Enare to Valgmyr, but she didn't remember him bringing her to a room, much less laying her in a bed and covering her with blankets. But she did recall the energy lacing within her body, attaching itself to her. As if in answer, it sang softly to her, and she gritted her teeth and tapped into its depths. This time, she penetrated the energy. Afton couldn't contain her feral smile as she extended her claws, going deeper into the alluring energy to lower her razor teeth. The energy no longer felt rotted or wrong—it seemed a part of her, more so than the magic in Ketill.

The room, in what could only be Valgmyr's castle, wasn't as she expected it to be. The space was colored in bright golds and stark whites. A wardrobe double her height was opposite the bed, and a desk and velvet chair were pressed up against the wall on the other side of the room. The space was organized, clean—the way she always kept hers. A notebook with a quill beside it on the desk in the corner were the only things out. She narrowed her eyes at the notebook. It was *her* diary. The one she would write in at night before falling asleep.

Afton swiped it up from the desk and flipped through the pages, seeing her handwriting, her words, her thoughts.

"I didn't read it," a deep voice said from behind her.

Whirling around, Afton dropped the diary on the desk and lifted her claws before even settling her gaze on Ragan. She hadn't heard him open the door.

He stood there, shirtless, his dark wings closed at his back, his horns curling at his forehead, his dark eyes blazing. Even though his features were exactly the same, the horns and the wings somehow enhanced that beauty.

Afton swung her clawed hand forward, gashing him across the chest. Blood blossomed at the surface of his skin, deep lines etched there, then they started to close, the crimson lingering.

"Do it again if you must." He sighed. "You did already stab me in the throat." From his pocket, he fished out her dagger, and tossed it onto the desk.

Afton wanted to grab the blade and hurl it at him, but what

would be the point? He would only heal again. She picked up the dagger and slid it into her dress pocket, where it belonged.

"You have me here. Now what?" she seethed.

"I know you don't trust me, and I deserve that. However, I want you to at least understand. So will you come with me?" he asked. "Then you can decide if you still want to rip out my organs."

"Javan died because of your energy," she said, unable to disguise the glimpse of emotion that came out. He may not have been dead when they left him, but she knew he was now.

Ragan's gaze softened. "It wasn't because of that. Like I said, his heart wasn't going to survive much longer. I'm truly sorry, Afton."

"What of the imps?" she spat, ending any more discussion about Javan. "One was hovering at the window."

"They don't come into the castle, but they will be where we're going." He turned on his bare feet and started down the hallway, leaving the decision up to her.

With a growl, she tightened her fists and followed behind him. She easily caught up to Ragan and gripped him by the arm. "What about my sister?"

"She's safe. The imps knocked her out with their energy, but she should be awake by now. Come on. You can ask me all the questions you want when we get there."

"So you can lie again?" she asked, incredulous.

"No more lies."

Sure, you ass… She released her tight grip on his arm, and he started walking again. Clenching her jaw, she padded behind him.

White and gold spilled down the hallway of the castle. In neat rows along the walls hung golden imps in kneeling positions, their hands at their knees, their faces shaped differently. From the ceiling, pearl lanterns dangled with green light burning inside. A flowery aroma swept through the area, and she inhaled the comforting scent.

Afton's gaze fell to Ragan's back, noticing his strong muscles, the way his back flexed around his tucked wings, remembering the way she'd dug her nails so deeply into him when her pleasure had struck. She peered down at the marble floor instead.

They reached what appeared to be a sitting room with a gray cloth settee and two cushioned chairs. A large fur rug rested in front of a fireplace, where flames the color of foliage burned. But there wasn't a log in sight. The walls were gold and white striped, empty of any decorations. She turned her stare back to the fireplace, wondering how many others Ragan had brought here to bed in front of it. She wanted to not care, but jealousy stormed through her, and she clenched her jaw tighter.

The front door pulled open, catching her attention. She hurried and met him outside. Her eyes squinted at the bright light, and a familiar scent washed over her. It was the same one from before—a smokiness combined with something grassy.

Her eyes widened as she followed him down the steps in silence to a wide-open area. The stories weren't wrong—there was so much green and brown *everywhere*. Above her, branches entwined with ivory roses and edelweiss. The edelweiss reminded her of the meadow beside her castle at home. Like in the story, Valgmyr's castle and everything within it was trapped beneath the weaved branches. There wasn't a single space she could fit through if she wanted to escape. She was like a raven trapped within a cage.

"It's protected by magic," Ragan said. "No weapon can pierce it."

"That's funny," she replied, "I distinctly remember it opening when we arrived before passing out."

"The imps can open it to leave. I can't." Another sigh escaped him.

Afton studied his expression hard, wishing he were lying

about that.

She surveyed the rest of the area, finding not a single tree in sight. Instead, there were topiaries and bushes of the greenest greens covering every inch of land. Perfectly-shaped stags that were at least five times taller than her, stallions that appeared to be running, ravens with large wings spread. Goats, chickens, griffons, and dragons were sprinkled throughout the space. More even farther. Vines ran up the walls of the limb barrier, and bushes weaved together along the bottom of it. It was … it was … the most beautiful thing she'd ever seen.

"All my life I've been trapped here," Ragan said, pulling her out of her staring spell. "After the true Thorin died down here, the imps gave me four months to bring you or your sister here. I wasted the first month by sending you letters, knowing you wouldn't show, knowing it would give me time away from here. But when you didn't reply to a single one, it only drove my curiosity. Then when I met you, I wanted to prolong this even more, wanted to prolong you hating me, until I knew there wasn't much time left."

He turned away from her and glanced up at the branches, then walked away again. This time leaving her with a pit in her stomach—she didn't want to feel sorry for him. *Couldn't* feel sorry for him. She had to go in a different direction, to clear her head for a moment.

Afton made her way toward one of the topiaries—a fierce raven with its wings frozen in mid-flight and its beak open. A rustling stirred, then it shuffled in her direction. The greens of its leaves darkened to black, hidden red orbs for eyes flaring to life, its wings lifting higher. But it wasn't only the raven, they were all edging toward her, their leaves completely black.

She moved. They moved.

She stopped. They stopped.

"Do not travel another inch," Ragan whispered in her ear, his warm breath tickling her neck. "I should have warned you beforehand not to go near them."

He stepped backward, taking her with him. The leaves of black returned to green, the topiaries retreating to their previous positions.

Nostrils flaring, chest heaving, Afton spun around to face him. "Perhaps if you'd mentioned there were garden animals willing to rip my head off, I wouldn't have."

He rolled his gaze to the branches above them, as if *he* were irritated with *her*.

"Why do you have that look on your face?" She placed her palms on her hips.

He pressed a hand at his forehead and shook his head. "This isn't the greatest of days. Just please come, Afton." The way he said her name seemed to hold regret, like he wished things could be different.

She did too.

They trekked through the grass, past tall and willowy trees laden with fruit. All Afton could think about was how Silver was faring. Keelen was with her, but she would discover Javan was dead, and Afton wanted to be there for Silver, to show her the emotions she always wanted to see. To tell her that she loved her and would do anything for her. But that wasn't an option.

"How were you able to disguise your eyes? Silver and I could never once alter ours."

"Valgmyr energy." He shrugged. "You could do it now if you wanted."

What would be the point of that?

As they rounded the castle, Afton took in the sight before her and halted. "What *is this*?" Her gaze widened as she peered at a lake. But they weren't the only ones there. It was surrounded by hundreds of other people. All still. All the same pose—both feet on the ground, their hands at their sides. Like statues.

Afton had slain enemies who had come into her territory in ways that would give others nightmares for the rest of their lives, but this was even more disturbing.

Blowing out a breath, Afton walked past Ragan to a short female. She wore a simple green gown with dark buttons down the center, her curly brown hair just past her shoulders. Reaching forward, Afton touched the woman's wrist, expecting to feel hardness. But the skin was as soft as hers.

She whirled around, lips parted. "Are they alive?"

Ragan shook his head as he stepped beside her. "No. They're all dead. Their souls are no longer here." He paused. "We're the only ones in Valgmyr except the imps. My brother used to be, but after you and I arrived, I found out he's no longer here…"

"Your brother? You really do have a sibling?" Her eyebrows shot up, and she thought about the day they'd had tea in Enare, when he'd said he would have done what she had to her parents to help a sibling. "And where is he now?"

"Rory's dead." He nodded straight ahead, his eyes growing glassy. "I don't know what happened. But I found him like this. I shouldn't have left him here alone…"

Afton's gaze settled on a male who looked similar to Ragan, only his brown hair fell just below his chin, his facial features softer, his body leaner.

"I'm sorry," she said, surprising herself. To lose a sibling would have destroyed Afton, could do the same with anyone. Even with an enemy she'd murdered, she knew people would mourn them. But choices always had to be made.

"He was all I had down here, and I didn't appreciate his company as much as I should have."

"What about the company of the others? Did you enjoy *them*?" She hated that she had to go there, when she knew how he was feeling, but with all the bodies surrounding them, it was necessary for her to know.

He closed his eyes, as though he was remembering each one. "Did I love some of them? Yes. Did I take some of them to my bed? Yes."

Her fists tightened, her claws digging in, drawing blood.

Then he opened his lids and gently turned her face to his with his fingers. "Did I stop after each one continued to die? Yes. Have I loved anyone as much as I do you? No. Has it been hundreds of years since I brought another to my bed besides you? Yes."

She swallowed … deeply. Hundreds of years? She had brought Aris to her bed only a day before she'd taken Ragan to hers for the first time.

"The energy," he continued, releasing her face, "has to stay here. You felt the rot inside it when we were in Enare. In Valgmyr, it isn't tainted, which is why the energy needs to remain this way, so it won't fester. I guard it. I protect it, while the magic you feel every day in Ketill gives life to the land. With the magic there wiped away, as it has been in Enare, the energy here will then slowly seep out to your lands, then spread and drain what it can. That's why there are so many bodies here. They were all temporary, and then there needed to be another and another and another. I'm not enough. There has to be two of us, which is why my brother was created, and even then, he wasn't enough either. But he never expired, not until I was gone. So perhaps it's my fault he's no longer here." A few tears slipped from his eyes, and she almost reached up to wipe them away, but he did it first. She still didn't want to give into him again. That was a lie—beneath all that anger, she did.

"And what happens when I expire? Then what? You collect *another*?"

He growled with frustration. Something she hadn't seen him do before. "I wouldn't have risked bringing you here if I knew you would end up like them. Only you and Silver will be able to last here."

"Why did you choose me over her when you met us?" If Afton had been him, she would have chosen Silver. What could he have ever seen in Afton that was worth loving over

Silver?

"Isn't it obvious?"

"I'm not likeable."

He released a low chuckle and covered his mouth with his fist. "You are to me."

Something in her chest warmed to him, despite his lies, despite everything. She didn't know how to feel about him anymore, but she knew she was trying not to smile. She met his gaze, her walls crumbling, but an instant before she could smile, an agonizing pain shot through her.

"What's happening to me, Ragan. I feel—" Afton gasped, falling to her knees as another flash of agony stormed through her, deep and hard.

Ragan was at her side, lifting her in his arms, and all she could feel was pain. That's when she noticed the garden had turned to black. Growls filled the air, drawing her attention in the other direction.

Along the castle's gold and alabaster arches, the imps sat, watching. The outside walls of the structure started to darken too, shadows bleeding across it, swallowing all of its color.

"You lied to me!" Ragan roared, his wings beating, lifting her from the ground.

Nothing made sense as he carried her through the air toward a balcony, her body jostling side to side. Tearing open the glass door, he rushed her inside.

Ragan dropped to his knees on the floor, anger written on his face. He didn't release her, only cradled her closer. "Rory and I were born with the energy, so it came naturally. The imps didn't tell me that it would do this to you. Your eyes may have been made from it, but you were never filled with the energy. They said you could survive, but they didn't tell me that it might not become a part of you. So you have to allow it. You can do this, not because I want you to, but because *you* want to. Because *you* are stronger than anyone I've ever met."

As the energy took and yanked and burned within her,

clawing and clawing, Afton screamed, "I can't!" She'd never said those words, never once thought she couldn't do anything. But this pain, this intensity, this sucking of her very soul was too much for her to grasp.

Rising from his knees, Ragan carried her to the bed as she writhed and howled in agony. He lay beside her, holding onto her, not once leaving her side. Even as she cursed him repeatedly.

She didn't want him to go.

And he didn't.

TWENTY-THREE

SILVER

"Try it again," Keelen urged, his brow furrowed. A dark, curled lock of hair fell at his eyebrow and he swiped it away, but it fell loosely there again. No, not Keelen. Rory…

"I am," Silver said between clenched teeth. She slammed her hand against the wall, the strength from her magic causing several jagged cracks to run up its length.

All that did was make her palm ache, not open even a sliver of the portal's entrance to Valgmyr. "I've been trying for *days*." He'd been right—this wouldn't be easy, even though she'd assumed she could do it in a couple tries, not hundreds of failed attempts. And not a single one had even gotten close.

"Only two." He sighed, his lids fluttering. He'd refused to sleep—because *she* wouldn't sleep.

"Rory." Silver's voice came out tired, frustrated.

"You're going to call me Rory now?" He lifted a brow, trying to appear playful, but there was something hidden in his tone she couldn't make out. If he remembered who he was, wasn't that what he would want to be called by anyway?

"It's your name, isn't it?"

He nodded, shrugging. "You can call me whatever you want."

"We don't have time to sit here and argue over names." She leaned her back against the wall, the stinging sensation finally vanishing from her palm. "Pick one."

"Keelen."

"You should have just said that to begin with then," Silver muttered, even though calling him Keelen felt more natural to her.

Closing her eyes, Silver concentrated, digging deeper as she ventured down into the magic of the earth, the way she had in Ketill when she'd located Keelen's soul from Valgmyr. Not Torlarah as she'd once thought. The magic in Enare perfectly matched that of Ketill's, in strength and in the way she could use it, but she couldn't grasp what she needed in order to open the damn portal and find her sister.

Silver knew how to maneuver through the different colors of energy, what strings to grab, how hard to pull them. The darkness was there, as it always was, a mixture of blacks and grays, muted hues, weaving together. But she needed to go farther, to find that pure obsidian where not a single drop of light or gray existed.

When sweat beaded her forehead, her upper lip, her neck, her back, and she couldn't sink into the magic anymore, Silver pressed her hand to the wall and pleaded with it to open. Just a crack, a sliver. Enough so she could squeeze through. Her hand shook as she inhaled the energy into her lungs, letting it spread within her. Beneath her palm, there was still only hardness, and she couldn't feel anything else, only the same amount of darkness she'd used to bring Keelen here over the years.

Silver yanked back her arm and slammed her hand against the wall once more. Pain radiated.

"Stop fucking doing that," Keelen demanded. "It isn't going to do anything except injure your hand, and you don't want any weaknesses once we get past the barrier." Not *if*. But *when*. His words made it seem like he knew she would get the portal open. She desperately wished she could. That it would happen *now*.

Silver turned to Keelen, her chest heaving. "Since Ragan and the imps travel through the portal easily, why can't you?"

"I don't know." He bit his lip, scowling as he seemed to focus on the wall, the ceiling, the floor. "It has to be because I'm not inside my own body."

Right… That part wasn't new to her. Silver had known every time she brought his soul to Ketill that the body he was in wasn't his. He wasn't a raven, and this male body didn't belong to him… But now that she knew where he truly was from, it felt different. Taking a deep swallow, she wondered what his natural form looked like. She remembered the imps slipping from the walls in her room and holding her down. Was that what he was? Skeletal, misshapen, soulless ivory eyes. Or did he appear more like Ragan did? She hadn't seen the Valgmyr King with his wings or horns, though.

Shaking off the images and straightening her spine, she told herself it didn't matter. Keelen had lied to her. Perhaps not in the beginning because he hadn't known then, even though he'd concealed that he remembered her after they'd kissed. But he had lied when he believed himself to be the Valgmyr King. He could have told her what he suspected— should have. Maybe then she might have been able to prevent her sister from being taken or willingly choosing to go. If the imps hadn't used their energy to knock Silver out, she could have stopped this.

"What should I do now?" She exhaled, locking her gaze with Keelen's.

"Now we go to Javan to say goodbye. Take a break. Think." His voice told her that she needed to rest before she hurt herself. Her body was starting to droop from weakness.

While she'd been working to get the portal open without any sleep, Keelen had taken a break to go outside and make a pyre for Javan. He'd gathered what he could from around the castle and hadn't asked her to help him. She knew he'd done it for her, and she didn't know if she would have had the strength to do that if he hadn't.

Swiping her arm across her forehead, Silver nodded. She didn't say another word as he led her outside to the front of the castle, near the rose garden that was no longer dead. The empty, withered branches were now healthy and blossoming with lush green leaves and deep red roses. Even the trees were in full bloom with oranges and pears—the returned magic had revived all the foliage around the castle.

In front of the garden were twigs, branches, and dried leaves that Keelen had collected. In Ketill, this pyre would have been considered pitiful, a shameful funeral, and it wasn't enough for Javan. But it was the best they could do.

Javan's body lay atop the cluster of limbs and brown leaves, his eyes closed, his sword and cane on either side of him. He was still, too still. His soul was no longer there, yet Silver could still feel his comfortable presence.

Keelen bent down, pressed his palm to the twigs, and a spark of orange erupted. Since remembering who he was, he had been able to dive into the magic, just as she could. She placed her hand at the opposite side of the pyre, trailing her fingers across several broken twigs and cracked leaves, letting flames ignite. Her veins thrummed as she pushed the flames forward to spread and conquer. Her fire became one with Keelen's, licking at every inch of the dead foliage before encircling Javan's body, cocooning him in its scorching embrace.

"Goodbye, Javan." He was her family, and would have been even if they weren't related by blood.

Silver and Keelen stood beside one another, neither saying a word because there was nothing to say in the moment. She watched until only ash remained.

Javan should have stayed in Ketill, then he wouldn't have had to have a funeral in a foreign land. But it was his heart that had taken him, and it wouldn't have pumped for much longer. She'd felt how weak it had become, through her magic, just before his last breath.

Silver couldn't spend any more time studying the disintegrated pyre, so she fractured the silence. "What are you? Are you like the imps? You said they created you."

"I do have wings. But I'm not an imp." He pressed a hand to his forehead. "I have horns here, and flesh like I do now."

"Oh." That part was a relief, but would it have mattered if he looked like those creatures? Maybe it would, maybe it wouldn't. It didn't matter right then anyway.

"So you've only left Valgmyr when I've brought you here?" she continued.

He nodded. "Only then."

"And you had no other companions besides Ragan? Only the imps?"

"I had you when you brought me out. I thought it would never happen again before you brought me back and into this body. But Silver..." Keelen sighed. "Every time I returned from being with you, I knew I could never truly stay in Ketill. The imps would bring humans home, and I would take some of the females to my bed. After hundreds of years of Ragan seeing females and males die, he refused to get close to any of them. I've only been alive twenty-two years. Most of the humans were lonely ... and I was lonely too. And then they would die, or I would end their lives for them when their time was drawing near. I didn't ever love them in that way, and they didn't love me either—only a mutual caring, a necessity to survive. And I wished you'd been there instead..." His voice trailed off.

Silver blinked, not knowing how to react. She'd been alive almost as long as he had, but she hadn't brought the entire world to her bed. There'd only been a few kisses. Something green and envious slithered inside her, even though he'd been trapped in a place with monsters and a brother who she wanted to slap again. "I see."

"It doesn't matter." He paused, his eyes flickering with something new. Hope? "I think I know what we've been doing wrong. You're not going to be able to open the portal. *I* need to open it. But I can't with this body."

Silver furrowed her brow in confusion. "Then how will we?"

"It still has to be you. You need to dip into the dark magic. Instead of directly opening the portal first, you're going to have to bring my body from Valgmyr to here."

A body? An entire body? Could she even do that? She had only ever been able to drag his soul from there. But it wouldn't be her alone this time—he would be working alongside her. His strength matching hers.

"Just tell me what to do," Silver said.

Keelen's eyes flashed with anticipation, his warm hand clasping hers. "We have to draw a circle on the floor, step inside, and then you're going to need to give yourself to me."

TWENTY-FOUR

AFTON

Ragan's warm body unraveled from Afton, causing her to blink. She parted her lips to protest, but only a whisper escaped her sore throat. He'd held her through each of her screams, her curses, her raging.

A cool gust of air spilled into the room, followed by the crack of an imp's wings, when Ragan opened the glass door. Afton tried to lift her head, but she was too weak to move after the energy took what it had wanted from her.

"Why is she suffering the same way the others had?" Ragan demanded, his voice a desperate shout.

Afton's gaze fell to a female imp hovering in the air outside, the same one she'd seen on the other side of the glass when she first woke in Valgmyr. The imp's white eyes glowed, her dark wings cracking against the night. Afton wanted to use her magic to burst the creature's blood vessels, but she didn't have the strength to do it.

"Tell me what I can do?" Ragan asked when no answer came.

After a few seconds ticked by, the imp shrugged and flew away from the open glass, the sound of her wings fading away.

A heavy breath escaped Ragan, his shoulders sagging as

he shut the door with a soft click. He slipped back in bed beside her, and she closed her eyes.

Before she could attempt to sleep and drift into a raven-colored world, the torturous pain came once more, shooting through her body like sharpened arrows released from bows.

Afton continued to take in deep breath after deep breath. She wished she could have traveled into a rooted dream and stayed there. Instead, she'd been lying here, after the sharp pains and biting aches had dulled then dissipated.

Even after that, she was afraid to move for fear she would feel like she was being ripped apart from the inside out again. But the vicious energy didn't stir.

She was still in the bed and not alone. Ragan's strong, comforting arm curved around her waist, and she'd pressed in closer to the warmth of his bare chest during the night. She'd been thinking for a long time while he slept. Debating whether to remain down here forever and hate him or take the chance and truly understand the things he'd done.

Slowly, so as not to wake Ragan, she rolled over to study him. His eyes were still closed, his long-curled lashes dusting his cheeks. He pulled her closer, and she allowed him to as he pressed his forehead on hers. But his lids remained shut.

"You still haven't slept?" he rasped, his voice tinged with guilt.

Afton lifted one of his lids so he was looking at her. She missed his brown eyes, but these ones were more truthful—they told her everything. They were the same shade as hers, yet they appeared so different in the way he observed things.

"No," she said. "I'm not sure if I'll ever be able to."

He winced and opened both eyes. "I knew you were going to hate me, but I also knew how much Ketill meant to you. If you were down here and understood that your energy could make sure nothing ever destroyed your home, then all of this would be worth it. I didn't take you here just for selfish reasons—although some were—but so the land you loved would be safe. Yet now…"

Afton hadn't thought about that. He'd explained to her by the lake how the tainted energy wouldn't seep into the land because she wasn't temporary. But she hadn't realized that it would mean Ketill would always be safe, as would Enare and every other territory. If she'd been in his place, she knew she would have done far worse. Would have lied to anyone she could to lure them to Valgmyr herself to try and save the world above. And he hadn't even done all of that—he'd used up his time to be with her, before he was forced to return.

"You didn't know, and I won't hate you for that." She exhaled softly. "But how can I truly let it in? I already feel it's attached, so I don't understand."

"When the energy is pulled from you again, I want you to only look at me. Focus. Focus on what makes you happy. Your sister. Ketill."

Afton couldn't lie to herself and say she hated him, couldn't even pretend to, didn't have the energy to anyway. And if the energy didn't become a part of her, then who knew how much time she really had left. But that didn't mean she wouldn't take down however many imps she could before that would happen.

"You," she whispered.

"Hmm?" Ragan's brows rose, and his breaths halted as he waited for her to continue.

"You make me happy too." She sat up and crawled on top of him, her face inches from his. "I may have wanted to rip your heart out at times and will continue to do so, but you do make me happy. I like a messy story better anyway. Besides, I did stab you, claw you, pretended to be my sister when coming to Enare…"

"I'd rather have you at my side wanting to rip my heart out than not at all." His lips pulled back into a radiant smile. "I love you. I should have told you before, and I wanted to, but I needed you to see the true me saying it. That was the one thing I held back on, even though I tried to show you in every way possible."

He loved her, and she'd known it, but she'd held back too. Kept those words trapped inside her mouth, let her kisses remain hers.

"I love you and I hate that I do, but I love that I do more. So, I'm giving you the one thing no other man has gotten from me. I had wanted to give it to you every time I was with you, but I'm also glad I held back until now." Afton leaned forward, slowly, her lips only a feather's touch away from his. Her heart pounded, roaring for her to do it, but she liked the anticipation it was bringing her, bringing him. Then she gave in to temptation, cradling his face and letting her lips mold to his. The kiss was soft, gentle, but it was as perfect as when they would ride each other to bliss, just as fulfilling.

"I've been hoping you would do that." He grinned against her lips. "Now, will you let me do something?"

"Only if you can make my toes curl."

Playfulness danced in his eyes, and she knew that look, her body yearned for it. Then his mouth captured hers, and her back arched as his hand traveled down to cup her backside. His tongue swiped up her lips and parted them. She mirrored his caressing movements, then moaned as his tongue plunged into her mouth. Afton matched him stroke for stroke, claiming every inch of his mouth. She hadn't known a kiss could be this bright, this satisfying. His warm tongue tangled with hers, and she ran her hands up his chiseled stomach, his naked chest, across his broad shoulders to the back of his neck. Her fingers entwined with his hair—it felt as it always did, like touching silk. His wings were tucked tightly at his back, and she removed a hand from his hair to trail her fingers over the leathery texture, then to one of his smooth horns. Her body heated even more as he growled with approval.

"Remove your pants," she demanded, her body rocking against him.

His mouth didn't miss a beat as she lifted up so he could unbutton his pants and shove them down. He kicked them off, becoming completely bare before her. She leaned back, taking all of him in, and even though they'd been like this together, he still made her heart accelerate. Afton wanted to stare at his naked form until the end of time, but she desperately needed him inside her.

Ragan's fingertips skimmed up the length of her spine, expertly loosening each button at her back, knowing just what she wanted. He peeled the dress from her shoulders, exposing her bare breasts, her peaked nipples.

"I won't ever get enough of you." He sat them both up, hungrily kissing her beneath her jaw and down her throat to one of her breasts. With his tongue, he drew circles around her nipple, then stroked and sucked. Her center pooled with her wetness from his rhythmic movements.

Rolling Afton to her back, he removed the rest of her dress and undergarments. He then took that impish tongue to her belly button and glided it down in between her legs to taste how ready she was for him. As he nipped, licked, and grazed her with his teeth, it was as though he was performing some kind of spiritual summoning with the combined brushing of his horns along her thighs.

"Tell me what you want?" His eyes met Afton's, his lips glistening from drinking her. He crawled over her until his mouth was inches from hers.

"You." She reached down and grasped his length, squeezing until his eyes fluttered.

"Have me." With one swift movement, she was off the bed and back in his lap, her legs cradling his hips, his hardness at her core.

She wrapped her hands around his shoulders and sank down on him. A moan escaped her as he filled her. Ragan gripped her hips, driving them forward. Her lips needed his once more and she kissed them, devouring them as her body's pace picked up.

He growled against her mouth. And she would never exhaust of that beastly sound.

"Show me everything you have," she purred with a grin.

Ragan knew exactly what she yearned for—he pulled out of her to flip her to all fours. She couldn't help admiring his strength while he hovered behind her. She was about to curse at him to get back inside her, but he must have read her thoughts as he slid into her, agonizingly slow. Then he pulled back and thrust forward. Afton groaned in ecstasy. He thrust again, harder, faster—she needed more and he gave all of himself to her, their bodies smacking, her breasts bouncing, his growls igniting everything in her. With each fierce movement, the exquisite feeling expanded inside her, coming closer and closer until a burst of energy barreled through her. She shouted his name, hoping the entire world outside the portal would hear her. Ragan panted her name in return while his body shook and quaked. He folded himself on top of her, his hands cupping her breasts as they breathed in and out together.

Ragan kissed her neck softly, trailing his hands down to her stomach. "I didn't think you would want me again once you discovered who I was and came here," he said.

"It was inevitable." Afton smirked, releasing a low chuckle. She turned so she was on her back, and he settled between her thighs. Drawing his head to hers, she pressed her lips to his. "Now—"

A sharp agonizing pain, harsher than before, shot through her. It felt as though all her organs were being squeezed until they burst. Afton could barely hear Ragan shouting her name over her own screams.

She didn't think she would ever stop screaming.

TWENTY-FIVE

SILVER

Silver's fingers fumbled as she unbuttoned the front of her dress. She wasn't an expert at this by any means, but she would give herself to Keelen so they could get into Valgmyr. If this had been before she discovered his past, she would have done it anyway. Although, her hands would have shaken then too.

"What are you doing?" Keelen's eyes widened, his lips parting as he reached forward and clasped her wrists, halting her movements at the button over her breasts.

Her gaze latched onto his, and she held it there firm, trying to keep her nervousness at bay. "You need us to be together, right? Flesh to flesh?"

"No!" He breathed and dropped their arms to her sides before releasing her. "That's not what I meant."

"Oh." She blinked and ran a hand through her tangled hair before refastening her buttons. "Then what *did you mean*?"

"I meant that I need you to pull dark magic from the earth and entwine it with mine so you can reach into Valgmyr and attempt to bring my body here. I know it will be tricky since you were never able to do it before, but I'm going to help you. And if I'm in my natural form again, then I should be able to open the portal and take you there. If that's what you want."

She studied him, his expression, and in that last note she knew he was honest and would do whatever she decided. "Yes, it's what I wish."

"Even if you end up trapped there?" Keelen swallowed. "If you die there?"

"Yes." Her voice was serious.

"Your sister won't be happy if something goes wrong. And neither will I."

Silver grasped his hand and gave it a gentle squeeze. "It's my decision."

"And that's why I'll do whatever you ask." He would. He truly would. Silver wondered what would have happened if she'd never drawn him to Ketill. Valgmyr's energy would have seeped into the land regardless of her actions. He wasn't like his brother—he hadn't concealed his identity willingly. And she knew if he'd been the Valgmyr King, he would have left her in Ketill while trying to save his kingdom without destroying or taking her in the process. She realized then that her feelings for him hadn't changed. Not in the least.

She looked at those gentle eyes of his, and she had to shift her gaze from them. "What else do we need? What is required for the circle? Just us?"

He bit his lip, his brow furrowing. "The setup is simple enough. We'll draw a circle, place four candles around it to represent north, south, east, and west. Then in between each candle will be a different herb, an offering of sorts."

"Any herb?" she asked, knowing she had plenty of different herbs stashed in her trunks.

"Any."

"How do you know all this?"

"We do have books in Valgmyr. It's not exact, but a combination of things to try."

Silver nodded and tugged him down the hallway. They went up the two flights of stairs leading to her room. When they entered, it was still in disarray. Not only from the imps, but because her things were already across the floor from when she'd tried to find out if she could make any spells to get to Afton.

Keelen bent down and lifted a jar of lemongrass that had rolled against the wall. She collected three other jars from her trunk containing rosemary, tarragon, and sage. From the desk, Keelen took one of the inkwells.

She started to head toward the door when Keelen grabbed her hand, hauling her back toward him. "We can do it right here. Anywhere should be fine. I don't want you to have to waste any more time." He placed a palm at her cheek, his voice soft. "Can you grab four candles from the wall while I make the circle?"

"Sure." Her heart pounded harder—they were getting closer to starting the spell, and she prayed it would work.

Keelen opened the inkwell and poured the liquid onto the floor. He dipped his finger into the spilled puddle and traced a misshapen circle. It was large enough to hold at least four people, so the both of them would fit comfortably inside.

Silver drew out four unlit ivory candles from their holders. Keelen then gathered the herbs she'd set aside on the floor and placed them in areas around the circle so they were perfectly diagonal from one another.

Taking a candle from her hand, he rubbed the wick and a flickering orange flame came to life. "Can you light the rest?"

Silver nodded, mirroring his movements across the wicks and handing the candles to him one at a time. He set them in the spaces between the herbs.

Raking a hand through his hair, Keelen straightened and took a step into the circle. He studied Silver for a moment, then reached out toward her. "Will you come inside with me?"

She gave a small smile as she clasped his hand, intertwining their fingers. He drew her forward and she was careful not to crush any of the surrounding contents.

After Silver slipped into the circle, Keelen released his grip on her and held his palms up. He motioned toward them with his chin, so she placed hers against his.

"I promise I'll keep you as safe as I can," he said, a deep line forming between his brows.

Silver liked that he didn't say he would keep her safe. That was a promise no one could truly keep. One would only be able to protect as best they could. "That's all we can do."

He lowered himself, nodding for her to do the same, their hands never releasing from one another as their knees pressed onto the floor.

"Ready?" he asked.

"As ready as I'll ever be." Silver would try her damned hardest to weave through the darkness, to get into Valgmyr so she could bring Keelen his body. If Javan were here, he would have told Silver not to trust him. If Afton were Silver, she would risk anything to try. But the truth was she trusted Keelen not to harm her, trusted in that with everything she had. For always.

Keelen closed his eyes, murmuring words in a language she'd never heard before. The magic around her thrummed, vibrating, shaking not only her insides, but the room's walls, the entire castle.

"Closer," Keelen said softly, not opening his lids. "Get as close to me as you can."

Silver inched toward him until her knees touched his. She reached down, down into the magic, through the wind, the dirt, the fire, the water, into that darkness from which she'd pulled Keelen's soul.

As before, the fog swirled around her. But she couldn't feel him there like she had in the past—because his soul was already here.

Silver had to go deeper for her magic to interlock with Keelen's. His energy still wasn't touching hers, even though she could feel it. She had to get closer to him physically first. "Sit back," she whispered, her breaths coming out deep.

He kept his eyes closed, holding his focus as he adjusted himself so that he was sitting on the floor. Releasing her palms from his, Silver scooted forward and sank down onto his lap, folding her legs behind his back. She pressed her forehead to his, her fingers at the nape of his neck, and absorbed his warmth. He wrapped his arms around her and drew her as near as he could.

Shutting her lids, she searched for Keelen's energy. But she didn't find him—he found her. Their magic circled around one another, then entwined, becoming one. And she knew he felt it too because he inhaled sharply. Silver now had his energy, and he had hers. She only needed to see past the fog and find his body in Valgmyr. But that white was all there was.

Keelen's fingers dug into her waist as though he saw it too, and perhaps he could. Silver didn't ask him anything because she didn't want to lose hold on how far they'd gotten. She still wasn't close enough to him to drift farther in.

Silver pressed her lips to his and caressed his mouth ever so gently with hers. He kissed her in return just as softly. She let her tongue slip into his mouth, stroking his. Their entwined magic became brighter, turning the fog into mist, but she still was unable to see anything else.

Then Keelen deepened the kiss. No longer were the kisses slow, but urgent, frantic. An outline in the mist formed. Silver stretched their magic forward until it grasped something firm—a shoulder. It had to be him, or at least she hoped. No other outlines were visible.

Silver let the magic weave in and out as if it was stitching something together. Beneath her, she could feel Keelen's arousal, and every ounce of warmth she had spread down to her core. She rolled her hips forward, their kisses growing wilder, his tongue tasting places she hadn't dreamed were possible.

A spark of electrifying energy blasted through her, followed by a gripping pain that squeezed her heart and twisted, causing her to shout. She lurched forward, her head falling to Keelen's shoulder, her body limp.

Then her chest heaved.

"Silver, are you all right?" Keelen asked, pushing her back, his hands cradling her face.

She slowly opened her eyes, trying to catch her breath. Her gaze landed not on violet irises, but pitch-black ones with glistening white pupils. And even though they were a different shade, the way he squinted was all him. They were her comfort.

Silver leaned back, lips swollen, then her eyes widened. Keelen barely looked anything like how she'd created him, besides his pale skin and build of his body. His hair was brown like Ragan's and no longer curled but fell just past his chin. His lips were lush, his cheekbones high. Two horns, like that of a ram, curled down from the sides of his forehead, dark wings folded at his back.

Otherworldly.

He was even more beautiful than before, more beautiful than anything she'd ever seen. While others may have been afraid, she wasn't. She would never be afraid of him.

Silver unraveled her legs from his back, beneath his wings. Liquid pooled around the two of them—the wax she'd used to create him had melted and unleashed this male.

"We did it," she said, her hands at his cheeks, her gaze not ever wanting to leave his. "You're you."

Keelen smiled, and her heartbeat increased at the familiar expression.

His lips pressed to hers, as though he just wanted to feel her one more time with his true mouth. "Now let me see if I can bring you to my home."

TWENTY-SIX

AFTON

"There has to be another reason why the energy is doing this to you," Ragan said. "I've tried to ask the imps for the past two days, and all I get are shrugs."

Afton hadn't attempted to talk to one yet—she was calming herself, knowing she would tear them apart if she did. Ragan had told her they could speak, but they elected not to most of the time. Well, she would make them speak today.

She'd been spending her time tapping into the energy, trying to get it to fully be a part of her, but instead, it seemed to be doing the opposite, unlatching. And each time Valgmyr pulled energy from her, the pain came in the same harsh waves. At night, she would entangle herself with Ragan and try to forget what occurred during the day.

Along the edge of the lake, Afton sat close to Ragan, studying the shimmery water, the frozen people. She wondered how long she would last before turning like them if the imps chose to reveal nothing.

"When we came here," Afton started, "I felt the energy connect. But with each passing day, it's loosening more and more. I won't die." It wasn't that she feared death. It was because she knew the imps would go after Silver next. And while Afton wanted to stay there, protect Ketill from behind these closed walls, it wasn't a place for her sister.

Silver would want to ride Midnight through the edelweiss fields, go to the shops to find unwanted objects to bring home, take tarts from the kitchens and share them with the servants.

Afton stood, looking from one unfamiliar face to the next. Curly blonde locks, straight black hair, pale skin, dark skin, tall, short, curvy, thin—so many people had come there and hadn't survived.

"What about Thorin?" Afton asked, continuing to drift from face to face, wanting to know which one belonged to the king she had considered her enemy all this time, when in fact, he had barely inherited the crown before trying to save his home. "Which one is him?"

Ragan rose from the ground and motioned for her to follow him. They circled to the back of the lake where he came to a stop in front of a figure that was only a little taller than Afton, his shoulders broad.

"This is the real Thorin," Ragan said, his lips pursed as if he was thinking about how he'd pretended to be him and hating it.

Afton stepped closer until she was directly across from the true King of Enare. His features looked nothing like Ragan's. His hair was several shades darker than Ragan's, and his face was handsome enough, rounder, his nose long, and his skin a deep golden hue. But if Afton had met him in Enare or Ketill, she wouldn't have given him a second look—she would have never been tempted by him.

"Was he like his father?" Afton asked, turning to Ragan. She hated his father, hated the way he had controlled Enare. And she knew she should have stepped in sooner, not only to have tried to keep her territory safe, but the rest as well. It didn't matter now, though, because the king was gone, and Silver would take Enare under her wing.

"I didn't meet his father, but Thorin truly wanted to save

his land. He was a good man, could've been a great king. But good people still die before they have a chance to become great." Ragan paused. "He was the last one to come down here before I was released."

Released from this cage... Freed for a time, but now shackled once again.

Afton would never know if Thorin would have been great—or if he would have fallen into a hole of cruelty, consumed by the control he'd inherited. But perhaps he'd been just like her, wanting to be nothing like his parents.

"I only pretended to be him to get you to come, as you know," he said. "But then once you came, I shouldn't have let you believe I was Thorin. I suppose I was trying to get you to hate me, to punish myself."

"It worked." Afton smiled. "Only briefly, though." She glanced from face to face, curious as to how long ago each person had lived outside of Valgmyr. None of them looked familiar. "Are they always going to be here? You can't make a funeral pyre or bury them?"

"No." He shook his head. "Once they die, their bodies come here. Their flesh won't burn and their feet stay planted to the ground."

None of them had survived. Not even Ragan's brother, Rory, was safe in the end. Afton's gaze drifted farther down to where his brother was frozen. She sucked in a sharp breath when her gaze met his *empty* spot.

"What is it?" Ragan asked.

"He isn't here!" She took off on a sprint to where she'd seen his form only days before, but now it was only a vacant area. The grass pressed down where his feet once stood.

"Where *is* he?" Ragan's wild eyes searched the faces around the lake. "Rory!"

Afton studied each one, seeking horns and wings, but there were so many bodies. None of them were Rory.

"Go check inside the castle, and I'll keep looking around

here." Afton nudged Ragan forward because he knew every nook and cranny. Could Rory still be alive after all? Afton's mind reeled, but a sliver of peace blossomed inside. Perhaps something good could come of all this. If she died, then Ragan might at least still have his brother... It may not be the same, but it would be something to help him stay focused, surviving. That wouldn't solve the issue he'd been facing for hundreds and hundreds of years, though.

Ragan took off in the direction of the castle while she ran beside the lake, verifying that each person wasn't Rory. All the faces blended together as she lost count. The beat of wings cracked above her, and she glanced up to find Ragan lowering himself.

As his feet touched the ground, he closed his wings at his back, his chest heaving and his eyes filling with worry. "He isn't in there."

They would have seen him out here—wouldn't they? He should have come when Ragan called him. Or maybe he wouldn't? She truly didn't know if he was decent like Ragan. Siblings could easily be like night and day—she and Silver were different in so many ways.

Before she could say anything else, he took off in the direction of the topiaries.

"Where are you going?" Afton called, barreling after him.

"I'm going to find out what *they* did to him," Ragan spat.

Afton's heart pounded, remembering the topiaries moving, the imps hovering on top of the castle. Ragan was heading to the one place where he told her not to go, where she hadn't wanted to go anyway.

But maybe she should have.

She took deep breaths, tapping into the energy that now only hung onto her by threads. Extending her claws and sharp teeth, she sprinted in sync with him. Skirting around body after body, she broke out from the collection and into red-berried bushes.

"You should wait in the castle or at the lake." Ragan sighed, slowing to a stop. He had to know she wouldn't listen, would only do what she wanted, which was to make sure he didn't get himself killed.

Grabbing his arm, she drew him closer to her. "It doesn't matter how long you've been down here, or that I've only been here a few days, I'm not letting you go there alone while I sit back and watch. Especially after you warned me not to go there in the first place. Yet here you are, risking *yourself*."

He raked his fingers through his hair, disheveling it. "Just stay close to me, all right? That's all I ask."

Afton supposed she could handle that. She nodded and released her hold on his arm.

Ragan slipped his hand into hers, interlocking their fingers, and gave her a gentle squeeze before releasing her. "Come on, then."

They leapt over round thorny bushes and stayed side by side as they entered the wide area filled with the lush green topiaries. A dragon, breathing fire, with its wings spread—a chicken, its beak pointed downward, nestled on the ground—a stag standing on its hind legs with antlers almost touching the limb barrier.

As she and Ragan edged closer to the center of the topiaries, the red eyes inside their leaf-covered heads ignited, burning brighter than the sun. Afton's heart thundered with a fear of the unknown. In Ketill, she always had the upper hand, knew what she was facing. But not here. Not this.

"Where is Rory?" Ragan demanded, his voice echoing throughout the green garden.

A rustling sounded from beside her and Afton glanced up to see the stag's movements. Grasping her hand, Ragan pulled her out of the way, just as the stag brought its hooves to the ground, inches from crushing her.

Afton bared her teeth, even though she couldn't take down everything around her if they all attacked at once. There wasn't much she could do to this massive beast either, but she would tear off as many limbs as she could before taking her last breath.

The wings at Ragan's back expanded, creating a light gust of wind. Before anything could happen to her, she knew he would attempt to fly them back to the castle. When she glanced behind them, there was absolutely nowhere to go. The topiaries were brushed up against the ceiling of the limb cage, and there wasn't a space Afton or Ragan could shimmy through. They were *trapped*.

"Rory's body is gone," Ragan growled through gritted teeth. "He was at the lake and now he isn't."

Afton thought there wouldn't be an answer after moments of silence had passed, but then a pattering stirred. Out from the branches and leaves of each topiary, one by one, the imps poked their small skeletal heads forward, their white eyes glowing, their pointed ears perking.

A deep crackle vibrated from the stag, its limbs drawing back. An imp pushed its entire body out, dropping to the ground. Female. Her feet landed perfectly, and her fragile wings opened. It was the same one Afton had seen at the glass door to her room on the two occasions. The female imp lifted her hand and pointed a single digit upward.

"You set him free?" Ragan furrowed his brow. "But Rory was dead—we saw his body out beside the lake, and you only shrugged when I asked you about it."

The imp shook her head to the first question, then shrugged at the second. Ragan tightened his grip on Afton—he must have felt her preparing to charge for the imp.

"Is he alive?" Ragan asked, his voice pleading.

Tilting her head to the side, the imp slowly nodded and her white eyes flashed.

"Where is he now?" Ragan asked, his voice low, deadly, but he still didn't make a move.

The imp's lips pulled back into a grin, baring teeth as sharp as Afton's. She again pointed up toward the barrier. Afton peered at the branches, expecting to see a body cocooned within the limbs and flowers, but it was empty.

"And what about Afton?" Ragan bellowed. "Every time I ask you about her, all you do is shrug about that too. Do you *want* this to continue? Is that why you're not giving me any answers?"

With a shrug, the imp turned back toward the stag topiary. Afton couldn't take any more shrugs from the creature or her turning her back on them. She lunged forward, out of Ragan's grasp, and caught the imp, just as the female was about to fly back in the topiary.

"Afton!" Ragan shouted, his voice more nervous than she'd ever heard him. "Release her." A flock of imps were already holding him back.

Hisses echoed all around her, the greens of the garden darkening to blacks. She squeezed the imp's throat, her nails digging in. "You're going to quit shrugging and tell us how we can fix this, or I'll make all your organs bleed," she growled, her energy stirring as she peered at the rest of the creatures. "You will not ignore me like you're doing with Ragan. And if you choose to kill me, my blood won't be the only one spilled before I'm dead. Now, where is Rory?"

Above them, the branches unraveled, as they had when Ragan first brought her there. A strong beat and swish sounded, resembling Ragan's wings, but his were unmoving. The heavy cracking drew nearer, a shadow of a form sliding into view. In his arms was another body with long, obsidian hair.

Her sister.

TWENTY-SEVEN

SILVER

With a deep inhale, using the earth's magic, Silver blew out a hard breath. The flames lighting the candles around Keelen's inky circle extinguished. Smoke curled up from their wicks toward the ceiling.

"Once we're through the walls, how are you going to get me to your home?" Silver asked, pressing her hand against the smooth texture. Even now, as she tugged at the magic, she couldn't push a single digit through.

"You'll see." Keelen smirked, motioning with his index finger for her to come to him. "I need you to hold on to me."

Silver's gaze roamed over him for a moment, taking in his beauty one more time. Those curled horns—his leathery wings with dark veins, creating a map of their own, running in different directions. She didn't think her heart could pound any harder as she stared at his half smile.

His arms opened for her to rest in, but she didn't want to be cradled when entering Valgmyr. Him sprinting her up the stairs to escape danger was one thing—this was another. It would also be more difficult for her to leap from his arms if he was holding her like an infant.

Stepping forward, she grasped his wrists and brought his

hands to his sides. Keelen's hair hung in his eye on one side, and she gently swept the locks behind his ear. She then placed her palms to his warm neck, her breath mingling with his when she leaned closer. Their earlier kiss came to mind, the way his lips had moved against hers, the way he knew how to do everything she could have ever wanted done to her mouth. And she couldn't stop thinking about it. But she forced the image back down, temporarily hiding it as Keelen gripped her waist and lifted her. She wrapped her legs around his narrow hips, his hands sliding down to her buttocks, holding her steady.

Her cheeks heated at his touch, and she rested her head against his shoulder while folding her arms behind his neck. She breathed him in, his woodsy and jasmine scent enveloping her. It was still there, same as before when he'd been a raven.

"Whatever you do, don't let go of me until I say it's safe," Keelen said, shuffling them forward.

"I won't," Silver promised. She trusted him with this—she trusted him with everything. Her stomach swarmed with flying imps as she prayed to the gods to let them pass through the portal and easily find Afton. She didn't know what would come after that, but she needed to bring her sister safely home. There wouldn't be a goodbye.

A strong gust of air blasted within the room as Keelen swung his wings forward. Her hair blew around her head when he pulled his appendages back and repeated the motion. They drifted upward, his feet completely leaving the floor. The sound of his wings was like true drum beats to her ears while he brought her toward the ceiling. She told herself she was going to keep her eyes trained on their destination, but at the last moment she slammed them shut, bracing for the hard impact in case it didn't work.

After a few seconds passed, she opened her lids and gasped at the sight before her. No longer were they in the castle, but flying across a dark blue sky. And it wasn't anywhere in

Enare.

Below them were entwined beige limbs, blooming with edelweiss and white roses, even though such flowers didn't normally grow on those types of branches. The barrier formed a dome, hiding a secret that she couldn't see yet. Valgmyr.

Outside of the barrier was nothing but the cerulean shade. Not a cloud, not a tree, not any homes, or even a sun. Only the sky, the branches, and the flowers.

Keelen pumped his wings harder, her body vibrating against his with each movement. Her stomach flipped as he descended, heading straight toward the barrier.

"How are we going to get through?" she shouted over the loud cracking of his wings.

"You'll see." And she could hear the playfulness in his words.

Despite the fear that they may crash into the branches, she didn't hold her breath. As soon as she was about to close her eyes again, the limbs unraveled, creating a sizzling sound. They peeled open to a space large enough for them both to fit through.

"This isn't good," Keelen said.

"Keep going." She bit her lip and continued to glance down.

Inside, she had expected to see the emerald greens of the story, yet there were mostly blacks. Above them, the limbs curled and wove back together, sealing shut. There wasn't even a sliver to peek out through at the blue sky. As they veered toward the ground, the topiaries were just like the tales, only not green. They were the dark shade she'd seen in the distance. The smoky, grassy aroma struck her nose, heavier than at Enare's castle.

Keelen's feet touched down, and Silver bit her lip as her gaze met Afton's. The expression on her sister's face was enraged, her jaw clenched. In her arms, she held a squirming imp, one hand at its throat, the other around its stomach.

Silver's gaze flicked to a growling noise—she found several imps holding another form back. The Valgmyr King—Ragan. He looked just the same besides his eyes, horns, and wings like Keelen's. Her blood boiled as she watched him, but she reeled her anger in, remembering everything Keelen had told her.

Still, Ragan had lied. Hid truths. Taken her sister.

"Not yet," Keelen whispered, holding her tight.

She stared at the imps, recalling the way they'd held her down, knocked her out with their magic, their blank white eyes boring into her. The Valgmyr energy swirled within her, yet it didn't feel tainted like before. She tried to tap into it, draw out her claws and teeth, but she couldn't.

"Rory!" Ragan yelled, trying to break free from the hissing creatures. "What the fuck are you doing? Get her out of here!"

"Get behind me," Keelen said, releasing her.

Silver untangled her body from him, and he quickly hauled her behind his back.

"Why is she here?" Afton seethed, taking a hand from the imp and thrusting it in their direction. Keelen grunted and fell to his knees, his body quaking, his eyes rolling back.

Oh no. Silver knew what Afton was doing. Same as what she'd done with the rats in the tunnel—break his insides apart, then burst every blood vessel and organ he had until he was dead.

"Stop!" Silver screamed and rushed for her sister, coming to a halt in between Afton's palm and Keelen.

Afton yanked back her hand before an ounce of magic could harm Silver. Her expression switched to one of confusion. "He brought you here…"

"It's Keelen," Silver rushed the words out. "He's Keelen. Don't hurt him. He brought me here because I asked him to. So we could try and bring you home."

"Keelen? Keelen is Rory?" Afton's nostrils flared as she turned to Ragan, both her hands gripping the imp tight again.

"Did you know he was her guard?"

"No." Ragan shook his head, still struggling to break free of the imps. "I didn't know. He never said anything to me, and he didn't look anything like my brother."

"He's good, and he didn't remember his past until Ragan took you from Enare," Silver said, turning to Keelen who was on all fours, his chest heaving, his eyes meeting hers. "I love him."

Afton made a choking noise in her throat, as though it was the most foolish thing Silver had ever said. She continued to stare at Afton, letting her see she meant it. Her sister's face fell and she blew out a breath, like she seemed to understand.

Silver realized something in that moment. She'd known Afton loved Ragan when he'd pretended to be a servant, she'd known her sister continued to do so even when he was Thorin, and after what Keelen had told her about his brother, she should have known there would still be a possibility.

"You love Ragan," Silver said softly, her arms falling to her sides. "And you didn't need me to come."

Her sister nodded.

Leaves rustled and imps flocked out of the topiaries, their wings flapping in a brutal manner. Afton held her hand up toward them, and they stopped mid-air, their wings still pumping. "Go near her, and I'll make it so your insides won't ever heal."

Silver met Afton's fiery gaze. "What do we do now?"

"You need to go home," Afton said. "Back to Ketill. Take Enare under your wing and rule them both. Be their queen, while I take care of our land from down here."

"That's why you truly want to stay here? In this prison?" she asked, incredulous.

"No, Silver." Afton's voice came out gentle, a sound she'd never heard from her before. "Haven't you realized yet that everything I do is for you? I would be protecting Ketill, therefore protecting *you*."

Silver's heart swelled—she loved her sister just as fiercely, but how could she be away from her forever?

"I don't know if they'll let her leave." Keelen was now standing and moving beside Silver.

Afton scowled at him and started to open her mouth to say something, when an ear-piercing scream tore from her throat. Her wretched sounds filled Silver's ears, and Afton's grip released on the imp as she dropped to her knees. Silver darted toward her sister, tears filling her eyes. She frantically looked from Ragan to Keelen, trying to find an answer.

"What's *wrong* with her?" Keelen shouted at his brother, anger rolling off him in waves.

"The energy didn't seep all the way down into her, only attached," Ragan said through gritted teeth, while trying to yank himself from the imps' hold. "And now it's loosening."

The imps surrounding them hadn't moved, their blazing orbs only continued to watch.

"If she dies"—Keelen's eyes widened—"that means they'll take Silver. And if the same thing happens to her, then she'll die and nothing in Valgmyr will change. They'll keep bringing new bodies here."

Silver's heart plummeted—not for herself, but because Afton could die.

Keelen looked at Silver with something akin to desperation before turning toward the imps. "I think I know what to do."

TWENTY-EIGHT

AFTON

As soon as the pain washed over Afton, it faded, and her chest heaved. Silver rushed to her side, helping her up.

"Why were you screaming like that?" Silver's eyes were wide, scanning her over, seeming to search for open wounds.

"It comes and goes." The longer episodes completely drained her of energy while the short spurts, like this, were only mildly better. Each one felt like her body was being cleaved into pieces.

Keelen's hand gripped Afton's arm as he studied her expression. She didn't have the energy to rip her arm away.

"Fucking release Ragan," Keelen shouted at the imps, his nostrils flaring. "No one is going to fight you, and I promise she'll leave you alone."

I promise no such thing.

The imps each peered at Keelen, their white eyes not revealing any of their thoughts. And then the ones holding onto Ragan released him.

"I don't understand why they always listen to you and not me," Ragan muttered and took Afton's face in his hands, his worried gaze expressing everything he felt.

"Because I don't take their shit," Keelen spat. Then his

voice softened as he spoke, "I don't think she's going to last more than a few weeks before they will require Silver."

"That isn't going to happen," Afton snapped, her hand clasping Silver's.

"You're right, it won't." Keelen locked his gaze on hers, and he looked just the same as when she'd seen his still body at the lake.

"How?" Afton asked, her shoulders sagging, a lost feeling washing over her. She didn't know how to save herself—she didn't know how to save her sister or her home.

"Silver and I used our magic together to retrieve my body from Valgmyr." Keelen paused and glanced at Silver. "As you know, when she last brought my soul to Ketill, she asked me to be your guard, your weapon. I had been drawn to her and agreed before I knew who I was, until the memories became clearer after the tonic you gave me. I'm meant to be hers, just as you'd wanted me to be. But that doesn't mean I can't be your weapon for a little while right now."

"Rory…" Ragan shook his head. "You're risking yourself to do this."

"Do you want to remain in Valgmyr?" Keelen asked, ignoring his brother.

"To protect our home, yes." She'd told herself again and again that she would do anything to protect Ketill, her sister. That hadn't changed.

The imp Afton had choked stood not far from them, watching, her sharp teeth still bared. All Afton would have to do is use her energy to murder the creature, but she held back for Silver, waiting to see what Keelen wanted to do.

"You and Silver have the capability of holding the energy like Ragan and I because of your eyes," Keelen started. "There's a reason I didn't die down here, a reason Ragan won't either." He glanced at his brother with a look that urged him to continue.

"We're immortal." Ragan sighed. "You know this. I think

I know what Rory is trying to say. It isn't only our eyes that makes us this way—it's our horns and our wings. And you and Silver only have one of the three which means you won't survive."

"What are you saying?" Silver asked. "That nothing can be done?"

Keelen turned from them and walked toward the imp, then knelt before her. "I want to ask something of you, Mother."

Afton arched a brow. *Mother*?

The imp tilted her head and held out her hand. A few other creatures shifted closer to their leader.

"I want to transfer my horns and my wings to Afton. She already has the ability to keep the energy healthy—she just doesn't have immortality. And isn't this what you wanted? Why you sent Ragan to retrieve one of them? You hoped a bond would form between him and one of the sisters, and that it could help in the process. Well, it did.

"No one else would love the lands like Afton. I don't want Silver to be destroyed by her sister not surviving. I don't want myself ruined by Silver dying. And I don't want to see my brother suffer any more either."

Afton kept silent, for once, too astonished to even gather the words screaming at her to argue or attack. She instead listened.

"If I do this," Keelen whispered. "I want Silver to be able to return home."

If Keelen gave up his immortality, that would mean he would be like her, and he would die down here.

"Wait!" Afton shouted, holding up a hand and stepping forward. "Only if Keelen can go with her."

The imp studied them both, the others behind her hissing. Afton would end the creature as soon as she said no—she waited for it. But the imp shrugged, allowing Keelen to do as he wished.

Afton narrowed her eyes, her heart accelerating—she

hadn't expected the imp to give in, even though she was Keelen's mother. Perhaps the lands were as important to them as they were to her.

"Are you sure this is truly what you want?" Silver asked Afton. "It would be forever."

Afton peered up at her sister's glistening eyes, the ones that matched hers, but were much kinder, gentler. "You are as much a queen as I am. You've always been. I only happened to be born first. You kill when necessary, you love fiercely, and you do what's best for others." Afton's own eyes pricked with an emotion she hadn't let herself dredge up often, and although the tears didn't fall, they were there.

Afton's gaze fell to Keelen's. "I'm ready when you are." She didn't care to ask him if he was certain because what he was sacrificing was more important.

He nodded and stood from the ground. "I have to touch you. Is that all right?"

She glowered and stepped toward him.

Keelen wrapped his hands around her shoulders and closed his eyes. "Open your magic to mine. That's all you have to do. I'll take care of the rest."

Afton placed her trust up front and took the risk—she'd seen the way he was with her sister, knew Silver would always come first for him, so she shut her eyes and did as he asked. Focusing on the spinning web of energy, Afton swept through it, brushing strands aside, peeling layer by layer open, until at the center was a gaping hole.

Keelen's fingers tightened and she could feel his energy within hers, searching for the chasm. She wanted to scream at him its location, yet she didn't want to disrupt his concentration. But then his energy was close enough so she could grasp it—she yanked it toward the dark hole.

She gasped as she felt it then, the whites and golds shining, the energy binding around her, attaching once more. But it didn't just rest against her bones and muscles, it penetrated every inch of her, like a soft caress through her veins.

A tingling sensation started at her forehead, her back, but she didn't feel anything burst free. She opened her eyes, expecting to find Keelen as he was, yet his horns and wings were no longer there.

Afton reached up to her forehead, her fingers brushing something solid—a curled horn. Glancing behind her, she discovered dark leathery wings protruding from her back. Her eyes widened, her heart pounding as she found her sister's face.

"You're the Queen of Valgmyr," Silver whispered, her expression filled with awe.

Afton blinked, her chest tightening when she looked to Keelen. She hadn't even liked him much, only found him a necessity, but he was more than that.

"Thank you," Afton said. A sinking feeling washed over her. "How can you both go home, though? I thought no one can leave here once they come."

"Their eyes." Ragan brushed Afton's cheek. "Silver's eyes are like yours, born with a bit of Valgmyr energy. So the imps will be able to take them home."

The female imp hissed, gesturing to Silver and Keelen that it was time for them to leave.

"Brother." Ragan wrapped Keelen into a fierce hug. "I know you never wanted to be in Valgmyr. But do know, I will always fight for you. Even when you're not here."

"And I would gladly stay if it was what you needed." Keelen pulled back with a smile. "You don't need me. You never did."

Afton turned to Silver and threw her arms around her, squeezing her tight. "Javan, he—"

"He's gone, and I know what he was to us. I always have," Silver murmured.

Her sister always could see through things better than anyone, and it should have come as no surprise that Silver had already known Javan was their grandfather.

"Make sure Midnight doesn't bother Ivory too much," Afton said in her sister's ear, trying to lighten the mood.

"I think she's starting to give in to his temptation finally." Silver chuckled, but Afton could hear the sadness in her voice. Then she squeezed Afton tighter. "I love you."

"I love you too." Afton drew back first, lifting her chin, desiring to be strong for Silver as she always had. "The imps once let Ragan out. Perhaps I'll see you again."

Before Silver could respond, out from the topiaries, the imps flocked forward, their wings pumping, their bodies arching. The creatures grasped both Silver and Keelen and lifted them upward.

Above them, the limbs unraveled, allowing them to pass through. She watched through the small space, studying her sister as she went up and up, until the branches drew back together, closing. The remaining imps tucked themselves within the topiaries, their stirring quieting.

Her sister was truly gone.

"Stay safe," Afton whispered, wishing Silver would somehow hear her.

Two warm arms circled her stomach. "I'm sorry."

"We all lost," Afton whispered. "But we gained more. This will just be another story to others, one which shall be passed down of a world that became better. People will continue to make mistakes, but they will have a land that won't darken and die. Sisters aren't meant to be together forever. But even apart, she'll still be with me." She whirled to face him. "And your brother better fucking make her happy or I'll rip his heart out."

Ragan rolled his eyes and slowly ran the tip of his finger across one of her horns. "They suit you."

"I'm sure they do." She didn't know when she would want to look in the mirror at them, when she wouldn't be reminded of all that had happened. That would be saved for another day.

"I want you to try something. Come on." He pulled her

from the garden and she walked beside him toward the lake.

They stopped in their tracks when they found what was laid out before them. She took a deep breath and smiled. The lake stood empty—all the bodies gone. Every single one. But across the ground was a fine layer of dust. Their souls had already left once they'd died, but now their bodies could have rest, too.

After a few moments passed, Ragan drew her to the ground. "Press your hands to the grass."

She knelt forward and placed her palms against the cool blades. Ragan did the same, his pinky brushing hers. A gentle tug came inside her, the land drinking her energy, but it didn't ache like before, wasn't the agony she had wanted to end. It was powerful and felt as though it was filling her instead of draining her. For the time being, the land halted its taking.

"I needed you to do that to prove it wouldn't hurt." He grinned, his hands grasping hers as they sat back. "You're forever by my side, if you choose to be, that is. Either way, you're the queen here, even if you're not mine."

She could still see the worry—the doubt—in his eyes, that maybe she wouldn't wish to be by his side in the way he wanted. "I think I rather like the quiet here, and if you truly don't mind my moods, then I'm yours."

"And I'm eternally yours." Ragan's lips captured hers.

"How about we go into the lake for a while? A little less clothing?" She smiled against his lips.

As she stood and helped him from the ground, she looked up one more time toward the barrier and repeated her earlier words.

Stay safe.

TWENTY-NINE

SILVER

Silver's heart thudded violently in her chest as the imps gripped her and lifted her in the air. She thought again about the night with the creatures in her room, when she'd been unable to defend herself, and wished their fingers didn't have to be on her. But she quashed that fear while watching the branches unfurl and the imps traveling through the open slit.

She peered down, and another group of the creatures were hefting Keelen into the sky. The cerulean color surrounded her, and she continued to study her sister below, until the flower-covered limbs stretched back together and sealed shut. The imps drew Silver farther away from the barrier. When she turned to look where they were going, she was pitched forward, a brief spout of gray concealing her eyes.

A loud curse tore from Silver's throat as her body crashed to a hard surface. She wanted to rip off the imps' appendages, but they, along with the flap of their wings and heavy breathing, had vanished. Chest heaving, she stared at the hard surface then back toward the wall where she'd been thrown out of.

Her eyes widened—Keelen wasn't beside her in the room. She jolted up and rushed toward the wall, just as his body barreled out from it and collided with the floor. He groaned, then pushed himself to stand.

They were back in the room they'd left from. Back in Enare's castle. It appeared the same with the drawn circle in the middle of the floor, the partially used candles and herbs surrounding the ink outline.

"Fuck, I wish I could have done more," Keelen said, gripping the back of his neck.

Why was he thinking he hadn't done enough? He'd given up so much to help her. "It's what Afton wanted. You did more than enough."

Keelen gave her a small smile, but she wasn't sure if he believed her. "What do you want to do now?" He peered out the window. A dark veil with a star-filled sky was already casting down on the castle.

She walked to the wall and rubbed the candle wicks between her fingers, lighting them with her magic. "We'll stay the night here then leave first thing in the morning. Ketill is going to be different with only us coming home. Not Javan. Not Afton. Enare's king is gone." Her stomach sank at the thought of Javan and her sister no longer walking the halls of Ketill's castle.

Keelen lifted her chin, his dark eyes meeting hers. "You're now queen of both territories."

She was. Enare had no other heirs so, as a queen, regardless of her territory, she could claim it as hers. "But will they listen to me?"

"They will." His serious expression told her he trusted in that. "I'll still be your guard."

Silver could be monstrous when necessary and kind when needed, but she'd always had her sister by her side. There would have to be the belief that she could do this, that she could bring two territories together and keep them safe. She would try her damned hardest. There would need to be time to heal, but at least Keelen would be by her side at home, as her guard.

Tearing her gaze from him, Silver took a seat on the mattress and removed her boots. She scooted back and crossed her legs. Keelen's feet shuffled against the floor as he headed for the door.

"Where are you going?" she asked, straightening.

He turned to face her. "I'm going to sit at the door. I wouldn't leave you alone in here."

Then what? Sleep on the floor? No. Silver slid back even more until she was almost touching the headboard. She patted the spot across from her. Keelen didn't hesitate and took off his boots before sitting in front of her. The mattress dipped as he crossed his legs too.

Both stared at each other, not moving, until Silver reached her hand forward and cradled the side of his face. A bit of red had gathered in his pale cheeks.

"I've loved you for a long time," she whispered, not being able to hold it in any longer. But he'd already heard the words when she'd spoken them to Afton.

"As have I." He leaned forward, his forehead kissing hers. "I've desperately wanted you to have my fucking heart for so long now."

Silver grinned, taking a quick peek at his lips, holding back the urge to kiss him. She flicked her gaze up. "I won't take it completely. You can give me half of yours and you can have half of mine. And if you ever want your piece back, all you have to do is ask."

"Mm, I think that sounds fair." A chuckle escaped his lips, and she grinned wider.

Silver tapped into Enare's magic, feeling its lightness, its life. It was all there, with no trace of the tarnished energy lingering. "Can you still draw the magic here?"

Keelen squinted, his brows inching closer together, and he pressed his lips into a tight line, seeming to concentrate. He shook his head.

Cupping her mouth, she took a deep swallow and her heart lodged in her throat. "So you gave up everything?"

"Everything." He took her hand from her lips and entwined their fingers together. "I don't need it anyway. I'm good with weapons. Ragan taught me how to use them when it was just the two of us in Valgmyr."

She didn't only lose a sister. He lost a brother.

Silver wanted to give him something that she'd never given to anyone—herself.

She pushed up from her position and crawled into his lap, his legs stretching in front of him so she could be on either side of them. Her palms cupped his face as she pressed her lips to his. "Show me," she murmured. Then softly kissed him again.

"Show you what?" His arms snaked around her waist, tugging her close.

"How to make love to you." Silver's fingers clasped the hem of his tunic.

Keelen's lips parted, his breath increasing. "Just follow my lead. Do anything you wish," he whispered, his pupils dilating as he helped her lift his shirt over his head. His mouth captured hers, and she arched into his touch. His tongue traced the seam of her lips, prying them open. As she kissed him, caressing, deepening, the stars from outside shone brighter into the room, alighting within her.

Keelen's hands skimmed up her dress, to her thighs, and she wanted them in all the places that hadn't been touched by anyone else.

"Unfasten me," she breathed, reaching down for the ties of his pants.

His fingers traveled up her back, loosening each button, his mouth never leaving hers, until they were all undone. Keelen peeled the dress from her shoulders, baring her breasts, her hardened nipples.

"You're everything," he murmured, craning his neck forward to kiss her scar. "Always have been." His head then dipped lower. Her heart quickened when his tongue circled her nipple. He gave it a soothing lick, and that small touch sent her over the edge, heating her, causing her to desire *more*. She drew off her dress and remaining undergarments while he shoved down his pants. As she peered up, she found Keelen already bare, and beautiful, before her. He helped her settle back into him—flesh against flesh.

Silver placed a hand against his chest and took a breath, letting her magic flow into his heart, showing him that she would always guard it.

Keelen's mouth crashed to hers, hungrily, desperately, allowing her to see that he would keep her safe too. He scooped her up and rested her against the mattress as his fingers trailed down her neck, to her scar, in between her breasts, to the area between her thighs that yearned for him. Keelen's true form was sculpted to perfection, lean and hard against her soft flesh. She'd fallen in love with him before she'd known who he truly was, when his soul could only temporarily visit while inside a wax raven.

Silver gasped when a sensual feeling ignited within her as his fingers stroked and rubbed her core, expertly, deliciously. A wondrous pleasure poured over her, and she couldn't hold back her moan. He nipped at her throat, grazed his teeth down her breast, continuing until his tongue was now between her thighs, kissing and licking and shattering her entire world into something anew.

"Show me more," she said when he lifted his head.

A mischievous grin spread across his face. "As you wish."

She tugged his hair and his lips met hers once more. With her free hand, she reached down between them, grasping his hardness.

"Silver," Keelen rasped as she pumped him. He threw his head back with a loud groan, even though her movements were unpracticed.

Her hand left his length and drifted to his back, their kisses harder, devouring. The tip of his hardness nudged her entrance. He took his lips from hers, his eyes questioning, and she nodded for him to continue. Then his mouth was back on hers, his chest pressed to her breasts.

Keelen pushed inside her inch by inch, and she sucked in a breath at the stretching, the ache, until she was full of him.

"Tell me when you're ready," he said, his voice low, his cheeks flushed.

"Now." She dug her fingers into his hips, urging him on.

Keelen's hips started to move, slowly at first. They watched each other for a few moments before he kissed her, like he didn't ever want to stop. His pace picked up, his hips rolling into hers. Over and over and over again. And she wanted him to show her even more.

As if reading her thoughts, he scooped her up and took her into his lap. His mouth descended to her other nipple this time, giving it equal treatment as his tongue flicked and tasted. She grasped his neck tightly, her body rocking with his, her center rubbing circular motions against him, his hands gripping her waist. A stack of stones built within her, growing taller and taller, reaching as high as they could go before they all crashed down, creating a rush of bliss through her unlike anything she'd ever felt. She moaned his name while her body shook from the sensations.

Keelen groaned, his body quaking as he spilled himself inside her, amplifying her magic. She allowed her energy to seep into him like before, only this time igniting the pleasure he was feeling—that she was still feeling.

His forehead fell to her chest, her hand on his, and they both breathed together, his heart beating beneath her palm, just as furious as hers.

"That was…" he trailed off, looking up at her, his expression content.

"It was." Silver smiled, still struggling to catch her breath, unsure if she even really wanted to. She folded her arms around him and he did the same to her. "Get some sleep, my raven. I'll be your guard for the night."

EPILOGUE

SILVER

A strong arm tugged Silver closer, and she opened her eyes and smiled. With a yawn, she rolled to face Keelen and brushed the lock of hair behind his ear that always fell into his face. She then ran her hand down his cheek.

He cracked an eye open. "Morning already?"

"No, we still have a while. Midnight requires your attention though." She wanted to mount him, but in her condition, she hadn't been able to do her nightly rides.

Keelen sighed. "That horse…"

"Midnight likes you."

He arched a brow.

Silver chuckled, her shoulders vibrating. A kick came at her swollen belly, and her hands pressed to her stomach. Any day now, she would give birth to their child. She didn't know if the babe would be able to draw energy, but she had a feeling her daughter would by the way more magic seemed to float around in her.

After a year, the castle still felt empty at times without her sister, without Javan, and even without Ragan. But it would soon be filled with a child, her cries, her laughter.

Something tapped on the window, and they both jerked

forward. With practiced movements, Keelen threw on his pants and grabbed his sword in one swift motion. The tapping came again just as Silver collected her nightgown from a pile of dresses on the floor.

She furrowed her brow, extended her claws, and met Keelen at the window. Nothing was there.

Pushing up the glass, she poked her head outside. The stars shone brightly in the night sky, and the silvery light from the moon highlighted the meadow, where the edelweiss was in full bloom. In the distance, she could see the silhouettes of Midnight and Ivory trotting across the field.

Just as she was about to pull back and close the window, a deep caw ripped through the night, and two black birds flew down from above.

Ravens.

One graceful bird inched closer to her and she held out her hand. The raven descended and landed on her index finger, lightly wrapping its claws around it.

With wide eyes, Silver turned to Keelen whose throat bobbed as the other raven sailed down to his hand.

Black eyes with white pupils peered up at them from both birds.

Silver froze, then took a hard swallow. "Afton?" she asked, wishing with all her heart that it was truly her.

"I thought it was time I came to visit you, sister. Even if it's only for brief moments," Afton said, her words spilling out from the dark beak.

Silver gasped and hot tears filled her eyes. She remembered the part about the stars, that when a loved one was meant to return with unfinished business after leaving this world, they would bring them back in raven form.

The stars weren't truly merciless after all—they were *merciful.*

Did you enjoy Merciless Stars?

Authors always appreciate reviews, whether long or short.

**Want another standalone romantic fantasy by Candace?
Then check out The Bone Valley!**

**He's a lover. She's a thief. A magic like no other will bind
them together.**

After the death of his parents, Anton Bereza works hard to
provide for his younger siblings. Love has never been in the
cards for him, especially after desperation forces Anton to
sell himself for coin. And he has no idea that, beneath the
city of Kedaf, lies a place called the Bone Valley.

When Anton's jealous client plots against him, he is cursed
to spend eternity in a world where all that remains are broken
bones. There, Anton meets Nahli Yan—a spirited woman
who once tried to steal from him—and his cards begin to
change. But as the spark between them ignites, so does their
desire to escape. All that stands in their way is the deceitful
Queen of the Dead, who is determined to wield her vicious
magic to break Anton and Nahli apart. Forever.

Also From Candace Robinson

Wicked Souls Duology
Vault of Glass
Bride of Glass

Marked by Magic Duology
The Bone Valley
Merciless Stars

Cruel Curses Trilogy
Clouded By Envy
Veiled By Desire
Shadowed By Despair

Faeries of Oz Series
Lion (Short Story Prequel)
Tin
Crow
Ozma
Tik-Tok

Cursed Hearts Duology
Lyrics & Curses
Music & Mirrors

Immortal Letters Duology
Dearest Clementine: Dark and Romantic Monstrous Tales
Dearest Dorin: A Romantic Ghostly Tale

Campfire Fantasy Tales Series
Lullaby of Flames
A Layer Hidden
The Celebration Game
Mirror, Mirror

These Vicious Thorns: Tales of the Lovely Grim
Between the Quiet
Hearts Are Like Balloons
Bacon Pie
Avocado Bliss

Vampires in Wonderland Series
Rav (Short Story Prequel)
Maddie
Chess
Knave

Demons of Frosteria Series
Frost Mate (Prequel Novella)
Frost Claim

Once Upon A Wicked Villain Series
Spindle of Sin

Acknowledgments

I've written a lot of things and the acknowledgments are always the hardest part for me because I never know what to put here. But what I can say is that I love these characters so incredibly much. This story is probably my favorite which is a hard thing to decide on since I love all my stories, but this one was just so special.

I would like to write an entire page to each of these lovely people for helping me with this story but I obviously can't. Amber H., Elle, Jerica, Hayley, Brandy, Amber D., Tiss, Didi, Ann, and SiriGuruDev, you guy seriously were my lifesavers on this project!

To my family who I love with every beat of my heart and to the hopes that one day we will all gain raven wings to fly, courtesy of our merciful stars.

About the Author

Candace Robinson spends her days consumed by words and hoping to one day find her own DeLorean time machine. Her life consists of avoiding migraines, admiring Bonsai trees, watching classic movies, and living with her husband and daughter in Texas—where it can be forty degrees one day and eighty the next.

Connect with Candace:

Website: https://authorcandacerobinson.wordpress.com/
Facebook: https://www.facebook.com/literarydust
Twitter: https://twitter.com/literarydust
Instagram:
https://www.instagram.com/candacerobinsonbooks/
Goodreads:
https://www.goodreads.com/author/show/16541001.Candace
_Robinson or ignore that and just try searching for Candace Robinson!